Willow Creek Valley Series
Return to Us
Could Have Been Us
A Moment for Us
A Chance for Us

A Moment for Us

NEW YORK TIMES BESTSELLING AUTHOR
CORINNE MICHAELS

To Kristy Garner, Marivett Villafane, and Ronyelle Baker. Thank you for always trusting me to make your broken hearts mend. You've touched me in a very special way and also made me laugh as you read. This book and all the tears are for you.

One

DELIA

I am the most pathetic person in the world.

There. I've said it. I don't want to be anymore and, therefore, I'm over Joshua Parkerson.

Over. Him.

He's not interested. He's made it abundantly clear that I'm not the girl for him, and that means I'm moving on.

Just as soon as I figure out how to stop staring into those blue eyes and wanting to weep.

"Delia?" my best friend, Jessica, snaps her fingers in front of my face. "You there?"

"Yeah, sorry."

She watches me, her lips pursed, and then sighs. "If it's any consolation, I believe he has feelings for you. He's just stubborn."

That really isn't any consolation because nothing will ever

change. We dance around our attraction, pretending we don't want each other—or well, he does. He kisses me, then leaves. He looks at me like he wants to devour me and then runs away, acting as though I'm crazy.

Well, I'm not going to be like this anymore. I'm so over him.

Yup.

It's his fault, really. If he hadn't been so damn sweet the night we talked for hours, I never would've loved him.

But he was, and these are the consequences.

It only got worse over time. He was older, smarter, funnier than all the stupid boys I met. Since Alex Parkerson was my best friend, I was also around Josh all the time, and that made my stupid heart his.

That time is over though. Josh doesn't want me, and I am done chasing him.

"It doesn't matter," I reassure her. "I'm over him."

That earns me a laugh. "You are?"

"I am."

"And when did this revelation happen?"

I shrug, looking down at the birthday cake on the table. "Just now. I've decided enough is enough."

"Well, I hope this one lasts longer than the last time."

I would love to tell her off, but the reality is . . . she's right. I've been down this road before, and I was doing fine until his broody, sexy ass showed back up in Willow Creek Valley. Since then, I've been back on the love train that always stops in the station of loneliness.

"It will."

Maybe.

But today is not a day for me to think or worry about Josh

and his issues. It's a really special day, it's Grayson's daughter's birthday. Today we celebrate Amelia and all her wonderfulness. Jessica has outdone herself planning this shindig for her new stepdaughter that she loves.

"Can you carry this cake for me? I swear I can't smell it without wanting to be sick," Jess explains as she pushes it toward me.

"Wasn't the sickness supposed to end?"

"It was," Jess says, rubbing her swollen belly. "I started to feel better, and then last week, it was hell again. The smell of vanilla is what's really killing me, which is a load of fun since *everything* has some hint of it."

I am so freaking happy I will most likely never have kids. Being pregnant looks miserable. Jessica's back hurts, she puked like crazy, and she has mood swings—really fun ones.

Amelia bounces in. "Jessica! Did we get vanilla cake? I love vanilla. It's my favorite cake. When my new sister comes, I'm going to feed her cake and help her with her homework."

Jess forces a smile, but she pushes her lips tight. "Mmhm," she hums without opening her mouth.

"Can we have it now? Daddy said it's time to sing."

Jess clamps her hand over her mouth. I laugh a little and step in to save her. "How about I carry it in for you, Melia?"

"Really?"

I nod. Amelia digs me. I'm the cool one who gives her treats when Jess and Grayson aren't looking. We also bonded over our shared hatred of the dance studio owner. Amelia is just mischievous enough to push her limits. If I ever did have a kid, I'd want her to be like this.

"Ready?" I ask as I lift the cake.

Melia goes off in front of me, yelling for everyone to come

sing to her. I walk into the dining room area, look around to make sure this is where we are going to sing, and Josh is right in front of me.

I shift to the left, and he does too—in the same damn direction, and there's nowhere to go. I try to twist, but it's too late. Instead of the cake going to the table, it ends up smashed between us, plastering both our shirts.

"Oh my God," I say quickly.

Josh's eyes move down as parts of the cake fall to the floor. "What the . . ."

"It's okay, right? I mean, it's not *that* bad."

He raises one brow. "We're wearing her cake."

I stay calm because that's the only option. "She's going to kill me."

"She's going to kill us both."

"Don't move," I say with my eyes closed. "Maybe we can salvage this."

I put my hands lower and lean back, praying to God that the cake is still sort of a cake.

When I look, it's worse. It's a disaster.

I groan. "Nope. Not a chance."

"I *was* her favorite," he says almost to himself.

"No, we all know Ollie is."

Josh huffs. "Well, this will solidify it."

"She loved me too."

Just then, Amelia barrels into the room. Her eyes go wide, and her little hands fly to her mouth. "My cake!"

"I'm so sor—"

"It was my fault," Josh cuts in. "I ran into Delia on accident and broke your cake, Monkey."

Her lip quivers, and I swear I'm about to break down in

tears. "It's okay, Uncle Josh."

"Oh, honey," I say quickly as more cake falls from our shirts onto the hardwood floor. Jessica walks up behind me and surveys the scene.

"What the . . ."

"We had a cake incident."

She gags and covers her nose. "I see that."

"Go into the other room, I'll clean it up."

She takes Amelia's hand and moves out of the room.

"What was that all about?" Josh asks.

"She has developed an aversion to vanilla."

Grayson walks in, looks at what was once the cake, and sets down a garbage can and a roll of paper towels. "Only you, Josh."

"Hey, it wasn't only me."

"I had a part too." I take my share of blame. Had I put the cake down before turning, none of this would've happened.

"Don't worry, Deals, I would never blame you. We all know it's always Josh's fault."

Josh flips off his brother. "Ass."

Gray ignores him and addresses me. "Listen, I need to help with Amelia since Jess is getting sick, do you think you can clean this up?"

"Of course," I say quickly.

"Thanks."

I grab the paper towels and get to work. First, I wipe everything off my shirt, noting that the pink icing stains will probably never come out. Great. And now I need to go home and change before I head to work in a few hours.

So, I give up on trying to clean myself off and kneel to start wiping up the cake splattered on the floor.

Josh grabs the garbage can and squats. "Here, I'll help."

Together, we clean up the mess that was Amelia's cake while Stella and Gray console Amelia.

Stella enters the room, a smile on her face when she sees us. "You both are a damn mess, but I fixed it. Have no fear. I'm back to being the favorite."

Josh scoffs. "That's what you think."

"I don't think it, Joshua, I know it. Auntie Stella, Uncle Jack, and Kinsley are going to the store to buy her six different kinds of ice cream and every topping they make since Uncle Josh ruined her cake."

He rolls his eyes. "Enjoy it while it lasts. I'll win her back."

"You better start saving because the only way that's going to happen is if you buy the girl an elephant." She waves with just the tips of her fingers. "See ya later, cake killer."

I laugh, and his eyes meet mine. "What?" I ask.

"Nothing, I just don't hear you laugh often. It's beautiful."

I'm over him. I'm over him.

"I laugh plenty," I say a little defensively.

"I didn't mean you don't, you just don't do it around me."

"Maybe I don't have any reason to laugh then."

His long lashes fall, and he sighs. "I'm sorry for that."

I want to rail at him, but I don't because it's not worth it. And I won't expend that much energy on Joshua anymore. "It is what it is."

We stand at the same time, and I sway. Josh's arms wrap around me quickly, helping to steady me.

He's so close.

So close, and God, he smells so good. I close my eyes, inhaling deeply as his cologne mixes with vanilla, which I happen to love. I commit all of this to memory—the heat of his body, the way his hands feel on my skin, and the sound of his deep voice rumbling in my ear.

Then I look up, bad idea that is, and see his beautiful face. The way his blue eyes are intense and piercing. How his jawline is covered in brown whiskers I wish I could feel as I kiss him and run my fingers over the sharp angle of his jaw. There's a scar above his left eyebrow that he got from Alex when he threw a rock at his head. Other than that, his cream-colored skin is unmarred and . . . touchable.

Josh releases me, and I clear my throat. "Thanks."

He nods and then glances at his clothes. "Well, this isn't going to work."

"No," I say with a laugh. "Not only because we're a mess but also because Jessica won't allow us to sit on any furniture or go near her because we smell like vanilla."

"Of course, I can't even change here because Grayson's clothes are two sizes too small."

Josh is the tallest of the Parkerson brothers and the broadest. Oh, and he's the sexiest.

Damn it.

I meant most stubborn. Not sexiest.

Okay, well, he's both.

"And Jessica is in her maternity clothes. Last week, I helped her move all her regular clothes over to her mother's since there's no closet space here. I'm going to head home now and change."

"Nice that you live close. You get to change and I have to stay in cake for an hour."

"Think of it as having your cake and wearing it too," I say with a grin and head out.

Josh's hand grips my bicep, stopping me. "I'll drive us."

"Drive us where?"

His big, blue eyes stare down at me, causing my breathing to falter. "To go get changed."

What I hear from that is . . . we'll get naked together.

I mentally slap myself. Not naked. Not we. No us. No nothing.

"I can drive myself. Thank you, though."

He looks out the window. "Well, you're boxed in thanks to being the first one here."

Damn it. "I'll just wear one of Grayson's shirts."

There is not a chance in hell I'm going anywhere with Josh alone. Not because I've had about a million fantasies of how this ends but because I will be surrounded by him.

I'm just not doing it.

Two

JOSHUA

"Where to first? Your place or mine?" I ask as she sits in the passenger seat.

"Ugh." She groans and then slaps her hand over her face.

"What?"

Delia shakes her head. "Nothing. I don't care. Not like this day can get any worse," she mutters that last part under her breath.

"Okay, yours it is."

I've had bad ideas, but this is probably rated the worst. I've done everything in my power to keep Delia Andrews from my life. I've pushed her away, pretended I see her as nothing but that doe-eyed girl who looked at me like I was a hero, all to no avail.

She's not that girl. She's a fucking warrior. That's what she is. She never backs down and always leaves me guessing.

And now, I'm driving her to her home, where she will get naked, which is something I've fantasized about since being in Willow Creek.

Bad. Idea.

Once the words were out of my mouth, it was too late to take them back. I'm nothing if not stubborn.

We drive through town, her staring out the window and me doing my best not to notice her. Not that I've ever been very good at doing that. I see her everywhere, and when she walks into a room, I feel like I can't breathe.

Then I remember that I will never put myself through this again.

I won't love another or let them love me, only to fail them when it matters most.

I've learned my lesson.

I just wish my dick would get the message.

"So, how's work?"

She smiles. "It's good."

"I heard you got the promotion."

"I did." Delia's voice is warm. "Ronyelle got the Operations Manager spot, and I got her old job. It's a really good thing."

"How is Ronyelle?"

I always loved her. She is sweet, has a sense of humor that you can't help but laugh at, and always gives more than she asks for. I'm looking forward to seeing her.

"She's great. She's improved the factory so much as just a manager that it was no surprise she got the promotion. I have a feeling she'll keep going higher too."

"Good. I've missed her."

"We'll be at Jennie's tomorrow. She has a breakfast with the managers each Sunday. You should come by."

"Maybe I will," I say with a grin.

"I'm sure she'll like that. Even though you're back in town, you're not really around," Delia adds.

It's true. I stay away from town unless I'm visiting Amelia. I like my time away. After busting my ass for my father for years, I'm enjoying taking time to do nothing but hunt or hike.

"Since Kinsley has been here, Stella asked us to give them some time without fear of bumping into them," I say as an excuse.

The other reason is her.

Delia stirs up too much. She's been like a shooting star in my life. She's bright and fleeting. Something you want to touch but always evade because it's not meant to be held still.

I had one of those once, and I know what it feels like to lose it.

"Makes sense, but now Kinsley is around you guys more, so . . ." Delia replies with a smile.

"So maybe I'll come around more."

"Good. To answer your original question, the job thing is great, thank you for asking. The extra money doesn't hurt either."

"Did you get a nice raise?" I ask.

"A really nice one. It's going to allow me to do some much needed improvements on my house. Gray was nice enough to get me in touch with someone who does renovations, and I'm going to have the floors redone first. After that, I think I can tackle the kitchen."

"Yeah?"

She nods. "My cabin is great, but it needs a little love.

You'll see it when we get there."

Yeah, and then I'll dream of her and me on that floor, doing all kinds of things.

I clear my throat. "I can't wait. You know I can help too?"

"Help renovate?" Delia asks with a hint of surprise.

I swear I just thought about how I avoided town because of her and now here I am, opening my big fucking mouth and volunteering to be around her more. "If you want."

"Don't you know that poor girls never turn away free labor?" Delia says with a grin.

"I didn't say I was free."

She laughs. "Like your sister-in-law would ever let you charge me."

"Yeah, yeah." That's not the only reason I wouldn't take her money. "Where to now?"

She tells me to make my next right and then directs me past the corner store.

It's a nice place, small, and looks as if it had the outside stained recently, but the flower beds are overgrown and one of her gutters is hanging on by a thread. No matter what it looks like on the outside or the inside, it's better than the RV I'm living in. I'm sure she at least has running water and electricity not provided by a generator.

"Like I said," her voice is higher than before, "it needs work."

"Everything worth a damn needs work."

"Even you?" she asks and then her eyes widen. "Shit. Sorry. I didn't mean that."

I let out a chuckle, not wanting to make her feel bad. "You're not wrong. I probably need more work than anyone."

Her face falls slightly. "I'm going to overstep here, but if

I don't say this, I never will. You have people who love you and will do anything to help you, but you have to accept their offer to help."

"I'm not good at accepting help," I admit.

"No one is good at it, but we learn that humbling ourselves is needed at times. Try it, Josh. And while you're at it, maybe work on not pushing people away. Love isn't a punishment. It's amazing and wonderful. It heals and allows us to move forward."

"I don't push love away. I love my family and my friends."

"Right. I know you do."

"That's not what you're talking about, is it?" I ask, but she bites her lip and looks away.

"I shouldn't have said anything."

"What do you want, Delia?"

Her lips part, and I can see the struggle warring within her. "It doesn't matter. I've never had a chance to get what I want."

"We don't get what we want in life."

She shakes her head and laughs. "No, we don't. But at least I've had the courage to want more." Delia exits the car without looking back, and I sit here, feeling like she punched me in the gut.

All these years, I don't know that she's ever been that bold. Sure, she says things, but it's always been more subtle. This was not. Before I know it, I'm rushing after her. I have more courage than she can ever comprehend. Does she think it's easy to want something and deny yourself?

I take her wrist, and she gasps, turning toward me. "What do you mean?"

"Mean?"

I look down in her coffee-colored eyes, searching for the

answers. "Yes, what courage don't I have?"

"Kiss me."

I blink, my eyes instantly moving to her lips. "What?"

"You heard me, Josh. Kiss me. That's what I want. It's what I've always wanted. I have the courage to ask for it, do you have the balls to do it?"

Our breaths grow just a little deeper. I move my hand up her arm as the other snakes around her back, pulling her to me.

Warning bells go off in the back of my head, but I am too pissed, too challenged, to stop myself.

"You want me to kiss you?" I ask, needing to be sure I'm not dreaming.

"Is that what you want?"

Fuck yes, it is. I want to kiss her and do a hell of a lot more. The thing I don't want is to hurt her or lie to her. I care too much about her to make her think there's any chance of there being an us. All this can be is lust. I don't have a heart to give her. "Yes, but you have to understand."

The breath falls from her lips. "Understand what?"

"That this . . . this kiss, it doesn't change anything. I can't give you more."

A soft laugh flows around us. "I never asked for more."

I take a step forward, pushing her back against the door, and then I do what I've wanted to since I stepped foot back in Willow Creek Valley. Hell, since the last time I held her almost fifteen years ago.

I kiss her.

Three

DELIA

He's everything I remember but tried to forget.

Josh's hands tangle in my hair, pushing my head to the side as his tongue slides against mine. He kisses me hard and then soft, playing with me like he's done my whole damn life.

I don't care that this will be all I'll ever have. I relish in it because now I'll know what it's like to be in his arms when there's no delusions between us.

I'm not a little girl, clinging to whatever desperate dreams I have about what our life could be. I already know—there is no life for us.

All there is, is this.

It's lust, lacing its way through us, binding us as our mouths stay fused together. I push down all my desires for more and take what he's giving.

My hands move up his back, gripping his strong shoulders, pulling him closer. The cool wood against my back is opposite of the heat on my chest. I moan softly as he kisses me harder.

Yes, God, yes.

He tastes like vanilla and mint mixed with sin.

Once, a lifetime ago, Joshua Parkerson kissed me, and he ruined me for years. Seems he's determined to do it again.

He moves his hand to the door and opens it, causing me to fall back, but he catches me quickly.

We stare at each other, my hands on his chest, my breathing sounding as though I've run a marathon. And I have. I've been running this same race for years, and now I see a finish line.

I know I'm over him.

I know that this is all it'll ever be, and . . . I don't care. I want this. I want whatever the hell this can be—once. I will finally know what it's like to be with him and then I'll be able to walk away.

He releases me and runs his hands through his hair. This is my only goddamn chance, and I can't let him talk himself out of this.

"Josh, please," I say, and that's all it takes.

He walks toward me in two purposeful strides, and then his hands are on my face, holding me before our lips fuse again.

I tear at his shirt, pulling it up and over his head. I don't even get a second to look at him because our mouths can't stay apart long enough.

Josh's fingers pull at the fabric of my shirt, and I help him, removing it as I back up toward my bedroom. We walk, kissing the entire way. A part of me worries that, if we stop, we'll come out of this fog and remember all the reasons this is a bad idea.

First being that I'm in love with him.

Second being that he does not love me.

But I'm not asking for more. I want what he offers now—sex.

"God, Delia." His voice is deep and feels like a caress.

"Stop talking," I tell him as we enter my room. "I don't want words. I don't want to talk. I just want to feel and touch and . . ."

"Fuck?" he finishes.

I nod. "There are no delusions here."

Maybe if I say it, I'll actually believe it.

"Good."

Josh lifts me, and I giggle as he drops me on the bed. "No words, huh?"

I shrug. "Dirty ones are fine."

"Yeah?" Josh grins. "Want me to tell you what I have planned?"

"I didn't realize you had a plan."

"I do. It's been a long time that I've thought about this," he confesses, and my heart rate accelerates.

No, Delia. Do not let that statement mean more. It's not that he's dreamed of you, just fucking you.

"I see," I say as nonchalantly as I can.

His denim-colored eyes turn almost liquid as he runs a finger down my chest, stopping at the button of my jeans. "I plan to strip you down."

"Good start."

"Then I'm going to lick off every bit of icing or cake left on your body."

"Now I wish I had bathed in it."

He grins. "I do too, but don't worry, sweetheart. I don't plan to stop there."

I like this. "No?" I ask, my voice low and gritty.

Josh hooks his fingers in the beltloops, pulling me so I'm against him. "No."

His lips hover over mine, and we breathe each other in. "What else do you want to do, Josh?"

"I want to taste every inch of you. I want to slide my dick inside you and fuck you until you can't think of anything else but me. I want to take you so high, you never come down. I want this to be the best fucking day of your life and nothing ever compares to how I make you feel."

I don't think he has to work too hard for that because there's not a snowball's chance in hell I'll think of another man after this.

"Well, I think this plan of yours has merit."

He unhooks the button of my pants, and our eyes don't break as the sound of the zipper sliding down echoes in the room. "Lie back and let's pray you had cake fall where I really want my tongue."

He pulls my pants off, finding that I don't wear underwear, making this much more efficient.

I lie here, panting, and Josh hovers over me, staring at my body. He lifts my hand, sucking my fingers one at a time, then moves down my arm where there's icing. I groan as he takes extra time there, sucking off the sugary mixture.

"You taste so sweet. I wonder though, are you sweet everywhere?"

My eyes close as he moves his mouth to my chest, licking my nipple before playfully biting it.

I look at him. "Well, is that spot sweeter?"

"A little bit, but I think . . ." he trails off as his finger swipes a spot of cake on my neck. "I think you will be much better lower."

"Do you?"

His finger swipes there, grazing my clit. "I do, and look, there's some cake."

I bite my lower lip. "Are you going to clean that up?"

"I'm a man of my word," he says before dropping down, pulling me to the edge of the bed, and then I feel his mouth on me. Josh licks, sucks, and flicks my clit, pushing me toward a climax much faster than ever before.

It's him.

It's always him.

When I make a noise, he refocuses on that spot again.

My breathing is labored, and I start to mutter words and his name. He obliterates my ability to think as the most intense orgasm of my life comes. Wave after wave of pleasure takes me under until I struggle to breathe.

Josh climbs up next to me, his hand resting on my cheek. "Hi," he says with an air of arrogance he's earned.

"Hi." I barely get it out between breaths. "That was . . ."

"Good."

"What's next on your plan?" I ask as I start to come back to reality.

He grins. "A lot of fucking."

I get up on my knees. "I have a request."

"What's that?"

"Since this is all we'll have, I want"—I lean down, pushing him back onto the mattress—"to do . . ." My hand moves to his pants, mimicking the way he stripped me of mine. I pull his pants off, his dick springing free, and I lean down. "This."

Josh's hands fly to my hair as I take him deep. I use every skill and trick I've seen to drive him crazy, which he seems to like because his hips start moving.

"Shit. Delia. Fuck. Baby. I . . ." Josh stammers, and I love that I'm driving him wild.

Another pump, and then he's pulling me off him and pushing me onto my back again. He grabs for a condom in his wallet and gets it on faster than I ever thought possible.

Our eyes meet, and it's as though the moment speaks louder than any words could. There is no going back. No pretending anymore that we don't know what the other feels like in the single most intense encounter two people could have. Josh will be inside me, in every way.

I reach up, pressing my palm to the scruff of his cheek. "Finish the plan," I say, somehow sounding confident.

I don't blink. I don't move or breathe or flinch as he lines up. The look of bliss on his face as he slides in is one I commit to memory. When his eyes close and he drops his forehead to mine, I allow the tear to fall.

Because I know, regardless of whatever lies I feed myself, I will never be the same again.

Four

DELIA

"Where the hell have you two been?" Jessica asks when we arrive back at the party.

"Sorry, there was traffic getting to Melia Lake," Josh explains so I don't have to lie to my best friend.

"Oh, I tried calling you." She looks to me, and I shrug.

"I didn't hear it."

Lie. I heard it blaring while we were having sex. Then when we were getting dressed. And again as I waited for him to get cleaned up at his place.

"Well, you're here now. Stella and Jack took Kinsley back since they only have a few more days with her. You just missed Alex, he said he had to handle something, God only knows what, but Oliver is still here."

Josh's hand moves to my back. "Excuse me," he says and walks away.

I watch him go, feeling the loss of him already. Ugh, I'm such a damn headcase.

"Still over him, huh?" Jess asks quietly, and I look back at her.

"Yeah, over him." It's not a total lie, I was on top for a period of time. So, I mean, it's true.

"Are you okay?" she asks, tilting her head a bit.

"I'm fine."

"I know that you've always had this thing for Josh, and since we're all going into business together, I imagine it's hard for you to have him in town full time."

A few months ago, Josh, Alex, and Oliver moved back to town because all the siblings left their father's company and decided to start their own venture. With Grayson owning a very large chunk of land, it was an easy decision for the five of them to build their own resort.

"It's fine, Jess. Truly. Josh and I . . . well, we know what we are and what we aren't."

"Still, your heart wants something different."

I smile at her. "I'm glad my head knows the truth."

She sighs deeply and wraps her hands around my arm. "You know, it wasn't all that long ago that I didn't know if Grayson and I would be together, but it worked out."

"You and Grayson are different."

"True, but I have to believe your heart will get what it wants."

Jessica is the sweetest. She has been through so much to get where she is now. I don't have the luxury she did when it came to Gray. He has loved her—always. Josh does not love me and never has.

"I have a great job, my mom is healthy, I own my home,

and my best friend is back. I think my heart has all it needs."

"You want a family too, Deals."

"Yes," I agree. "I also want a man who thinks the sun shines from my ass, but that's a fantasy. I am totally fine being an amazing aunt to your kids."

She rubs her belly. "You'll be the best."

"I'm sure Stella will fight me on it."

Jess snorts. "Stella works on bribery, that's a short game."

We enter the living room where the three remaining Parkerson brothers are watching the football game. Amelia sits on the couch between Josh and Ollie, pulling their attention whenever she demands it.

It's sad because, if Josh would allow himself the opportunity, he would be an amazing father. The way he dotes on Amelia shows it.

Not my problem, though. We are nothing other than two people who had fantastic sex.

My phone alarm goes off.

"I have to go," I explain to Jess.

"Already?"

"I have work."

She gives me a sad smile. "You're leaving me with the three of them?"

"You married one."

Jessica groans. "Fine. I guess I'm stuck with him."

"I can hear you!" Grayson yells from the couch.

"I wasn't trying to be quiet," she says back.

"I'll give you a call this week, and we can have lunch," I say as I grab my purse off the counter.

"Okay."

"Bye, Amelia. Happy Birthday, Monkey!"

"Bye, Aunt Delia."

I love that in the span of a few months, I gained what feels like a whole family. My mom and I have been on our own since my dad died when I was four. We've done all right, but it's been lonely. Jessica moving home was like getting my sister back, and with her came a whole family.

I kiss Jess's cheek, wave to the guys, and head out to my car. Since everyone else has left, I can actually get out of the driveway now.

When I get to the driver's side, Josh calls out, "Delia, wait."

I turn, plastering a smile on my face. "Hey."

"You're leaving?"

"I have work."

"Right, which was why you needed to change . . ."

I don't know that I've ever seen Josh flustered. This is a nice change. "Did you need something?" I ask.

"No, I wanted to make sure you were okay."

"I'm fine, Josh."

He kicks the ground, sending a pebble flying. "I know that. It's just . . ."

"That I've had a thing for you for, well, ever and now we've had sex?" I finish the thought.

"That's one way to put it."

I press my hand to his chest and smile. "I'm good. I'm a big girl who has no delusions of what happens now. It was sex, really great sex, and . . . well, thank you."

"Thank you?" he asks with a lilt to his voice.

"Yeah, I appreciate it."

Josh's eyes widen for a second and then he looks almost pissed. "I didn't do it for appreciation."

Well, well, if I weren't seeing this firsthand, I wouldn't believe it. He's mad. Good. I've been mad and frustrated with him for years. "Right, but I asked you to kiss me. I practically egged you on."

"Is that what you think?"

I shrug. "It's the truth. I'm not stupid, Josh. I know how guys are."

"Do you?"

There's no mistaking the hard edge to his voice. "Look, I have to go. I'll see you around, okay?"

Josh, being a gentleman, takes a step forward and then opens my door for me. "Yeah, we'll see each other around."

I force a casual smile and enter the car. "Bye, Josh."

"Bye, Delia." He closes my door, and I feel like doing a fist pump as I drive off.

Delia one.

Josh zero.

I enter the building on cloud-fucking-nine, whistling as I walk.

"And why are you so happy?" Ronyelle asks with her head tilted to the side.

"I . . . had sex."

Her smile grows wide, and she tosses her black hair to the side. I start walking toward the office, and she laughs. "That's right, strut!"

I do as she says and walk with a little bit of a swagger I didn't know I possessed.

When we get to the manager's office, she points to the chair. "Who did you have sex with?"

"Joshua Parkerson."

Ronyelle's eyes go wide. "I'm sorry, did you just say Joshua *Parkerson*? As in the man you've been in love with since we were in grade school? *That* Joshua Parkerson?"

I lean back in the seat. "Same one."

"Are you stupid?"

My jaw drops. "What?"

"Delia, I love you, but you are. You can't have sex with Joshua Parkerson and pretend like it isn't a big deal."

"I'm not pretending."

She purses her lips and raises one brow. "Is that so?"

"I'm fully aware that it's a big deal. But don't you see? This is a good thing."

Ronyelle crosses her arms. "Oh, I can't wait to hear this bullshit."

I love my friend, but right now . . . not so much. "It's not bullshit."

"You randomly hook up with the guy in the bar, not the guy you've been dreaming of marrying for over a decade." She moves to sit beside me, and her rich brown eyes are filled with sympathy. "You know I love you."

"I do."

"It's why I need to tell you that you're going to have your heart trampled."

"My heart is out of this," I reassure her.

The sound that escapes her says she doesn't believe me. "Okay, let's say that is true, you think having sex with him doesn't complicate things?"

I groan. "You're killing my post-sex buzz."

"I'm killing your delusions, that's what I'm killing."

I grab her hand, squeezing it softly. "I know that you're

just looking out for me, and I love you so much for it, but we had sex, I'm fine, and that's that. It'll probably never happen again, so let me have my day of triumph."

Her dark brown hand covers mine. "Fine, but when you fall apart, which will happen once this haze you think you're in clears, don't say I didn't warn you."

"I won't."

"And don't be stupid enough to do it again."

At that, I pull back. "I just said I wouldn't, but why the hell would I turn him away if he offers?"

"Oh, Lord," she says under her breath. "Because you're going to get hurt. Not him. He is probably well equipped to deal with sex without strings. He's been single for a long time, and you can't tell me that a man that good-looking has been a monk."

I grimace. "I don't think about it."

"Of course, you don't." She laughs. "No one wants to think about it. I pretend my husband has never been with another woman. I know it's a lie. But he lets me have it. Why? Because it's better for all of us."

I sigh deeply. "Buzz is dead."

"Is the haze gone?"

"Yes."

Ronyelle nods once. "Good. Now, you have two people who called out, and the general manager wants you to increase production this shift. Happy welcome to being a manager."

I grunt and get to my feet. "*I* should've called out."

She stands and moves to sit behind the desk. "But then you would be in your haze and living in la-la land."

I walk to the door. "I like la-la-land!"

I hear her laugh as I walk out, and when I get to the end of the hallway, I stop, lean against the wall, and replay what she said. Then I close my eyes for a second and curse to myself. "She's right, I'm stupid."

Five

JOSHUA

My family is falling apart, and I can't fix them.

I hate that feeling. I'm a fixer. The oldest brother who was always the one they turned to. It's my job to make things better, but I can't do it this time.

Stella and Jack are dealing with an impossible situation with their daughter, and all I want to do is make it all better.

This gnawing in my gut has me restless, which leads me to needing to get away from the RV. Somehow, when I got in the car, I drove to Willow Creek, down through the town, past Grayson's house, Stella's loft, and down a side road I have no business being on.

In front of a house I shouldn't be in front of.

I don't pull into the driveway because I'm not sure what the fuck I'm doing here. All I know is that I want to see her again.

We slept together four days ago, and I didn't call, which makes me a dick.

So, now I'm here.

Like a goddamn idiot.

I put the car in drive, but then I see Delia open the door, a mug in her hand, and she smirks as she leans on the doorframe.

No getting out of this one. I park the car again, exit, and wave. "Hey."

"Hey, how long were you planning to stay outside for?"

I laugh. "How did you know I was here?"

"I saw you pull up." Then she points to the corner of the house. "I have cameras."

"Has crime gone up in Willow Creek while I was gone?"

She smiles. "No, but I'm a single woman who lives in a wooded area."

"Yet you don't lock your doors," I say with a brow raised.

"True, because I have the cameras. When I bought the house, Grayson installed them so I would feel comfortable."

Now I know who to thank for my stupidity being on tape. "I'm glad you're protected."

She laughs. "They do nothing but let me know someone is here. We all know how worthless the sheriff is with his stellar response time."

I walk up the steps, standing in front of her, hating the urge that rises, wanting to kiss her again. Delia's gaze is locked on mine. "What's wrong?"

My head jerks back a little. "What?"

"Something's wrong."

"Nothing is wrong."

"Josh," her voice is soft, "I know you, and something is eating at you, which is why you're here."

That gnawing feeling in my gut grows more insistent. I hate that she can read me. I came here for . . . hell, I don't know what, but it wasn't this. Talking about how Stella and Jack are suffering or how my father is a piece of shit who is trying to destroy my mother won't change anything. Then there's the stress of being here again, seeing Delia and knowing that, if I let her in, I'll fail her, just as I've done with everyone else.

"I'm here because I wanted to see you," I tell her the half-truth.

"For?"

"To make sure you were okay."

Because I missed you.

She nods slowly. "I'm completely fine."

I'm not.

I step closer. "I'm glad."

Delia's pupils dilate slightly. "Are *you* okay?"

I will be once I kiss you.

My hand moves to her face, and I brush my thumb against her bottom lip. "I shouldn't be here," I confess, reminding myself of how stupid I am.

"Then why are you here?"

Delia's hand moves to my wrist, her brown eyes gaze up at me. They're filled with something I can't name. I study her, wanting to know all her secrets and praying she never learns mine.

Being with her that one time was a mistake. It didn't sate the urge to have her, it made me want her more. I know what it's like to be with her, to feel her heat around me, and I need to do it again.

I love the taste of coffee on her tongue, the sounds she makes as she kisses me deeper. Everything about her is alluring. Delia has always been my siren, and now that I've answered the call, I won't be able to stop.

"I don't know," I say without thinking.

She pulls my hand from her face, lacing our fingers together. "Do you want to come inside and figure it out?"

"Figure what out?"

Delia's lower lip slides between her teeth. "What you want."

"I know what I want."

"Yeah?"

I nod. "I shouldn't take it though."

I should get in my car and leave. I should turn around, drive back to Melia Lake, and do whatever I can to keep my ass there. That's what the right thing to do is. But then I look into her eyes and want to drown in them.

I stand here. Touching her, holding her hand, allowing her to comfort me when I don't deserve it.

"What if I'm giving it?"

"Who said it was you?" I counter.

She laughs once. "It certainly isn't because of your charming personality." Her back is against the doorjamb, and she pulls me closer. "But go ahead, lie and tell me you don't."

I shake my head slowly, moving in toward her lips. "I shouldn't."

"But here you are."

"Why are you doing this?"

"Because it's what I want."

My forehead rests on hers, our breaths mingling as the pull to kiss her grows with each second. "Tell me to leave," I implore.

"Why would I do that?" Delia asks huskily.

"Because you should."

She lifts her face, her hand moving to my jaw. "Take what you want, Josh. What we both want."

Without another word or thought, I kiss her, and I take everything because I'm a selfish bastard.

"And you young bucks don't know nothing about women," Fred says. He and Bill have been sitting in these same chairs at the diner for as long as I can remember. They're old and offer opinions with or without you asking.

Bill nods. "Not like in our day."

"And what days were those?" I ask before taking a sip of my coffee.

I'm not sure why I'm encouraging it, but who knows, one day this might be me and my brothers. We'll be the old guys, sitting around our favorite place, talking shit to the younger generations.

"The days when men weren't a bunch of pansies. We went up to a woman we liked and asked her out."

"I don't want to ask anyone out," I counter.

Today's topic is the Parkerson brothers who are still single. Fred and Bill have decided it's time I hear their lectures, and Jennie, who I normally love, is hiding on the other side of the swinging kitchen doors, listening and laughing.

"The hell you don't, son. Listen here, you might think you know what you want, but you don't," Fred tacks on.

"And *you* know what I want?"

Bill laughs. "We have eyes, don't we?"

"You don't have sense," I mutter.

"We also have our hearing, so watch yourself, Joshua Parkerson. I am not above taking you outside and teaching you how to fight," Fred threatens. The sad part is, I don't think he's kidding.

"My apologies."

He humphs and looks at Bill, who continues. "Our point is that you like the Andrews girl. She's a sweet one, that Delia. Took care of her mom when she was sick, not even a hesitation."

Fred lifts his mug. "That's right. When a woman will give up her own dreams to care for another, that's a good woman there. He's a fool for not seeing that."

I'm aware of how wonderful Delia is. She's just not in my future. The last four days have made it hard to remember that though. I've thought about her constantly. The way she gave herself to me without any hesitation. After we had sex, we sat at her table, had a cup of coffee, and then I left. No strings. No issues. No regrets.

"And what about her wants?" I ask. Because Delia seems completely fine with this arrangement. We hook up and we ask nothing of the other person.

"Aren't you listening to a word we're saying?"

I look at Fred, feeling as if we're in some weird circular conversation. "I'm listening." Just not understanding why they feel the need to say anything.

"I wonder if it's their dad," Bill muses.

"He's an idiot too," Fred says.

"Had a wonderful woman and ruined her."

Fred purses his lips as he nods. "Eveline was a sweet one before Mitchell came along."

"So, we're thinking the stupid comes from his side."

"Must be."

Bill and Fred turn to me. "Maybe it's better he stays away. Best not to risk it."

I roll my eyes. "Thank God I have you two to set me straight."

Bill grins. "You should thank us because we're a blessing. Now, are you going to take our advice or continue being a nincompoop?"

I hadn't realized there was advice somewhere in there. So far, all I've heard is that I'm a pansy and stupid. "And what advice was that? I thought you just said I was stupid."

Fred huffs. "You're clearly not listening, stupid."

"I have no idea what you're saying."

"To ask the Andrews girl out!" Bill exclaims and then lets out a long sigh.

"I don't want to ask Delia out. If I did, I would have done it."

"Then it's a good thing I'm not sitting around waiting for you," Delia says from beside me.

Shit.

Bill turns quickly toward Fred so his back is to me, proving they are all talk. Delia is wearing a huge smile, but under it, I can see I hurt her. "I didn't mean it that way."

She shrugs. "Relax, Josh, I'm just teasing." She leans over the counter. "And you two know better than to try to get me a date. Last time you tried, I almost moved to avoid having to see him."

Bill and Fred give her warm smiles. "We just want you to have what we have."

Delia raises a brow and points her finger. "I will, when I'm good and ready to find that. Until then, no meddling."

"We don't meddle," Bill says a bit defensively.

"No? What the hell has the last twenty minutes been?" I ask.

"That was us setting you straight."

She laughs, and I turn to her. "You think it's funny?"

"Of course I do. For once it's not me having to listen to them tell me how, in their day, I'd have been married and raising a brood of kids by my age. You're the one getting their unsolicited and usually bad advice—well, other than them telling you to ask me out, which we all know won't happen, but it's actually good advice."

"I could ask you out," I challenge.

Jennie walks over and hands a bag to Delia. "Here you go, honey, tell Jessica I hope she's feeling better."

"I will," Delia says with a smile. When she turns to me, that smile vanishes. "You could ask, but . . ." Her voice drops low so that Bill and Fred can't hear. "I might not say yes."

She turns and saunters out the door, leaving me stunned. A second later, a hand lands on my shoulder.

"She sure showed you."

I blink. "Yeah."

"Fool," Fred mutters.

Bill squeezes a little and chuckles. "He's got it bad."

No, I can't.

I won't.

I never will.

Six

DELIA

Jack has outdone himself. Not only has he brought Stella's entire family out here to witness him proposing but also he has somehow made things right for Kinsley and her foster father, Samuel. It's been hard on Stella, losing her daughter, but he found a way, and I really pray it works for them.

For today, we're all going to pretend it will and celebrate their love.

"I'm so nervous you'd think I was the one being proposed to," Jess says as she sips her ginger ale.

"It wasn't all that long ago that it was you."

She laughs. "I know, and these woods are magical. That's all I know. Two people who are destined to be together, step foot in them here, and poof . . . they become a couple."

I don't miss her pointed stare over toward Josh. "Subtle."

Jess shrugs. "I wasn't trying to be."

"Good, but we're not having this discussion."

"Fine, fine." She raises her hands. "I won't say a word."

I don't believe a word of that, but I let it drop. "How are you feeling?"

Her hands move to her belly. "Good. Tired, but good. Amelia is running me ragged, but she's amazing. I'm ready to have this baby so we can know everything is fine."

She's been so stressed since the fire. Thankfully, Jessica wasn't injured too severely, and she hasn't had too many complications with the pregnancy.

"No matter what, you and Grayson will handle it, but so far, all the tests have been good?"

She smiles. "They have. And I have to trust it."

"You do."

Jessica jerks her head over. "What is going on with Alex?"

I turn to see him standing there, staring out at everyone. "I'm not sure. He's been different since he's been back."

"I noticed the same."

"Do you think it has to do with the whole thing with their dad?"

Alex was closer to Mitchell than his brothers were. I don't know if the closeness was reciprocated, but we used to joke about how his father did no wrong in his eyes. I can't imagine it's easy for him to know just how low his father would go for his own gratification.

"It could be. Gray hasn't mentioned anything, but that doesn't mean anything. His father is basically dead to him."

I nod. "I don't blame him."

Regardless, it can't be easy. Leaving the family business, the financial security that came with it, and the future they had laid out is a difficult choice. It probably was the best thing that could've happened though because it brought the family back together.

"Me either. I'll make sure I have Alex over soon."

Jessica would win awards for her kindness. It's a miracle she's friends with me. "I swear, you're the only reason people still like me."

"Me?" she asks in high-pitched disbelief.

"Yes. You're the sweet one and balance out my sass."

Jess laughs. "I balance none of that. You haven't lost an ounce of it."

"No, but it's why guys always loved you. You were sunshine where I was a thunderstorm."

She bumps my hip. "Since you brought up the topic of guys. I heard a rumor."

Of course she did. "A rumor?"

"About a certain car outside your house the other day."

Jesus. This town is so damn predictable. "He came by."

"For a few hours?"

"It wasn't a few."

"And what were you doing in your time together?" Jess asks with a smirk.

"Seems you already made assumptions."

"I know that you're a grown-up and are capable of making your own decisions."

I take a sip of my champagne and then sigh. "I am. Thank you for the trust."

"I trust you not to be that stupid. Plus, we all know sex complicates things, and you wouldn't do that to yourself."

"Nope," I lie.

"Good. I'll set people straight. Gray heard it too, and Josh assured him there was no validity to the rumor."

Oh, he did? How nice of him to give me a heads-up. "There you have it." My tone is a little clipped.

"What's wrong?"

"Nothing, I just . . . I hate that people are talking about me. It's stupid and petty, you know? I walked in on Fred and Bill giving Josh a sit down about how he needs to be smart and ask me out. None of that is needed, you know? I am over Josh. I don't want to date Josh. I'm . . ."

Jess laughs softly. "Over him?"

"Yes."

I don't know why I'm bothered by all this. People love to mind everyone else's business while ignoring their own. It's human nature, but I don't understand why they're invested in this. Josh and I are adults and there is no misunderstanding about what we are or what we're doing.

I'm someone who is madly in love with him, in denial that I'm not, and sleeping with him as often as I can so that, when he leaves, I have something to hold on to.

That's all.

Josh is a guy who feels nothing for me, other than lust. And . . . I'm okay with that.

Mostly.

Not really.

Okay, not at all, but I'm good at lying about it.

As if summoned by this conversation, all four Parkerson brothers approach.

Grayson's hand slides around his wife's back, resting on her belly. "How are you?"

She looks up, adoration so thick in her eyes it steals my breath. "I'm good."

"No sickness?"

Oliver gags. "I'm going to be."

I laugh, but Gray does not look amused. "Shut up."

"All I'm saying is that the two of you should be over this phase by now."

Jess sighs. "One day, the three of you are each going to meet a woman who makes your heart flutter, and we'll see how long it lasts."

"Great, now we get advice from our sister-in-law too," Josh says under his breath.

"I don't give advice," Jess counters. "I tell you the truth."

"Which is just another word for advice," I tack on.

"Hey!" she admonishes my way. "You're supposed to be on my side."

"I'm so glad I don't have to deal with any of this shit," Alex says, lifting his beer bottle.

"What shit?" Jess asks.

"Nothing."

"I think Alex is feeling left out," I say, knowing that is absolutely not what he's saying. He huffs, which I take as permission to carry on. "See, I think Alex likes someone, but he's too stubborn or stupid to say anything."

Oliver perks up at this. "Really?"

I nod.

"And who might our brother be lusting for? Please tell me it's someone we can give him shit for."

Alex clears his throat. "I don't have feelings for anyone in this town."

"What about Odette?" Grayson so helpfully asks.

"I don't feel anything for her. We actually talked last week and both agreed to let this shit between us stop."

I loop my arm through his and smile. "A truce for the

woman you love?"

"Ohhh." Jessica beams. "You want me to talk to her about what a great catch you are?"

His eyes widen. "Are we fifteen? No, I don't want *you*—or anyone else for that matter—to talk to her."

Odette is the owner of the company that's building the Firefly Resort. She's beautiful, smart, and unequivocally attracted to Alex. When I asked him about it, he said they hooked up but it was one night that he's tried to forget.

"I promise, love isn't what's on my mind. It's more about how being back here . . . it's making me itch."

"Itch for the woman you love?" Jess teases.

"Absolutely not."

"I'm not sure about that," I say with a teasing grin.

"I used to love you."

"You still do."

Alex shakes his head. "We should be talking about why Josh was at your house the other day." Josh's glare should cause Alex to combust, but he smiles back at him. "What? Don't like the subject change?"

"What does it matter?" Josh asks.

I clear my throat. "It wasn't a big deal. I don't get why you care."

Alex's brow raises and he turns to me. "Oh? You don't get why? Maybe you forgot that I was your best friend when we were kids." He turns to Josh. "Well, what were you doing over there?"

"He came to see the floors," I answer Alex.

"I was picking something up." Josh speaks at the same time.

"Which is it?" Alex prods.

I can feel Josh's anger radiating, and I'm sure everyone else can too. He doesn't like to be questioned, and he definitely doesn't like lying, so this situation is going to come to a head very quickly if I don't defuse it.

"Odette!" I call her name, waving at her. "I wanted to ask you something."

She comes over, smiling at everyone. "Of course, what can I help with?"

"It's a decorating thing, actually," I say quickly. "I was telling Josh the other day about how I'm going to be remodeling my cabin soon."

"Oh! That's wonderful."

I smile. "Yes, I'm really excited. Josh was saying I should do the kitchen, but it's a huge undertaking. Grayson is going to do the floors in just one room for me, right, Gray?" I shift to him.

"Yeah, this week." He looks to Josh. "Are you helping too?"

"Yes. I told Delia when I took her home after the cake debacle that I would."

I release a heavy sigh. The mood and discussion changes as the brothers start talking about the best way to rip up the floor and lay the new one. I couldn't care less if they talk about this for hours because it means they're not discussing me or Josh.

Just then, Alex turns to us. "Okay, we have a plan."

"Oh? Should I be scared?"

"Don't worry. We've got this. Josh is going to stop by tonight to re-measure since Grayson is known to be a bit of a dumbass when it comes to writing things down, and then we'll get to work."

"This all sounds promising," I say with a smile.

"It is. Take a walk with me?" Alex asks with his hand extended.

"Umm . . . okay." I follow him out, walking toward the bar area. "Is everything okay?" I ask.

"I'm not sure, Deals."

Alex has always been hard to read. He's not like his siblings in so many ways. Josh is the protector, always looking for ways to help everyone. Grayson is the provider, who ensures things run smoothly. Stella is the manager in every freaking way, and Oliver is the playful one. He makes sure that everyone remembers to relax a little, but Alex, well, he's serious and a little broken.

"Just start at the beginning and go from there."

Alex runs his fingers through his dark hair. "Being back in this town is like a fucking time warp. Do you ever feel that way?"

I laugh. "Yes. I think everyone here does."

"I love my siblings, but . . ."

"But?"

He sighs, looking out at the trees. "I don't belong here."

"What about the resort?" I ask.

He shrugs. "I'm not going to leave, but I hate this damn town. I hate having to see my mother and worry about running into my father. But it's like nothing has changed, and yet, everything has . . ."

His eyes move over to where Winnie stands. A long time ago, Alex had feelings for Winnie, but he never acted on them.

"Still?" I ask.

He shakes his head. "No, not still. I'm happy she's happy. But that's the thing, it's like everyone fits in here."

"You do too, Alex. You're a Parkerson."

"I know, and when I came back, I didn't really think about it. Gray needed us, and I would never leave my brother hanging." I take a sip of my champagne, waiting for him to say more. "Forget it," he says with a laugh. "I'm being a fucking idiot. Willow Creek is my home, and my siblings are what matter."

There's more he wants to say, but my asking him to elaborate won't help. So, I just smile.

"You're a good man."

"I'm also smart."

"And humble," I add.

"My smart comment was because I see what the hell is going on with you and Josh."

I take another sip, not wanting to implicate myself. He's as good at waiting as I am, though. "There's nothing with me and Josh."

He tilts his head to the side. "Really?"

"Yup."

"Okay then."

"I'm over him," I say again for the benefit of both of us.

"Right."

"I am."

I look over at Josh, who is staring back at me. My heart is pounding, and I feel dizzy. God, he's so damn hot. I want to run to him, pull him into the woods, and get dirty in a whole other way.

I need a shrink.

I look back to Alex, and he chuckles. "Right. You're completely over him."

I wonder how long it'll take before I start believing my

own lie.

Seven

JOSHUA

S ometimes things are just perfect. This is one of those times. I was tasked with coming over to Delia's home to measure.

That's not all I plan to do on the floor here.

She's still wearing the dress she had on at Stella's party, and I fight back the urge to maul her.

"Hey."

She swallows deeply and lets out a slow sigh. "Hi. Look, you don't have to do this. I'm sure you have better things to do."

I grin at the opening. "I can think of a few things that are better for the floor than measuring."

"That's not what I meant."

Now I feel like a dick. "Right. Of course not."

"It's not that I don't want to have sex again," Delia says

quickly.

"Okay."

"It's that it's stupid, Josh. We're going to have to explain this to your brothers or sister. I don't . . . I don't want to have to hear about how dumb I am."

"Why would we have to tell them anything, but more importantly, why do you think you're dumb?"

"Because . . . every single person who has accused me of sleeping with you has told me so. And maybe they're right. Maybe I am and deluding myself into thinking I'm okay with just a random hookup."

"We're not random, Delia."

She huffs and keeps going. "It's not like I've done a good job at being over you. I mean, I am. I'm over you. If you didn't know."

"That's reassuring."

"But that doesn't change the fact that, for a very long time, I was not over you."

I purse my lips and nod slowly. "But you are now?"

"Yeah. In the sense that I'm not secretly writing *Mrs. Delia Parkerson* in my diary anymore. We're friends who just happen to fuck, right?"

"Yes, we're friends, Delia. Plus, we're not doing anything wrong."

"Oh, I know that. I'm a thirty-two-year-old, grown-ass woman. I'm not looking for love—not from you, at least. I get it."

I try not to be offended by that last part, but I am. "Nope. Not from me."

She lets out a laugh. "Don't even. You know you don't love me, and you won't."

She's wrong. It's not that I won't or don't love her. It's that loving her doesn't change my feelings toward relationships. I can love her and also keep that part of me at a distance.

"It's not because of you."

"It's you," Delia says without pause. "I don't understand it, but it's fine."

I wish, for just one moment, I could lay it all out there. To share the pain and the heartache of my past, but it won't change things. It won't heal me. Some days, I don't understand why I can't just let go of the past, but I can't. The one thing I do know is that I will never, ever love someone just so they can be taken from me again.

No fucking way.

It's better for everyone involved if we keep things like this.

"It's not fine."

She rubs her temple and steps back. "Maybe it's not, but it's reality."

"Yeah, it is."

Delia's eyes turn watery, but she forces a smile. "I'm sorry. I am being emotional, and you don't deserve it. I think seeing Stella so happy today just made me a little off. Why don't you come in and measure so we can actually do the floors?"

I enter the cabin, and Delia heads off to another room. I grab my tape measure and get to work, writing down everything so that my brothers and I can order the material and get this done for her.

When I'm finished, I walk toward the bedroom and find her half-dressed. "Hey."

She turns, pulling the shirt over her head so I can no longer stare at her perfect breasts.

"Hey. You done?"

"Yeah."

"Okay."

"Are you heading to work?" I ask.

"No, today is my day off. I'm going to Jess's for pizza night."

My sister-in-law is a menace who I'm going to throttle. Well, I would if she weren't pregnant and in love with my brother.

Still, she did this on purpose. I know it.

"How about I drive you over?"

"You're going too?"

"I am," I say, and then Delia bursts out laughing. "For the first time ever."

"When did she ask you?"

"Two days ago."

She laughs harder. "God, she's so damn transparent."

"Meaning we're being set up."

Delia nods. "I love her and all, but . . . they really need some skill when it comes to being sneaky. She called me two days ago, asking if I wanted to do pizza night because Amelia was sad that Stella and Jack hadn't been over in a while."

"She said the same thing to me, but she added that Alex and Oliver were busy so I had to come."

"And we all know you can't say no to anything for Amelia," Delia says with a grin.

"I'm putty in that little girl's hands."

I love Melia and would do just about anything she asks. This is especially true if I know it's going to piss off Grayson, which was why she got a violin for Christmas last year. Nothing says holidays like the screeching of a violin at five in the morning.

"Well, seeing that we're both going, how about I drive?"

"You want to go there together?" Delia asks. "Not in separate cars?"

"Is that a problem?"

She bites her thumbnail. "No, it just means you have to drive me home."

Where I will pray she asks me to come in . . .

"I figured as much."

Delia sighs. "Okay. Sure. Why not?"

I have a hundred reasons, most of them are sexual, but I keep my mouth shut and follow her out to my car.

"Do you think my new sister will like dolls?" Amelia asks, dumping a bucket of plastic people on the floor.

"I'm sure she will."

Amelia ponders that as her head tilts to the side. "Lauren Bennett says dolls are stupid and she hates them. She likes to read."

"Everyone likes different things. When we were little, your dad hated baseball and liked football, but I loved baseball."

She hands me a doll. "Did Daddy like dolls?"

Oh, this is just too easy. "He did. He still does too. Especially the blow up ones. You should ask him to see it."

"Josh!" Delia walks in at that exact moment. Her eyes are wide, but she's trying—and failing—to hide her smile.

"What?"

"You know what."

I shrug, pretending I have no idea why she'd think I said something wrong. Delia drops down beside me. "Which is your favorite?" she asks Melia.

"This one."

She holds up a doll that looks like it's been through a meat grinder. There are chunks of hair missing, the face has magic marker makeup all over it, and someone must have chewed on her hands. I'm slightly horrified at my niece.

"That is your favorite?" I ask in disbelief.

"She's the nicest of them. She's had a rough life."

"Yes, I can see that."

Melia hands the doll to me. "Daddy says that even though she's a mess, she needs to be loved."

"He's a smart man," Delia says with a hint of reverence. "I think that, sometimes, those who look the most damaged have the kindest hearts."

"And this one?" She holds up a perfect-looking doll. "She's the mean witch."

"But she's wearing a pink ball gown! How is she a witch?" I ask Amelia, thoroughly confused.

"Uncle Josh!" she whines. "Don't you see? Her insides are rotten."

"Oh, yes, now I see it." I turn to Delia, wondering what the hell is wrong with this kid.

Delia smiles, taking the doll. "Maybe she needs more love. Maybe her insides are rotten because her heart is broken."

Amelia sits back on her heels. "Can you love someone better?"

"I sure think so," Delia says as she brushes the doll's hair. "I think that we can offer kindness, love, and friendship to everyone." She drops her head and whispers the next part. "Even the grumpy or mean ones like your uncle."

The giggle that escapes Amelia is musical and sweet. "He's

not grumpy!"

"No?"

She shakes her head. "No. He just needs a lot of hugs."

"I do not."

"I think you might be right." Delia grins and then takes a sip of her wine.

Melia jumps forward, and I catch her easily. Her arms wrap around my neck, and she kisses my cheek. She pulls back, holding my cheeks in her small hands. "See, you're smiling."

"How can I not? You give the best hugs."

Her head rests on my shoulder, and I close my eyes for a moment, imagining a different child. A different life. A different time when I thought this could be me.

Back when I was full of the blissful ignorance of youth.

I could've had a family. I should've had this, but that life wasn't in the cards. I was dealt a different hand. One that is dark, black, and lonely where I choose to stay. I will never again move toward the light because, at least here, there's no pain.

There's a comfort in knowing how it feels to have lost it all and there's nothing more that can be taken.

My brother enters with a wide grin painting his face. "Are you playing dolls with Uncle Josh?"

Melia lifts the doll that looks like it went through the shredder. "Yes! Uncle Josh told me that you love to play with dolls too, Daddy."

I hide my laughter, muffling it as a cough.

"He did?"

"Blow up ones."

I can't help it, I burst out laughing, thankful I came to dinner.

Eight

DELIA

I haven't had a migraine like this in over a year. The pain is so bad that it hurts to keep my eyes open, so I sink down on the bathroom floor and close them.

It hit so fast and seemingly out of nowhere.

I rest my head against the cabinet, letting the darkness and silence do whatever it can to ease it.

"Delia?" Josh's voice is on the other side of the door. "Are you okay?"

I reach for the door handle. Thankfully, it's a lever one, and I hit it hard enough to open the door. "Shhh," I say as I press my palms against my temples.

"Are you all right?"

"Headache. Get Jess," I rasp.

The door closes softly, and a moment later, I hear Jessica's voice.

Jessica was in a terrible plane crash and had a traumatic brain injury that left her with crippling headaches and trouble speaking. She'll know what to do.

"Headache?" she whispers, pushing my hair back.

"Yeah, it's bad."

"Do you have your meds?"

"No," I say softly. "I don't carry them because it's been so long since I needed them."

When I got my migraine medication, it was a gift from the heavens. I was down for an hour or two instead of the days it would take me to function again. I don't know what triggered this, but it's already raging, and I know enough to know that nothing short of the prescription will stop it.

"I can have Josh go to your house or you can take one of mine."

While I know taking another person's medication is frowned upon, Jessica was on the same exact medication and dose that I was. "Yours," I say, tucking my head in my knees.

The water turns on, and even though I know it's not loud, it sounds like a train moving through my ears.

Jessica takes my hands, placing the glass in one and the pill in the other. I swallow the medication, and then she takes the glass from me.

"Bed?" she asks.

I move to my side, letting my head rest on the bathmat, not caring that I'm on the floor of the bathroom. "No."

"Okay. I'm going to let you lie down in the dark and quiet for a bit, I'll be back."

I hear her leave, and a second later, someone lifts me and warmth surrounds me. I know these arms. I know the scent of the man who has me wrapped in his embrace. The sound of Josh's heartbeat and breathing fills the room. He tucks me against his chest, securing me tightly.

"Josh," I start to protest.

"Shh, just close your eyes."

I do as he says and allow myself to settle against him, wrapping my arms around him and resting my head on his shoulder. His lips touch my forehead, and I sink into the moment. The feel of him caring for me, giving me his protection in a way I never thought possible.

We stay like that for God only knows how long, and the medicine starts to work, granting me a reprieve.

I stir, and Josh shifts a little. "Are you okay?"

"It's better."

"Do you get these headaches a lot?"

"No. Not for a few months. It was bad when I was working nights, but since my promotion and the stress levels have decreased, it hasn't happened. Why did you come in here?" I ask.

"Because I was worried."

I sigh while tucking my hair behind my ears. That's great that he's worried, but we should be pretending we are nothing, and that's going to be harder now that his brother and my best friend know he came in here. My heart wars with my very tired head. "And what are Jessica and Grayson going to think?"

"I don't give a fuck what they think," he whispers. "You're my friend, Delia. Above whatever else has happened between us, I'm not going to sit out there, drinking a beer, while you're curled up on the floor in pain."

"I'm sorry. I just . . . I don't want people to start asking more questions." Ronyelle knows about what happened, but she'll never say a word to anyone. She'll let her disdain of my life choices be known, but she'll only say it to me.

"No one's going to say a thing," he says, cupping my cheek.

"And how did you explain you coming in here?"

His thumb brushes my cheek. "Simple. You're my friend, and that's what friends do. Let them assume whatever they want."

That's easy for him to say. He's not the one answering a million questions about the rumors in the town. Or maybe he is, but whatever. It's always worse for the girl.

If he's trying to convince anyone that he's unworthy of someone to love him, he's doing a piss-poor job of it.

Instead, he's like a knight in shining armor that I want to mount.

Stupid.

I'm stupid.

Years of longing has amassed into this need to take whatever Josh is offering. To turn him away would be impossible and I'm not sure I can survive it.

But then I think about the other things in my life that people have endured for love.

When my mother was diagnosed with cancer when I was sixteen, she fought hard, beat it, and then had a recurrence right before I was supposed to leave for college. So, I stayed, and I watched her, listened to the stories of regrets she had when she thought she wouldn't survive.

Only, she did survive, and since then, she's spent every day doing things she dreamed of. She's traveling, going back to school, and learning to love herself so that maybe one day she'll be able to love someone else again.

Me? I'm learning how to fuck things up and use whatever flimsy excuse I can find to hold on to the crumbs he's offering.

"I'd like to go home," I say around the emotions raging inside me.

"Okay."

His hand drops, and he stands before helping me to my feet as well. A long, slow breath eases from Joshua and then we exit the bathroom. The lights are bright, but thankfully, they're not painful.

"Hey," Jess says, pushing herself out of the chair when we enter the living room.

"Hey. Josh is going to take me home. I'm sorry I ruined dinner."

"You didn't ruin anything," she replies quickly. "I know all too well how bad a migraine can be. I'm just glad the medicine helped."

"Me too."

Grayson walks over and places his hand on Jess's back. "Are you going to come back after you drop her off?"

Josh clears his throat. "No, I'm going to head back to the lake. We have a busy few weeks coming, and I want to be sure we're ready."

"And you're going to accomplish that at night?" Jess questions.

"First thing in the morning. Alex and I are going to the build site to see what Odette has done and then, I think, out to fish."

"Right." Gray's voice is quiet, but it feels like he's shouting. Not because of the lingering headache but because of the look in his eyes.

He clearly doesn't believe that.

Jessica looks to both of them, shakes her head, and moves toward me. "Call me tomorrow?"

"Sure."

"And the doctor."

I smile. "Yes, Mom. I will."

"Good."

I give her a quick hug, and then Josh and I head out. The ride to my house is quiet. I lean my head back, watching the houses and trees we pass. Today has not gone how I thought it would. I'm tired, and my mind is a minefield of questions. I keep skirting them, afraid one will detonate if I step on it.

Josh pulls into my driveway and exits the car when I do.

I struggle to open the door, and he takes my hand, turning the knob. The heat of his body envelopes me. I really wish I didn't feel so much when we touched. It would be great if, just this once, I wasn't weak to him.

He stays like this, even though the door is now unlocked. I imagine what we look like in a statue form. His body wrapped around mine, one arm around my belly, his hand on top of mine, and his chest against my back.

I shiver.

"Are you all right?" His voice is low, vibrating through me like a tuning fork.

I don't turn to him. I don't move a muscle as I work to calm my heart. "I'm fine."

"Delia."

"Yes?"

"I'm just . . ."

"You're just?" I ask, urging him to say something. Anything. To kiss me. To pull me into his arms like we're in a damn movie and tell me how it's always been me.

"I'm so goddamn conflicted when I'm around you."

"Why?" I ask, wanting to know the answer as much as I

fear what it will be.

"Because I'm not good for you. I will hurt you and . . ." He steps back, sighing deeply. "I don't want to. I don't want to be the man who breaks your fucking heart."

I go toward him because I'm an idiot. There's really no other reason than that. I want him. I want the scraps and the pieces that he's throwing my way. It'll all suck soon, but I can make it feel good for now. Nothing in life is guaranteed anyway, so I might as well take what's offered.

Maybe I can love him enough for the both of us.

"Josh," I say softly. "What if you can't break me? What if I'm much stronger than that? What if it's not your decision, but mine?"

I move to him, my hand pressed against his chest, feeling the thrum of his heartbeat. "What does that mean?"

"I'm not asking you to love me, I'm just asking you not to leave tonight."

I may love him. I may never be able to lie to myself that I want the entire fucking world from Josh, but I'm not naïve enough to believe I'll ever have it. That's my cross to bear.

"Don't . . ." My hand falls, and I turn toward the door.

"I'm not going to beg you," I say. "I deserve better than that. If you don't want me, then go."

I feel him behind me, his hand moves to my stomach. "I want you. God, I fucking want you." My eyes close, heat flooding through my veins as I feel his lip touch the back of my neck. "I want something that is far better than I should ever get to touch." Another kiss, now a bit to the left. "Tell me I can't have it."

If he were any other man in the world, I would. I clench my teeth together, knowing I'll never deny myself the opportunity to have him touch me.

His hand moves up, cupping my breast. My head falls back to his shoulder as he moans against my neck.

"Delia, tell me to stop."

I can't tell him that. I want to weep at the fact that I know those words won't leave my lips. Instead of crying or feeling sadness, I step forward, his hand falling away. I started this with him. I decided that my heart could handle this insane agreement. Josh has been a dream to me, something that would never be attainable. He won't think of the stupid future that I do, but that's not his issue, it's mine.

Joshua Parkerson has given me no false pretenses, and I jumped into this anyway.

There's not a chance in hell I'm jumping out.

I want him far too much. I love him even though I shouldn't, and I can't tell him no because it's not what I want.

Both of us are breathing heavy. "Come inside," I say, and his eyes widen.

"No."

"No?"

He runs his hands through his hair. "You had a migraine, and . . . I'm a fucking bastard."

"No, you're only a bastard if you leave me now."

"You don't deserve this."

I laugh once. "I don't deserve to feel desired? Wanted? Sexy? I don't deserve to have someone see me that way?"

Josh's lips part, and he steps forward. "You are more desirable and sexier than any woman in this world. You have no idea how much I want you. I walk around here, trying to come up with ridiculous reasons to have you again."

Oh, those words, I've seared them in my head and plan to

call on them many times in the future.

"Then come inside and show me."

"Not now. Not with you having a migraine."

There's a lot wrong with my head, but the migraine is the least of it. I reach my hand out, resting it on his chest. "Don't make me ask again."

I watch as the storm rages in his eyes. The desire to do what I'm asking against the fact that I was literally curled in a ball an hour ago in pain.

My head is fine and the only thing I feel is desire.

I want all the tiny seconds I can get, hold on to, and remember after he leaves.

He steps forward, reaching behind me and turning the knob.

And then he lifts me, carrying me inside.

Nine

JOSHUA

This is wrong.

This is wrong.

And I don't have the willpower to stop it.

Why does this woman make me so fucking stupid? It's as if every promise I've made myself disappears when she touches me. Hell, when she looks at me.

I'm a damn idiot, that's what I am.

Still, the sound of Delia's soft moan seems to seep through my soul, hardening my dick even more.

Our tongues fight against each other, moving deeper, wanting to take everything the other will give.

I move toward her bedroom and then stop, remembering all the things I wanted to do to her on this floor.

"I want you here," I say as I stop between the dining room and living room. "I want to lie you down on the cold wood floor, taste you, make you scream."

Her lips move to my ear. "Then stop talking and do it."

I put her down, standing above her, as she waits. God, she's so fucking gorgeous. Everything about her is perfect. The way her blonde hair flows around her, and the cognac-colored eyes staring up at me with so much trust that it threatens to bring me to my knees.

She watches as I grab the blanket off the back of the couch for her to use as a pillow. "Lift your head."

She does.

I place it under her. Her headache may be gone, but I'm not taking the chance.

Delia smiles up at me. "And they say chivalry is dead."

"There's nothing chivalrous about what I want to do to you, sweetheart."

"Promise?"

"Absolutely."

"Good." She grins.

I lift her skirt up, and when I find she doesn't have any underwear, I stare up at her.

Delia's grin hasn't faded. "What?"

"You had nothing on all night?"

"Or at the party."

"Fuck." I groan deeply as I spread her legs, taking in the view I've come to dream of. "And did you think about this?" I ask as I kiss her ankle.

"What?"

I nip her calf as I move higher, eliciting a giggle. "Did you think about me lifting your skirt, sliding my tongue against your clit, making you moan?"

Her eyes flutter closed, and she nods.

I wait until her gaze meets mine. "I think about this all the time. I ache to feel you," I confess, knowing this is a risk. "When I saw you at the party, I wanted to take you behind a tree . . ." I kiss her thigh.

"And do what?" Delia's words are like silk against my skin.

"Sink into you, take you right there where anyone could hear you moaning my name. I wanted to watch you fall apart in my arms."

She leans up, taking my face in her hands, and I swear she can see all the things I'm not saying. How I want to love her. How I wish I could have her for a lot longer than I will. How much I would give to be a man worthy of her, but will never be.

"I wish you had."

I close my eyes, feeling too much desire for this girl. "You shouldn't want me."

"Well," she says with a laugh, "it's too late for that."

"One day, you're going to meet a man who will give you the world, Delia. He's going to love you like you deserve and provide the future you should have."

"That day isn't today, so give me what I want now."

"And what's that?" I ask, willing to give her anything I can.

"You."

The sound that comes from me is more animal than man. I push her legs up higher as her head falls back against the blanket. Within seconds, my mouth is on her pussy. I lick, suck, and slide my tongue in and around her. I can't get deep enough or hard enough, needing to ruin her for that man in her future.

A primal urge to destroy that image is so fierce it makes it impossible to ignore. My tongue laps at her, making various shapes, and she moans louder. I keep going, wanting this moment to be burned into her brain for eternity.

She calls to the devil in me, who is intent on claiming her even though I'll have to release her after.

"Josh! Yes! Jesus!" Her voice is strained as her hands slap the wood ground.

When I slide a finger into her, the heat and tightness has me aching. I've never been this hard or this desperate to be inside a woman.

I need her to come. I can't wait much longer.

I move my finger in time with my tongue and suck hard.

Delia falls apart. Her moans, mingled with her labored breathing, fill my ears.

I sit up, pushing my pants down as a hazy smile plays on her lips.

"I need to be inside you," I tell her, already rolling on the condom.

"Yes, God, yes."

I line up at her entrance and push in. She gasps, her hands clutching my shoulders. We're not even halfway undressed. She's in her dress, and my pants are around my knees, but I feel exposed as we stare at each other.

"Josh." She sighs.

The quiet reverence in her voice breaks me. I pull back, loving the sound of pleasure that falls from her lips. I push in again, my heart racing, and a chord that I severed years ago starts to wind back around me. Deeper I go, feeling that pull to her. The need to have, care, cherish someone again beckoning.

I shove it away. I can't do that. Not again. I won't when I know the pain of loss scars so deeply it disfigures.

Delia rocks her hips up, pushing me to the hilt. Our gazes lock, and when I see the one thing I'd been hoping to never see again, I snap.

I go harder, faster, needing to chase away the demons of my past. Wanting to vanquish the love that I saw in her eyes. She can't love me. I won't allow it.

With each hard, steady thrust, lust and desire fill her expression. That's allowed.

She starts to tighten around my cock again, and it's too much.

"I'm close," I warn her. "Let go, Delia."

She grips my arms tighter, her eyes close. "Yes, harder!"

I do. I slam against her, the sound of skin slapping and labored breathing fills the room. She moans again as I fuck her with abandon. "I . . . can't hold back. You feel so fucking good!"

"Yes! Yes!" she yells, and then her head turns to the side as she screams my name.

And I'm done. I can't stop myself. I let go to the most intense orgasm of my life.

My arms give out, and I use every ounce of strength I have not to collapse completely. Both of our breathing is ragged, and it's long moments before I'm aware enough to shift off her.

It's then that I feel it.

The difference. The stickiness and heat that is far more intense than it should be.

The strength I had lost returns as I push up.

"Fuck!" I say as I pull out, seeing the tip of the condom empty and the rip visible. "Fuck."

Delia sits up. "Hand me something."

I rip my shirt off, giving it to her. My mind goes in circles, freaking out and thinking of how to handle this. "Delia . . ."

There's nothing I can say that either won't make me the biggest asshole ever or change the situation.

"Relax, Josh. It's okay," she says as she stands. "I'm on the pill. I have been for years."

I run my hands through my hair as I pull my pants up. "I just . . ."

"I know. You don't want a family, and believe me, this is not what I want either. I want kids with a man who wants them with me."

"Okay. Yeah, no. I just . . ."

"I get it. I won't lie and say there wasn't a moment where my heart stopped right then."

I let out a deep breath and nod. "Yeah, it was . . . a . . . moment there for us."

"It was." Delia smiles softly. "Listen, I'm clean as well. Just so you know. I get tested yearly and all that."

"I didn't think—" I stutter because now I do feel like an asshole. "That didn't cross my mind, but I'm the same. I get tested, and I've always been careful."

Delia leans in, kissing my cheek before heading off to the bathroom. Shirtless, and unsure, I press my hand against my temple and pace. What the hell? I've never had a condom break like that.

She's on the pill, which is basically the only thing keeping me sane right now. She didn't seem worried—at all. That has to be a good thing, so I'll follow her lead.

Delia returns, and she hands me a sweatshirt. "It's probably going to be a little tight, but it's the best I can do. It was . . . a friend's."

She's giving me another man's shirt. "I'm fine."

"Josh, it's cold out."

There's not a chance in hell I'm wearing some other guy's shirt. Some guy who was here, who touched her, who has felt what it's like to be with her.

I'm a fucking mess. So many conflicting emotions swirl through my head. I'm pissed off about the condom breaking, beyond speechless about how good it felt to be inside her bare, raging at the idea of her being with other guys, and all I want to do is pull her into my arms.

"I should go," I say, contradicting what I want.

"Yeah, sure."

"I have things to do."

Delia nods. "Okay."

"Things for the resort."

"Things. I get it."

I run my hands through my hair. "I can stay, if you need me."

"No. I feel my headache coming back. I'm going to lie down."

Her head. Fuck. I really am a piece of shit. I step toward her, but she retreats. "You're pissed at me?"

She plasters on a fake smile. "I'm not. I just want to lie down and process the day. Thanks for driving me home and"— her eyes move to the floor—"that. So thanks for everything."

"You're thanking me for sex?" I ask with anger laced in my words.

"Isn't that what we're supposed to say? I mean, I'm not sure of the protocol here. You're clearly upset about the events of tonight, which I'm not jumping for joy about either, but . . ."

"But?"

She throws her hands up. "I don't know! My head is a mess, and . . . you and me and us and this. It's like it doesn't add up. You cared for me, Josh. You sat on that floor and held me as though I was important. Then we get here, and I can't turn you away. I can't stop myself from touching you and soaking up any chance I have at this. Then you put a steel wall up around yourself when suddenly something happens, and I'm sorry, but I don't know how or what the hell to think!"

I take two strides before I hold her in my hands. "I'm just as fucked up about it as you are."

"How? How are you so fucked up, Josh? Why?"

"Because I don't want this! I don't want to care. When I saw you in the bathroom—fucking hell, Delia, all I wanted was to make you better. I do care about you, and that's the problem!"

She shakes her head. "That doesn't make sense!"

"I will never love again. I can't. I literally can't. There is no way I will let myself hurt you or get involved further than this."

"I'm not asking for you to love me."

"Then what are you asking?"

She shoves out of my grip. "I'm asking you to be what you promised. A guy who comes over, hooks up, and then leaves without looking back. I need you to be *that* guy, Josh. That way, that when you walk away, I won't be broken and obsessed with the time you held me. Or the times you kissed me and my heart raced. Be the asshole because I can hate him in a few weeks when this is completely over."

If that's what she wants, then that's what I'll do. Regardless of the fact that she deserves better than that. She's not some random girl—not to me. However, I hear what she's asking, and if that's what she needs, then I'll do it.

I grab the sweatshirt of whatever asshole fucked her last, throw it over my head, and walk out the door, hating myself with each step I take.

Ten

DELIA

"I'm going to head to Mexico next week and then stay in Florida with your Aunt Lou," my mother says.

"Nope."

"Right. And then maybe I'll paddle around the world in a canoe."

"Sounds great," I answer.

"I'm thinking about shaving your head before that, though."

I nod. "Yup."

A french fry hits my forehead. "Delia Parker Andrews, are you even listening to me?"

I sigh as I wipe the salt from my skin. "No. I'm not."

"At least you're honest. What's going on? Is it work?"

If it were, that would be a nice change. "It's nothing, Mom."

"So much for the honesty thing."

My mother and I have always been more like friends than parent and child. When I was in high school, I confided in her just as much as I did with Jessica. It speaks volumes that I haven't told her anything about what's been going on with Josh.

However, if there's anyone in the world I can tell without them judging me, it's her. Even if she's very old fashioned about relationships.

"I slept with Josh."

Her eyes widen. "Parkerson?"

"Yup."

"And?"

"And?" I mirror her question.

"And . . . how are you? Clearly, the answer is on your face, but I'd like to hear the details. When did it start? How long?"

I fill her in, glossing over just how many times and how fantastic it is. Although, knowing her, the question will come anyway.

"And you're both okay with this casual thing?"

"I thought I was—or, at least, I was pretending I wasn't in love with him."

She nods with a smile. "But you, my darling girl, have a heart that was meant to love."

"I didn't think I still loved him. Not like that. I mean, I was fine because I was stupid and young." Mom takes a bite of a fry, and I can all but hear her calling me a big, fat liar. "I'm really not in love with him. How can I be? He's been gone for years. I've dated and whatnot. It doesn't matter that I fell for him when I was a stupid girl."

"Yet here you are."

"He and I have no misconceptions about what this is," I

say a bit defensively.

Her hands go up, and she shakes her head. "I'm not saying you do. I'm not even saying that what you're doing is wrong. Hell, I got married young and look where that got me."

"Mom," I admonish.

"You. It got me you, and I love you more than anything, but I've spent the last twenty-eight years alone. Losing your father was the hardest thing I've ever gone through. I'll never love another man, and some days, I wish I had dated and found out who I was before I settled down. If I had known I would have only a few years with my forever man, then I would've lived a little more before I found him. Maybe you being with Josh is just you living your life as a single woman before your forever comes along."

That's the problem. When we're together, it's easy to forget that Josh isn't that guy for me. And the sex is . . . off the damn charts. Then he broke rank and took care of me when I was hurting, and I saw him, really saw him for the man he is.

I got to be in his arms, feel his strength and comfort.

Now, I'm screwed because I want it all.

I want the stupid man and his stupid arms and his stupid heart.

"I just need a few days, Mom. I know what we are and what we'll never be. It's . . ."

"Josh."

"Yes, Josh. I thought we were both talking about the same thing."

Her head jerks to the side. "No, it's Josh."

"Hi, Mrs. Andrews," Josh says as he scoots in beside me. "You look beautiful as ever."

"And you're just as charming as I remember."

I bite back the urge to gag. "How are you feeling?" he asks her.

"I'm doing well. I was just telling Delia a few friends and I are heading off to travel for a month or two. It's all very exciting."

"Where to?"

While he and my mother talk, I listen, feeling a hundred variations of awkward. The last time we saw each other was two weeks ago, and things were strained. He hasn't called, and neither have I.

As I look around at the diner, I can hear Alex telling me about how it's as if nothing has changed, but to me, the world feels different since Josh returned.

His hand moves to my leg, squeezing gently as he keeps talking to my mother.

I move his hand off me and scoot a little farther away. Josh grins, and I can't tell if it's at me or whatever has my mother giggling.

I turn to face him, making it harder for him to touch me. "What brings you here?" I ask abruptly.

Josh's smile doesn't falter. "Food."

"Yes, but your brother said you were at Melia Lake this week."

"I live there."

"I know this," I say with a huff. "Which is why I'm wondering why you're here."

"We break ground tomorrow, so all of us are having dinner at Grayson's tonight," Josh answers.

"That's great. I'm happy for you guys." I really am. Their parents are assholes. Mrs. Parkerson has always been . . . a bitch with Jessica. She made it very clear that she did not approve of her son dating one of the poor girls in town.

God forbid.

Since they got married, though, she's trying, and Jessica, being the forgiving human she is, is doing the same.

I don't know that they'll ever love each other, but Jessica knows Amelia loves her grandmother and she wants her own daughter to have the same relationship.

I would never be that nice.

"So, I'm in town for dinner tonight but was supposed to grab lunch with Stella, who just blew me off."

"Really?"

He nods. "Yup. She completely forgot. She and Jack are working on the cabin for Kinsley and Samuel."

I smile, warmth flooding my heart. "I'm so happy for her and Jack," I say almost dreamily.

"Me too. No one deserves happiness more than Stella."

I nod. "And I think it's kind of beautiful how it's all happening."

My mother dabs at her eyes. "I have always loved that girl. It's nice to see things falling into place."

No one has a heart like my mom. She cries when things are good because she is genuinely happy for them. When I told her about what Stella and Jack were going through, she wept and prayed for them. If she could heal the world with love, she would.

"Don't cry," Josh says quickly, handing her a napkin. "It's all good things."

"That's why I'm crying." She laughs. "It's so nice when things go the way they should. Kinsley is a lucky girl to have so much love around her."

He looks to me, and I just shrug. "She's a tender soul, this one."

"And you?"

I laugh once. "I'm a frigid bitch."

He leans in while my mother riffles through her bag as her ringtone blares. "I know that's not true." His velvet words wrap around my heart.

"Do you?"

"I do." Josh lifts his hand, brushing his thumb along my jaw. "We need to talk."

"Found it!" my mother exclaims, breaking the moment. "I need to take this call."

She gets up, leaving me to deal with Josh.

"We don't have to have this conversation," I assure him.

"I think we do."

There's nothing he could say that would change things unless it's: I love you, want you, and need you to be in my life.

Then, yeah, that changes everything. However, I'm not an idiot, therefore, I know this will not be what comes out of his mouth.

Josh leans forward, his voice low so that none of the walls, meaning the nosey ass people in Willow Creek, hear. "I want you."

I blink.

"I want you in my life."

Okay. I might die now.

My breath hitches. If he says the first part, I hope someone can call for an ambulance because I will perish on the spot.

"You're my friend, Delia. Above all else, I've always respected you."

"Right . . . and you don't now?"

"No. Yes, I mean, of course I do. I'm saying that I can't

treat you like you don't matter. Whatever we're doing, it's . . . you're . . . not nothing."

"I know I should take solace in that, but you fail to realize something, Josh."

"What's that?" he asks.

"I have spent the better part of my life loving you, wishing that you would love me back. Then, the day I decide I'm *really* going to be over you, we have sex. I thought I could do it, but I don't know how to fully compartmentalize what we're doing. That leaves me with two options—either I keep you at a distance when we aren't sleeping together or we stop sleeping together."

"I don't like either option."

And I don't know how to do both.

My mother returns, a wide smile on her face. "I have to go, can you drive me home, Deals?"

"Of course."

Josh gets up and extends a hand to help me. I take it because I know if I don't that'll cause more of a fight.

"I'll walk you out."

Before I can refuse him, my mother loops her arm in his. "Thank you, I appreciate that."

I pay Jennie, and she winks at me. Great, so much for keeping gossip to a minimum. When I get outside, Josh is leaning against my door.

Steeling myself from making a fool of myself, I walk over. "Excuse me."

He moves, but his fingers wrap around my forearm. "I meant what I said."

"I know you did. So did I."

His thumb rubs the sensitive skin of my wrist. "What

now?"

I look up into those blue eyes, hating that he can't just love me. It would make it so easy. We'd be happy, I would give him my heart, and I would care for his in every way. Something changed Josh years ago, and I am not going to break down the walls he's ensured are thick.

"Now, we're at an impasse. It's up to you whether we can ever bridge it."

"What the hell is your deal?" Ronyelle asks as she walks into my office.

"Umm, what the hell is yours?"

"You haven't said a word about your love life, and I've been left wondering for the last month."

I laugh. "I have no love life."

"Fine. Sex life."

"I thought you didn't want to know?" I ask, leaning away from the reports.

"I don't."

I raise one brow. "Really?"

"This is me, asking you, for your benefit. I imagine you haven't told Jessica you're sleeping with her brother-in-law, so I'll be your best friend for this."

"How kind of you." I love her.

"That is what I am. Kindness incarnate. Now, spill it. Are you still sleeping with Josh or have you gotten your head on right?"

It's clear she still feels that it was a mistake. Should make this conversation fun.

"We did . . . a few more times, but I'm done."

"You're done? Or is he done?"

I sigh, shaking my head. "I'm done. I was stupid, you were right."

"I know I was right, but I'm curious what, exactly, I was right about."

"I am not very good at pretending I don't love him while having incredible sex."

"No shit. Did you really think otherwise?"

"I tried to."

Ronyelle grins. "Well, what made you see the light?"

The fact that we had an incident and I threw down the truth and Josh is avoiding it.

"I realized I deserve someone who loves me back."

The fire that lingers in her eyes dims, and instead of her brutal honesty, I see empathy. "Oh, honey, are you okay with ending things?"

"I don't think so."

She sighs. "You need Jesus."

"You need to fix me."

"How do I fix you?"

I shrug. "You're smart, you'll figure it out."

We both laugh. "I wish you had listened to me when I said it a month ago."

Me too, but I thought I could handle it. She sits beside me, and I lean my head against her shoulder. "I'm a mess."

"You got that right."

"How did I fuck this up so bad?"

"You fell for Josh's soul and there's nothing wrong with that."

"Other than it's ruining my life."

"That's your choice, Delia. You don't have to let what you feel dictate the future. You can decide right now that you're not going to lie to yourself anymore."

I want to believe that, but I'm not sure I can. "When I see him, all I think about is how good we feel together. It's like this part of me can't stop it. I want whatever I can get of him, and that's so damn stupid."

Ronyelle leans forward. "And what about you? What will be left of you if you keep lying to yourself about what you really want?"

A tear falls down my cheek. "I don't know, and that's what worries me."

Eleven

DELIA

They say time heals all wounds. They . . . are fucking liars.

I got a text from Josh this morning saying he missed me and wants to stop by. That was it. Two weeks of radio silence and . . . he misses me. What does that even mean? Does he miss the sex? My smile? My glowing personality? And why come by? Why keep torturing ourselves like this?

Because I miss him, and I am so damn tired of it. Yesterday was so bad that I had to put my phone in Ronyelle's office to keep from texting him. At night, I dream of him. During the day, I think of him. The freaking man is taking up my brain while I'm trying to eradicate him. I have ached. Stupid, grumpy bastard he is.

He may miss me, but he doesn't feel the same way I do. Which, hello, my brain already knew, but my dumb heart didn't listen. Well, hope is dead and I am tired of waiting for a miracle.

Each mile to his RV, I get more worked up. I mean, who does this? Stupid men who have commitment issues, that's who. I'm not going to allow this to happen. I need to end this right here and now. We are friends and that's all this will ever be going forward. The friendship we had before didn't have texts about missing each other.

I knock on the door to the RV. "Delia . . ." he says, his eyes wide. Josh steps down, closing the door behind him. "What are you doing here?"

"You wanted me to stop by and miss me?"

"You got my text."

I cross my arms over my chest. "What do you miss?"

His gaze moves to the window of the RV. "What does that mean?"

"I'm asking what you miss. I'm asking why you would text me that after I told you how I felt."

Josh sighs. "I missed you. I wanted you to know that."

"Why?"

He moves closer to me. "Do you miss me?"

"No." I lie.

He smirks. "Not even a little."

"Nope."

"Not the slightest amount?"

"I am going to punch you in the throat if you keep this up."

Josh's eyes flicker in the moonlight. "If you didn't miss me, then you wouldn't be here, but more than that, when we started this, I told you that I have wanted you for a long time. I wasn't lying. You're asking me to treat you like you don't matter, and I can't."

Before I can come up with a response, there's a loud thump that comes from inside the RV.

"What was that?"

"Nothing," Josh says quickly.

"Is this a bad time?" I ask because he's awful shifty.

Then he looks again, and it dawns on me. He has someone here and doesn't want me to see. Why else would he be acting so weird, keeping me outside, and checking to be sure the woman he's hiding away in his RV doesn't hear. That bastard.

I am a complete and total fool.

My jaw is slack as the realization of just how dumb I am punches me in the face. I take a step back. "You have someone here?"

"What?" Josh blinks a few times. "No. Who would I have here?"

"Did you get a cat?"

"Is this a trick question?"

It doesn't matter anyway. I can't get mad because he's not my fucking anything. He doesn't owe me fidelity and whatever is happening here is just too much for me. I wanted Josh, but I don't want to force him into it.

"I shouldn't have come here. I'm sorry that I interrupted your night with whoever you're with."

"There's no one inside," Josh says.

I huff, and it's almost a laugh. "Please, Josh, don't lie."

"There's no one in there."

"Right," I sneer.

"There is no one else I want."

"You don't want me either," I say with a mix of defeat and acceptance.

"Go ahead and see, Delia. Open the fucking door and see."

In the back of my mind, there's a voice telling me that I'm crazy. I mean, I am outright losing my damn mind. I drove out here—to break up with the man I'm not even dating—all while he has some woman in his RV.

If this were a story Jessica was telling me, I'd call her a maniac.

But here I am, going up the steps.

I open the door, waiting for Josh to either stop me or the girl to come out.

But there's nothing.

No one is here.

I move a little farther in, and there, on the floor by the table area, is a book.

A book I recognize the cover of.

It's lying face down, which is a crime to any booklover, but there is no mistaking it for anything other than the romance novel I was reading last week.

I turn, and Josh pulls the door closed, watching me the entire time.

"Find anything?"

I raise my brow. "You know I didn't." I grab the book. "Well, other than this."

He smirks. "Now you see what I was hiding."

I lean against the table. "That you like romance novels?"

"I've never read one until now."

"And?"

"I see why women like them."

"Yeah? And why is that?" I ask.

Josh steps forward, his strides long and confident as he eats up the space between us. "Because, in the book, the guy is smarter and more intuitive about what the woman wants. He's not afraid of love. Hell, this guy wants it so bad he's willing to do anything for her. Is that what you want, Delia?"

I shake my head. "No. I know the difference between reality and fiction."

"I didn't ask about reality. I asked if this is what you want."

That's exactly what I want. I want Josh to give in. To take what I'm offering—my heart, my love, a chance—and love me.

His nose brushes against my cheek, and I fucking hate my body for the shudder it releases. "Josh . . ."

"I can't give you that. If there were ever a woman who could make me crave it, it would be you."

I close my eyes as the heat of his breath warms my cheeks. "But you can't."

"No." A single syllable that says a million things.

"I wish you could."

His lips move along my jawline. "I do too."

I want to slap his chest and demand he try. Instead, I grip his shirt, tugging him against me, and fuse my lips to his.

My plan of telling him it was over goes to shit.

After the most sexually gratifying experience of my life, I'm in his bed, proving myself to be an idiot who can't tell the wrong guy no.

Seventh time is the charm. This was it. It has to be.

"This is the last time," I say.

"If you say so."

I turn my head to him. "I do."

"Okay."

"You're not even upset?" I ask, feeling a little miffed.

"I would be if I thought that were true."

Ugh. I get up, pulling the sheet off the bed—and him.

Which is a mistake because, damn that man is glorious when he's naked. Or dressed. Really, it doesn't matter.

"I came here with a plan," I say as I drop the sheet and look for my pants. "I was going to tell you I didn't want to do this anymore, get back over you, and start my life." I shove my leg through the wrong pantleg and groan. "But no, you have to be reading . . . my book!" I keep ranting, again starting to wonder if maybe sex with Josh has done something to my sanity. "So, what happens?"

"You sleep with me?" Josh so unhelpfully answers my rhetorical question.

"Not again, buddy. No more sex for you and do you know why?" Josh puts his hands behind his head, staring up at me. "Because I need more, Josh. I need . . . I need to go," I say now that I have my pants fully on. "I'm not doing this again. We're not doing this again."

"If you say so."

I grab my book and sweater. "I do. I say so."

"Okay then, as you said the last time, thank you for . . . this."

I glare at him. "You are so not welcome."

And with that, I make the dramatic exit I have dreamed of doing, with one arm in my shirt, which is still mostly bunched up around my neck.

Perfect.

Twelve

DELIA

Oh my God. Oh my God. Oh my God. Oh my God. Can one say that too many times while staring at a pregnancy test?

A positive one.

No, I don't think one can.

Oh. My. God.

This is false. It has to be. I'm on the pill. I've been on the pill for years, and . . . I can't.

I let out a deep breath, fighting back the tears that are building, and decide that, today, I am not going to deal with this because I'm not pregnant.

I'm not.

That would be so much easier to believe if my period weren't two weeks late.

I'm never late. Ever.

If there's one thing about me, it's that I'm so regular it's not normal. Each day, I've pretended that it was fine, and it was nothing, but . . . it's . . . not. Maybe.

Stella laughs loudly in the dressing room, and I hear Jess sigh deeply. This is supposed to be a day of stress-free fun. In a few days, Stella and Jack will have their second wedding, and it's all amazing things.

Except now I want to cry, more stressed about those two little lines than I want to admit.

I peek out of the stall, making sure the coast is clear before I exit and toss the test into the trash. Winnie exits right after me.

I wash my hands, splash water on my face, and force a smile as Winnie does the same.

Stella enters, heading for the sink. She gasps. "Shit!" She stares at her hand. "My ring!"

"Relax," Winnie says, "we'll find it."

Jess comes rushing in. "You lost your ring?"

Stella nods. "I had it on when we did toasts."

"Okay." Jessica is calm. "Did you have it when you got changed?"

She looks around, and we all do the same. "Yes. It has to be in here." Stella's panicked voice breaks.

We all search, getting on our hands and knees, looking over and under. I hear Stella yell. "It's here! It must've flown off."

Jessica stands there, holding something in her hand. Her gaze moves to each of us.

It's my test. Oh, damn it. She must've looked in the trash, thinking Stella's ring could've fallen there.

"Why are you holding a pregnancy test?" Winnie asks.

"It was right here," she explains. "I'm . . . I mean, I'm

seven months pregnant so we know I wasn't taking it."

I have to cover and not let anyone know it's mine. Not until I know the truth and see a doctor. Jessica will . . . God, no one even knows Josh and I slept together.

"Is it positive?" I ask.

"Yes," Jess confirms. "So, which of you guys is pregnant?"

Stella looks around and shakes her head. "How do you know it was one of us?"

"Because this room was spotless when we came in, and we've been the only people here." Jessica looks at Winnie, me, and then Stella.

I can see the confusion in everyone's eyes. There's not a chance I'm making it out of this without them figuring it out. Winnie is with the new guy, but she doesn't seem worried, and Stella could be, but well, we both know she's not.

Jess puts the test on the counter and turns to her sister. "Is it you, Win?"

"No!" she says quickly. "I have an IUD, and Easton wraps that shit up."

"Deals?" Jessica asks.

I have to lie, and I don't want to, but I can't admit this. I shake my head, doing my best to act the same as the others. "No, definitely not. I'm not having sex, so I can't really get pregnant."

Stella stares at me, and I know she knows. Somehow, Stella Parkerson—well, O'Donnell now, knows the test is mine. And if she knows that, then she probably knows who the father is. Tears start to pool, and I beg her with my eyes to please just cover for me. I'll figure everything out, but if it's her, no one will question it.

Something passes between us, and Stella turns to Jess.

"Yeah. I mean, you found out. It's me. I'm . . . pregnant."

"Oh my God!" Winnie yells and bounces up and down. "I am so happy. Does Kinsley know?"

Her eyes widen with genuine fear. "No, no one does, and you can't tell her. Please. Not until I figure things out."

"This is amazing." Jessica smiles, her watery eyes brimming. "Our babies are going to be just a few months apart, and they'll be best friends."

"For now, can we not talk about this—at all?" Stella begs.

Jess grins. "Of course, we'll be quiet."

"Thank you."

"Come on, let's get back before Kinsley gets curious," Stella says, already moving to pull the door open.

Jess and Winnie head out first, both of them smiling and giggling. My heart is racing, and I don't know how to extricate myself from this—or Stella, but I will. I start to go, but as soon as I step, Stella's hand grips my arm.

"We are so going to talk about this," Stella warns.

The tears that were threatening before return. "I know, just not today. Can you give me a few days?"

"Is it Josh's?"

I nod and wipe away the tear that finally fell. "A few days, Stella. I just need a few days."

She hugs me, and the resolve I was holding on to threatens to break. "A few days."

Not that anything is going to change, but I need to at least get an appointment with my doctor and find out why my body is lying.

"You're pregnant."

"No. Run it again."

Not that the sixteen pregnancy tests I took the last four days have been different, but still.

"Delia, I promise, you're pregnant."

I shake my head and groan. "How? How is this possible! We use condoms, and yes, we had one break, but I'm on the pill. What the hell are the odds? Because we had like a one hundred and ninety-eight percent chance of no baby. We should have a negative percent chance between my birth control and his condom . . . literally . . . no baby!"

Dr. Locke smiles sympathetically. "It doesn't exactly work that way, but I understand what you're saying with all the precautions you took. However, something failed."

"You think?"

She laughs. "I don't mean it that way."

"Can I sue someone?"

"No."

"Well, I want to."

"I'm sure you do." She attempts to be understanding.

"Then answer this because I need to know, how? How did my birth control, which I take at the exact same time every day, fail me?"

She places my paperwork down and exhales. "You didn't miss a pill?"

"No."

"Okay, what about being sick? Sometimes if you're throwing up a lot, like with a stomach bug, the pill may not have had a chance to get into your bloodstream."

I shake my head. "None of that."

"St. John's Wort?"

I scrunch my nose. "No. Don't take that."

"Okay, well, any antibiotics or . . . anything?"

"No, I've been . . ." I trail off. Medication. That day. The day the condom broke. "I took migraine meds."

"Which one?"

I pull out the list of medications and vitamins I take. "These can lessen the effects of birth control, and we highly encourage you to use a condom."

Jesus. I remember that now. It was what the doctor mentioned when I was given them. At that point, I wasn't having sex, so it didn't matter.

I laugh because, really, what else can I do? "I did use a condom! It broke! This can't be happening. This just can't."

Dr. Locke clasps her hands in front of her. "I'm not sure what to say. I know a child wasn't exactly in your plans, and I don't know about your situation, but there are options."

I close my eyes, feeling the weight of the world settling around me. "I need to talk to the father first."

"Of course."

There may be options, but there's only one choice for me. I'm going to have a baby. I may not have planned for it, but the reality is that I've always wanted a family. This isn't exactly how I thought I would achieve that, but it doesn't change the fact that it's how it happened.

If I were younger, I may do what Stella did and allow another family to give the child the best life possible, but I'm not eighteen. I have a great job, a home, and I have support. My mother will be over the damn moon once she recovers from the shock.

It's Josh who's the unknown.

Thirteen

JOSHUA

The last time I saw Delia was not my finest moment, but the woman fucks my head up. She says we're done, then comes around, we have sex, and then she storms out.

I'm not sure what the hell to do about it.

"What's got you all screwed up?" Alex asks as he heads toward me.

Alexander and I both live at Melia Lake. Our RVs are far enough apart that we don't feel like we're on top of each other, and I like it that way.

"Who says I'm screwed up?"

He laughs. "You're clearly thinking about something intense. Is it because we just broke ground and it's already a nightmare?"

"That's par for the course, isn't it?"

Alex shrugs and then hands me the box of pizza he was carrying. "I guess. It's been a while since I was on site during construction."

The way he says it causes me to pause. "Do you miss it?"

"Miss what?"

"Architecture. I know you had a plan."

"My plan didn't fit into Dad's." Alex's voice is hard.

"Still, you never wanted to run the family business."

He sits in his chair, grabbing his beer. "I definitely didn't. I sure as fuck never had dreams of being back in Willow Creek either, but . . ."

"But there's nothing we wouldn't do for family."

Before he answers, he takes a long pull from the bottle. "At least, for you guys, there's not." He leans forward, bracing his elbows on his knees. "Did I tell you that Oliver called and asked if either of us would give up our RV?"

I chuckle. "No, I guess things aren't so great at Grayson's?"

"Would you want to live there?"

"Hell no," I say with a grin. "I love Amelia, but that can't be fun twenty-four seven."

"He said he woke up yesterday and found a mangled doll staring at him."

I burst out laughing. "I want to feel bad for him, but . . ."

"It's Oliver."

I nod. "If anyone deserves this, it's him."

"Right, with all the practical jokes and hell he caused when we were kids, I'm enjoying this torture."

"Plus," I say after I swallow a bite of pizza, "he likes to go on and on about how everyone in the family loves him the most."

Alex leans back in the lawn chair with a sigh. "Still, it's

going to be cold here soon, and I'm not looking forward to that."

"Yeah, but we have a pretty good setup."

He looks over at me. "You think living in a portable home is a good setup?"

I shrug. "Do you think about settling down at all?"

Alex shakes his head. "Not really."

"Maybe we should look for a place that's more of a home than an RV."

Maybe then Alex wouldn't feel so out of place. If we had a place that was ours, it would give us a sense of normalcy.

"For who?" he asks.

"The three of us. You, me, and Oliver. We could find a much nicer cabin if we go in together."

"I hadn't thought of it."

In a way, we've all been in denial that we actually moved back here, so it isn't shocking that one of us thought to actually buy a place. I don't want to live in a shithole, and Willow Creek is a strange area to buy. You have the insanely expensive homes or the small ones that no one wants to share.

Yet there's something about buying a home with my two brothers that has me hesitating. I don't want to be this guy. The one who lives forever with his brothers because it's easier that way. They should get married, have kids, be happy.

"Don't you want a family?" I ask.

"Me?"

"Come on, Alex, we both know you're not like me. You've always been more like Gray."

He laughs and lets out a long sigh. "I guess. I want kids and all that, but my life's a fucking shitshow right now."

"How?"

He shakes his head quickly. "Nothing, it'll be fine. I don't know that I want to rush into anything, and buying a house sort of locks us into staying here."

"I think opening the resort did that," I say with a laugh. "I'm not going anywhere."

Alex shrugs. "Then you buy a big house, and Oliver and I will live with you."

"Gee, thanks," I say with sarcasm.

"Well, you're never getting married or having a family."

I've said that a hundred times—more than that, but when he said it with that finality, it bugged me.

Or maybe it upsets me because, when he said it, I thought of Delia.

No, this is what women do. They get in your head, make these stupid ideas seem possible, and then tragedy strikes washing the dream away.

I shove all of it down and use a different angle to decide against this.

"Why would I buy a big house for you, me, and Oliver to live in when I know you'll both leave?"

"Investment."

I point over at where the construction is happening. "I have one of those."

"This is different."

"Listen, I did this RV thing because, once the resort is built, I plan to live on the property. I don't need to buy a house for you and Oliver, my stupid brothers who have their own money."

Alex rubs the back of his neck. "I get it. I just don't want to be living in the RV during winter. A foot of snow does not equal fun when trying to run the generator."

He has a point. "Maybe we rent a house during the winter."

"We could. Delia mentioned her extra room the other day. I'm thinking of taking her up on it. At least then I'm not locked in."

My anger surges so quickly I don't have time to temper my response. "Yeah, that's not a good idea."

Alex's gaze snaps to mine. "Why the hell not?"

"Because you'd be in her way."

"Last I checked she and I were still best friends," Alex challenges. "Not sure how the hell I'd be in the way. She's not dating anyone and she offered. What am I missing, Josh?"

He and Delia have been friends since they were kids. I know my brother doesn't see her that way, and still, I want to punch him in the face at the suggestion of him being in a house with her.

I get to my feet, needing to move and get control of myself. "I . . ."

"You?"

Hate him.

I glare at Alex, who just smirks. "I'll answer that for you, Josh. You are a fucking asshole. You have liked her and wanted something with Delia for years. You're afraid of love, human relationships, anything that can hurt you. But, the best part of that is, you're afraid of someone else stepping in and doing what you can't for her. Let her fucking go. She deserves better than you."

"I know that."

"Do you? Because that woman has a heart bigger than any of us knows. And for some unknown reason, she fucking loves you when you've done nothing to earn it."

I move back to the chair and sit. "We slept together," I

confess.

Alex just stares at me. After a few times of opening and closing his mouth, he groans. "Jesus. When?"

"A few times over the last few months."

"Josh, I'm going to kill you if you hurt her. I'm telling you this as your brother and someone who has looked up to you my entire life, I will never forgive you if you hurt her."

There is anger in his voice, and I deserve it all. For my whole life, I've tried to be more of a father than a brother. I did everything I could to be a good man because we all knew our father was incapable of it.

Hearing Alex makes me wonder if I'm any better.

And right now, I don't think he believes so.

"I care about her."

He shakes his head, looking down at the ground. "If you did, you won't lead her on."

"I'm not. We were both fully aware of what we were doing. I never made her promises. She doesn't expect anything more."

This time, he gets to his feet. "She. Loves. You! She has *always* loved you. Of course she expects more!"

"If she did, she wouldn't have been the one to put an end to it."

He moves out of my view, standing at the edge of the tree line. When he turns back a few seconds later, the anger seems to have gone out of him a little.

Before he can speak, headlights shine from the access road and head toward us.

Alex lets out a low laugh. "Well, it seems you're about to eat your words, Josh."

I turn and see it's Delia's car.

Fourteen

DELIA

I should've called first. Maybe then I wouldn't be scrambling with what the hell to say to Alex.

There's no way in hell I'm going to tell Josh I'm pregnant in front of Alex.

Josh walks over to the car, opening the door. "Hey."

"Hi."

"Are you okay?" he asks with concern.

Oh, shit. Maybe Stella already told him. No. She said she wouldn't, and if she had, he would have probably hunted me down to find out if it were true. "Why do you ask?"

Josh looks over to where Alex is standing. "Just that you didn't call, and it's late."

My pounding heart slows a little. He doesn't know.

"Yeah, we just have to talk."

He gives me a soft smile and extends his hand, helping me

out. When we get closer to Josh's RV, I wave at Alex. "Hey."

"Hey."

"What's wrong?" I ask, noting the way his jaw is clenched and he keeps shifting his weight.

"Just a disagreement with Josh."

That's nothing new. Since Alex moved back to Willow Creek, something has been bothering him. He hasn't confided in me about it, but that's the way he's always been. He has to fix the problem a hundred ways—usually the wrong ways—in his head before he can talk about it. I've learned that pushing him is not the way to get him to hurry up and spill his problems.

"I see."

"I'm going to head back home, get a fire going, and have a beer. Want to come?" he asks.

"Not this time." My eyes move to where Josh is leaning against the door to the RV. "I need to run some things by Josh—about the renovation."

"Okay." Alex's voice indicates he doesn't believe me. "I'll see you later." He walks over and kisses my cheek. "Call if you need me."

I wink at him and smile.

He gives his brother a mock salute with two fingers and then is gone. "Did you and Alex fight?" I ask, breaking the silence.

"He's not happy with me."

"I could see that. Why is he mad?"

Josh looks out at the woods. "It doesn't matter."

Okay then.

I sigh deeply, knowing that if I don't just get this out, then we're going to be in a whole other world of hell. I am already nervous and on the verge of puking, which is a feeling I might as well get used to. However, this isn't hormones, this is fear.

Josh goes to open his mouth, and I beat him to it.

"I'm pregnant."

His head jerks back, eyes wide, and even in the dark, I can see the color drain from his face.

"I just found out a few hours ago. Apparently, the night the condom broke, my birth control also failed because of the migraine medication I took. I wanted to tell you once it was confirmed, and . . . well, it's confirmed. I'm pregnant, and I don't need or want anything from you. In fact, we don't even have to tell people it's yours if you don't want." I wring my hands together and then rest them on my stomach. "I know you . . . don't want kids. I get it. I do, but I thought I'd have a husband or at least someone who loves me. Silly, I know. But this is the reality, right? We're having a baby. I'm having a baby, I guess is what I should say. Again, I don't want anything. Not money or commitment." I stop my rambling, waiting for him to say something.

Josh takes a few steps toward the chair and then sits. "You're pregnant?"

"I said that. Yes, I am."

I also can't seem to speak without it being a large burst of words or just a few.

"And you didn't plan this."

I knew it was coming. I knew, and I prepared for it, and yet, it still feels as though I was slapped. Tears fill my eyes, but I don't let them fall. Instead, I swallow the hurt and focus on being pissed. "No. I didn't plan this. I didn't want this. In fact, I prayed it wasn't real as it was all happening. Also, how does one plan for the condom to break?"

"I didn't mean . . ."

"Yes, you did. You meant it because you know I have been in love with you, wanted whatever I could get of you, but I didn't want this, Josh. I didn't want a baby that you didn't want."

He sighs and then runs his fingers through his thick hair. "I really didn't mean that, Delia. I don't think you planned this."

"I swear, I was just as shocked as you are when I found out. Well, maybe not as much as you since I took about fifteen pregnancy tests over the last few days."

"Why didn't you tell me then?" he asks, his voice more concerned than angry.

"I was in denial. I thought—more like hoped—the doctor would confirm the tests were wrong and it was some weird thing that was not, in fact, a baby."

"But it is." Josh says it like a statement but it sounds like a question.

"Yes."

The new reality of our lives shifts into place as we stand here. I'm going to be a mother, and Josh, regardless of his plans or wants, is going to be a father.

When the silence becomes uncomfortable and my anxiety builds, I shift from foot to foot and reiterate, "You don't have to do anything."

His head whips quickly to look at me. "What?"

"I just mean that you don't have to be a part of anything. I know how you feel about kids, and . . . I can do this on my own. Financially and emotionally. Of course, I want you to be. You're a great man, and I know you'll be a good dad. It's your choice, and I won't force you into anything."

There. I've said my piece. He can be a part of things or not, but I won't push his choice either way. I have a great support system, and if he doesn't want to be a father to our child, then so be it. There will be enough uncles and aunts that the baby will never go without love or a male figure in their life.

"I'm not going to abandon you or the baby." His voice is hard like granite.

"I didn't say you would. I'm just telling you that I make no demands."

He shakes his head. "You should. You should demand everything, Delia, because you deserve no less. I am just as responsible as you are, and while this wasn't what either of us wanted, it's not that child's fault."

And my stupid, untrustworthy heart falls a little harder for him.

He isn't changing his mind on wanting to be with me, but at least, he'll be there for the baby.

"No, and I appreciate that. However, with our newfound circumstances, I think we should be smart."

"Okay, what does that mean?"

"It means that whatever fun we were having, really and truly ends now. No more."

"Afraid of pregnancy?" he jokes, and I laugh a little.

"Afraid of never moving on from you. I can't raise a child with you and keep my heart out of it. So, we're friends only from this point on."

Josh smirks. "I thought you already drew that line."

"I think we both know better."

When he stands and walks toward me, his eyes are soft and assessing. I do my best to conceal the myriad of emotions inside me. I'm angry that this is happening. Happy that I'll be a mother. Sad that he doesn't love me. Hopeful that we can at least raise this child with love. And disappointed because it'll never be together.

"I understand."

"I just need . . . I need a chance at a future with love and family. I know you're not the man who wants that. I would never ask that of you."

His eyes close, telling me this is the case. "I wish I was different."

"Me too, but then you wouldn't be you. The thing is I want what's best for our child. If you want to be involved, that's great, but it can't be half measures. The baby deserves all of our love and commitment."

"As much as this wasn't what I wanted, I would never do that. I'll be here for you and the baby. There's no half any-thing, and I don't need time to know what the right thing is. I would never abandon my child."

"I never thought you would."

Josh has always put family above all else, and I never truly thought he'd do anything different when it comes to this.

He nods. "Good."

"So, now what?" I ask, feeling lost.

"Now we figure the rest out."

Figuring the rest out apparently means a knock on the door at six a.m. so he can start on renovations of my place.

"Do you know what time it is?" I ask.

"Yes, time to get the floors done and take care of any other repairs you need done."

"What I need . . . is sleep."

He grins, holding out a cup of coffee from the shop down the road. "I can't do that, but I can caffeinate you." I go to grab it, but then he pulls it back. "Wait, can you have this?"

"Do you want that hand?"

"Yes, but is it okay for the baby?"

I snatch it out of his grasp. "It's necessary for me so, therefore, it's fine." Once I've taken a few sips, I open the door a little more to let Josh in. "But, yes, the doctor said I could have coffee, just in moderation. Believe me, I asked."

"Good."

He grabs his tool bag and walks over to the living room, which is where they decided they wanted to start.

"Why did this have to start today?" I ask.

Josh shrugs. "I want everything done for you before the baby comes."

"That's sweet, but we have a lot of time. I'm barely pregnant."

"And you have a lot that needs to be fixed."

I look around the house, feeling a little defensive. "I just want the floors done."

"And I want to fix the bathroom sink that's leaking, the backsplash in the kitchen should be replaced, and I think we can refinish the cabinets in the kitchen."

I lift my hand. "Stop it. I don't need all that. I like my house."

"I do too." He nods in agreement, then adds, "Grayson said those were some of the things you wanted done."

I blink a few times. "Yes, as in one of those . . . if I had an unlimited budget, then I'd do them all, but I don't."

He grins. "Well, you have free labor, and between my brothers and me, we have all the connections to keep your costs down. So, let's say you were going to pay five grand for the floors, now you'll pay a thousand. Your dreams just got bigger."

While this is amazing, I feel uncomfortable. "I don't want charity."

"I didn't say it was charity."

"So, I have to pay you?" I ask.

The look in his eyes tells me he doesn't find that humorous. "I would never take your money."

"Because I'm pregnant with your kid?"

"No, because you're my friend."

I take a sip of the coffee and let my head settle. He's being nice. Nice at six in the morning, but still, he's here and doing something I want done. "I just . . ."

He takes a few steps toward me. "It's not because of the baby. I mean, it is partly, but we were going to help with the renovations before that."

"Josh, there's so much uncertainty. Seriously, I don't feel comfortable with this."

"Uncertainty with what?"

"I'm really early in this pregnancy. In fact, we probably shouldn't even tell people yet."

"Why not?" Josh asks.

"Because sometimes, in the beginning, the pregnancy doesn't always stick."

"We're not going to lose the baby," he says as though he can demand it to be true. "Plus, you need the repairs done anyway, so what's the harm in starting?"

"None, but we don't have to start right now. There is time."

"Time slips away, sometimes faster than we think." His brow furrows, and he quickly turns, stopping me from trying to decipher his meaning. "I *need* to do this. I need to do something, and . . ." His eyes meet mine as he turns back. "I want to do this."

I really want to ask him why it's so important, but instead, I nod. "Okay."

Josh comes close, kisses the side of my head, and then walks off, leaving me stunned and confused. How does this man scramble my brain so easily?

He grabs a prybar, flips it before catching it, and walks over to the edge of the floor. The muscles in his arms contract as he leans down, and I feel the heat burning through my cheeks.

Damn he's hot when he's looking all manly with tools.

Get a grip, Delia. You are not going to cross that line ever again.

Yeah, I don't even believe my own lies.

Well, standing here is a bad idea if he's going to flex and start ripping things up, getting hot and sweaty and . . . nope. Not going there.

"I have to get ready for work," I say quickly.

"Okay. I'll be here."

Here in my house. Fun.

I head off into my bedroom to get ready for the day. Work starts in two hours, and there's no reason to go back to bed for twenty minutes. I turn my music on, not wanting to hear the sounds of my floor being torn up, and step in the shower. I put the fact that I'm naked while Josh is in my house far from my mind.

It doesn't matter that I want him. That I always seem to want him. We're not doing anything sexual again. So, who cares that, as I wash my hair, I imagine it's his fingers sifting through my blonde locks? Or about the way the pads of my fingers move against my scalp as I picture him in here, naked, touching me.

It's me who imagines that he is here, watching, directing me as I rub the soap down my body and across my breasts.

With my eyes closed, I can hear his voice, calling my name, the way it's deep and muffled because his lips are against my neck.

The heat, steam, and increased hormones are making me crazy. I want him so badly. I want to feel him, taste him, let him touch me everywhere.

I hate that I'm this weak when it comes to Josh.

My hand moves lower, and I wish it were his rough fingers touching my clit. I moan, rubbing circles. "Yes, yes," I say with my hand on the wall. I'm so turned on, and I need to release.

I let out a heavy sigh, listening to bass pumping through my speakers, echoing off the walls.

"Jesus fucking Christ."

I squeal, my hands flying to try to cover up whatever bits I can. "Josh! Turn around!"

He does, his head shaking back and forth. "You're trying to kill me."

"No, I'm trying to shower!" I turn the water off and grab the towel as shampoo drips down my cheek. "What are you doing in here?"

"I knocked twice, called your name, and I heard you say yes."

Oh, kill me. Please. "What do you want?"

Josh faces me, his eyes are full of lust. "You."

The word is like a bullet to my chest, and each breath is a

struggle.

He continues to speak, his voice husky. "You have no idea how much I want you. How watching you like that, touching yourself, wondering if it was me you imagined, makes me ache."

I don't have to imagine because I can see his erection. "We shouldn't . . ."

Shouldn't say these things.

Shouldn't feel this way.

Shouldn't want each other.

But what we should and shouldn't do doesn't make it easier to stop.

"No, we probably shouldn't." He moves closer. "You should tell me to get out, slam the door, and fucking lock it. You should hate me because I can't be the man you need."

My heart slams against my chest as he takes another step. "I don't hate you. That's the problem."

His hand lifts, pushing the suds away from my cheek. "Tell me to go, Delia. Tell me because I'm not strong enough to go without you pushing me."

I open my mouth to say the words, to stand by the convictions I had not even twenty-four hours ago when I put my foot down that I couldn't do this.

But he's here.

He's here, and God, I want to feel his hands on me. He's here, and he's looking at me like I prayed he would for years.

Strong enough? I'm the one who isn't strong enough.

The lie slips from my lips as I reach up, taking his face in my hands. "Just this once . . ."

"Yes, just this once."

And then he kisses me, and we find a whole new way to

shower.

Fifteen

JOSHUA

"Earth to Joshua!" Stella says as she waves her hand in front of my face.

"Huh?"

She rolls her eyes. "What's your vote on the changes?"

I have no idea what changes she's talking about because I can't pay attention to anything. All I keep thinking about is Delia and that we're going to have a baby.

Secrets are things we don't keep, and it's killing me not to tell them.

"I'm with the majority," I say, and Stella claps her hands.

"Okay, that's all."

Grayson gets up, gripping my shoulder. "I need to get back to Jess, she wasn't feeling great this morning, and the doctor said it could be any day now."

Alex is next. "I am going to have lunch with Mom in case

any of you would like to join."

Oliver, Stella, and I put our fingers to our nose. "Not it."

Alex flips us off. "Chicken shits."

"Give her a kiss for me," Ollie says with a shit-eating grin.

As glad as I am not to be going, I'm now stuck with the twins. Stella and Oliver are great. I love them, but when they're together, they're a goddamn nightmare. Stella is all too observant, and Oliver is a shit stirrer.

If they key into my mood, I'm screwed.

"All right, I'm going to head home," I say, and Stella grabs my wrist.

"Stay."

"Why?"

"Humor me, big brother."

I let out a long sigh, and then sit again. "What's up?"

"Why don't you tell me, Josh. You're not like your normal self."

Oliver laughs. "Right, he's usually more opinionated than anyone wants him to be. Today, he's all broody and quiet."

"I'm fine."

Stella shakes her head. "That's a lie if I've ever heard one."

Some days I wish my sister weren't so smart. "I appreciate your concern, but I promise, it's nothing."

She looks to Oliver and jerks her head to the side.

"What?" he says, his voice going high. "Why do I have to leave?"

"Because you're a pain in the ass, and I want to talk to Josh without you."

"So, you don't want me here?" Oliver asks.

"Clearly not if I'm telling you to leave."

He huffs but gets up and heads toward the door.

"I *know*, Josh," Stella says as soon as he's out of earshot.

"You know, what?"

She gives me a soft smile and then loops her arm in mine. "About Delia."

I jerk my head back, knowing Delia hasn't told anyone, not even Jessica. She was clear that she wanted to wait a few weeks and be sure there weren't any complications, and I don't think anything has changed about that in the last three days.

"I don't know what you know, Stella."

"That she's pregnant. She took the test when we were all at the spa, and . . . well, I took the fall for her when Jess found the test in the garbage. I played it off that it was me and then said it was a false positive and the doctor said I was not pregnant."

"Does that happen?" I ask, wondering if maybe there's a glimmer of a chance we're not really pregnant.

"Yes, but if she told you about it, we're going to assume Delia went to the doctor. Blood tests don't lie."

Right. Delia did tell me that she had it confirmed by her doctor.

"So, you know."

Stella's smile is more like a thin line. "How are you?"

"Confused," I admit. "I don't really know. It's been four days, and I'm still in a haze."

"I remember what that feels like," my sister confesses. "When I found out I was pregnant, I really couldn't process much. It was like someone had taken everything from me while also giving me a gift. Then, well, then it was completely different from what you two will go through."

I don't know that I'll ever forgive my parents for what they did to Stella. Forcing her to give up her child like that is unthinkable. She should have known that we all would've been there for her, helped however we could've. Sure, I was living in New Orleans, but that wouldn't have stopped me from doing whatever I could've for my sister.

"You never should've had to deal with that."

"We're not talking about me." She elbows me and gives me a real smile this time. "I'm just telling you that Jack and I understand what you and Delia are going through. If you want to talk to us, we're here."

"What do I even say?" I ask, the question meaning a hundred different things.

Stella, in her infinite wisdom, laughs once before speaking. "About what part?"

"I don't want kids."

Saying it aloud makes me feel like shit. I hate that I feel that way, but there are many reasons for it. I've seen how hard it is, and I've had the worst role models.

I don't want to be anything like my father. I don't want my kids to grow up feeling like we did—pawns.

Stella grips my arm, resting her head on my shoulder as we walk. "You have always been the brother who never made sense to me."

"Yeah?"

She nods. "You were the *best* big brother. You always were more like my dad than anything. I didn't worry when you were home because you made sure that things were good. I remember when I got pregnant with Kinsley and was so afraid you'd be upset with me. Jack was worried about Grayson, but me? It was you I feared disappointing."

"You would've never disappointed me, Stella."

"I know that now. I'm just saying that you, of all of us, should be a dad. You'll be a great one."

She doesn't know that. "What if I fail him or her?"

Stella's eyes widen. "How would you fail them?"

"I don't know. There are a hundred things that can go wrong. I'm not good at this. I'm not like Grayson who altered everything in his life for Amelia. I'm not like you, who gave your daughter up so she could have the best life possible. Even now, you're sacrificing to make the best decisions for her."

The words don't make sense to her, she doesn't understand me. None of my siblings do. I've spent the better part of twelve years being closed off and alone. In New Orleans, no one pried into things or asked why I didn't want love. It was easy to come up here for short visits where I could pretend.

But now I'm here, and my siblings don't abide by boundaries.

What worries me more is that I want to tell them the truth, but I'm not ready yet.

"Josh"—Stella squeezes my arm and steps back—"you are that man. Fear is normal when it comes to being a parent. I don't know that it ever goes away either. I spent every day of the last twelve years worrying and wondering about Kinsley. I would go back and forth about what the right decision was and talk myself in circles. We make mistakes as parents. We stumble along the way, and I think that's just life. What matters is your intentions." Stella rests her palm on my cheek. "And you, my dumb, amazing, and closed-off brother, have no malice in your heart."

Said heart would be slamming against my chest so hard it would bruise if it were actually still in my damn chest. If it hadn't drowned twelve years ago when I failed someone I loved.

"Good morning, beautiful," I say to a very unhappy Delia at six in the morning. I learned my lesson last time and brought two coffees.

"It's my day off."

"Then you can go back to sleep."

She gives me a very hostile stare. "No, no I can't. Do you know why?"

"Not really."

"Because you'll be tearing up the damn floors, which is loud. Do you know how I know that?"

"Not a clue."

Delia huffs. "Because Mrs. Garner, who is on the other side of the wooded lot, came over to ask if everything was okay. That led to her staying here for an hour, telling me about the break-in down the road. That turned into her opening her police scanner app, which I didn't know was a thing, and listening to it to be sure she was safe to head home."

There's so much to unpack in that tirade but only one thing that really matters. "What break-in?"

She moves her jaw back and forth and then grabs for the coffee, but I sidestep her. "Answer and you can have your coffee. I'll hire a barista if you want."

"Oh. I want."

I shake my head. "What break-in?"

"I don't know. She said someone had their car broken into a few days ago, and then there was an attempt at the house a few doors down."

"Did they catch the guy?"

She shrugs. "I assume not, Jeremy is the sheriff."

Yeah, that doesn't sit well with me. "Was anything taken? Anyone hurt or has Jeremy increased patrols?"

"Again, no idea. I'm not worried."

Of course she's not. She's a lunatic who doesn't lock her damn doors but has a camera . . . because that's really going to stop someone. "I don't like this."

She extends her hand, opening and closing her fingers as I move the cup around. "I'm not particularly happy about it either. Coffee . . . now."

I hand it over, and she sighs in relief as she brings the cup to her lips. "I'm calling Jeremy."

"Why would you call him?"

"Because he's a cop."

"Not a good one," Delia counters.

"He's the only one the town has, so we're going to start there."

She rolls her eyes. "We have a new guy too."

"Oh, good, now we have two cops. I feel better."

"I can't believe you're worried about this. Mrs. Garner is a crazy old lady! She and Mrs. Villafane sit on that porch and gossip all day. If anyone is going to catch the guy, it's them. Plus, they could be wrong and this didn't even happen."

That's the worst deflection I've ever heard. "Right. I'm sure that's it. We both know it happened and those two women know everything that happens in this town. If the two of them teamed up with Fred and Bill, they'd be unstoppable."

She shakes her head while grumbling. "Call Jeremy, learn nothing. I checked the camera after she left. No one has been around the house."

"That you know of. What if they just didn't walk in the camera's view?"

Delia purses her lips and then turns away.

"I'm going to call and find out," I inform her.

She waves her hand as she enters her bedroom and shuts the door behind her.

I don't waste a second. I dial Jeremy's number. We went to high school together and played football. He'll tell me everything.

"Hey, Josh," he answers on the first ring.

"Hey, Jer, listen I'm calling to ask you about the break-in by Delia's house."

"Oh, that . . . dude, if I was friends with her, I'd be worried . . ."

Well, that's all I need to hear.

Sixteen

DELIA

"You are not moving in. No. Nope. Not . . . *no*," I say again, wondering what second dimension of reality I'm living in.

"It makes sense."

"It does? How?"

Josh nods. "I live in an RV. I hate it. Oliver hates living with Grayson and needs to move out before Jess has the baby, and . . . you're not staying here alone."

He's lost his fucking mind. They say that women go crazy when they find out they're pregnant, but I've never heard of the father losing his damn mind.

"I'm perfectly fine living in my own house alone."

He crosses his arms over his chest. "Do you know what Jeremy's first words were when I called him?"

"Where are the donuts?"

Josh's brows lower. Apparently, he doesn't find me amusing. "No, it was that if he were friends with you, he'd be worried. Then he said he wouldn't let you be alone if he were me."

Now that pisses me off. "*Let* me?"

"Yes, let you. He'd protect you."

"Jeremy can't protect himself, let alone someone else."

"Delia." His voice is low with warning.

"I'm not alone. I have cameras. Plus, I'm not some damsel in distress."

"No, you're the mother of my child, which is far more important."

My jaw falls open, and I blink. "You're taking this a little too seriously."

"By wanting to protect you? By caring that you're out here alone and without a neighbor close enough to hear you if you need help. If you stopped for a second, you'd see how my moving works out well for everyone."

I laugh once because none of this works. Him staying in my home does not bode well for the no sex thing since we had sex not even five days ago. Not that there's much of a chance of that at the moment since I want to shake him until the sense he has comes back.

"You're not moving in with me. It would never work!"

"Why?"

"Are you *insane*? What do you mean *why*? I want . . . I can't have you living here!"

"But you're over me," Josh reminds me.

I glare at him. "So, you're going to be fine if I bring a guy home?"

His jaw clenches, and there's fire in his eyes. Exactly.

He may not be able to love me, but there's feelings beyond

friendship. A man doesn't react that way if there are no feelings.

"Do you have plans to bring someone home?"

I shrug. "I could."

"Right. So, is that a yes?" The steel in his voice goes
straight to my core.

Oh, I like jealous Josh. He's a lot a bit sexy.

No. No sexy. No anything with sex in it.

"I don't, but that doesn't mean I won't at some point.
You've made it clear that you don't want a relationship, and I
get it, but I want more."

"Delia." He says my name with a hint of pain in it.

"No, you living here would be a mistake."

"You have two bedrooms."

"Yes, and the second one will be the baby's."

He sighs. "We have about seven months before that room
is needed. It works, Delia. I'm here every day to work on the
floors. Once I finish with those, there are other projects as well
as the baby's room that will need to be redone. I can give Oliver a place to stay and be here to help with the renovations and
make sure you're not alone. What if someone breaks in? What
if you're here—by yourself—and this crazy person gets past
your state-of-the-art alarm system?" The sarcasm is thick on
that last part.

"Grrr." I am really getting annoyed. "I have neighbors!"

"Oh, yes, that's reassuring. I'm at least thirty minutes away
now. If I stay here, I'll be thirty seconds."

I cannot believe I'm even listening to this, but he has a
point about the break-ins. I may joke that Jeremy is a horrible
cop, but Mrs. Garner was completely freaked out, and I can't
dismiss that. If Josh is here, it might bring a little comfort to

her too.

"I don't know . . ."

He walks over, taking my shoulders in his big hands. "Think about it. It works out that you'd have me near if you needed me. We'd have some time together to get to become better friends before the baby comes, and you'll have your own personal errand boy for when you get a craving in the middle of the night. But we're about to be parents. So, if for nothing other than the baby, we should figure things out before he or she arrives."

I shake my head, refusing to listen to his reasoning that sounds so damn appealing. "I don't know. I have to think about it."

"It's not a no."

"It's not a yes either."

"Where do you want me to put this?" Oliver asks as he carries in a box for Josh.

"The second bedroom," Josh yells from the car.

Two days. That's all it took before the man was moving into my house. I am so damn weak.

Oliver walks over to me and then kisses my cheek. "Bless you. You're doing the Lord's work."

"Shut up."

He laughs. "I'm serious. You're giving me a place to live, free from Amelia and her way-too-fucking-early play time. Not to mention Jess is seriously about to burst and so, so cranky because she can't sleep."

"You're a horrible uncle."

"That's just it, I'm not. I'm the best, and it's because I don't live with them."

I roll my eyes as he passes me. Josh walks in next with a much bigger box. I huff and then walk into the kitchen to get myself something to drink, wishing it could be vodka.

Today, I've felt so nauseated. I've been lucky in that I haven't had any morning sickness before now, but I've been on the verge of puking all day.

Might be stress of having a tall, hunk of a man sleeping in the room opposite of mine for a while.

The first thing we agreed on was that he will not be sleeping in my room. I am not remotely strong enough to turn down that temptation. The second was that we have to be respectful of the other person's life. If he wants to date, I will pretend not to give a shit while secretly wishing her a lifetime of diarrhea. If I date, he will not say a word to intimidate or be rude.

"Delia?" Josh calls from the door of the kitchen.

I turn, letting out a low breath. "Yeah?"

"Oliver is done, he's going to head to Melia Lake and then meet us at Grayson's."

"Why are we going to Grayson's?" I ask, not aware of this plan.

He smiles. "Jessica's water broke."

Seventeen

DELIA

"**S**he's perfect."

"She is, isn't she?" Jessica says with tears in her eyes.

"Did you decide on a name?"

Jess's gaze moves to Grayson, who is out in the hall calling his siblings. "No. Grayson doesn't like the names I picked, and I really hate his."

"What's your top choice?" I ask.

"I like Adeline, but he says it's going to be hard having two girls with names that start with A."

I smile. "He might be right, especially if you have another one after her."

She sighs deeply. "He likes Ember."

I purse my lips and think on that. "You know . . ."

"I know, I know. It has meaning, and it's pretty. But, like, do we need to immortalize the fire?"

I rub my finger against her daughter's cheek. "She's not the ash from the fire, but the ember that remains warm. I think it's beautiful, just like her mother."

Jessica looks back down at her, a tear falling. "She is, and you're right. She stayed alive, enduring and fighting to be here. I . . . I . . . ugh. I hate that you're both right. She is Ember, isn't she?"

I let out a soft laugh. "I think she is."

"I think so too."

"I'm so happy for you." I look at the sweet little girl in her arms, and my lip trembles. This is going to be me soon. Maybe not the girl part, but the holding a baby part. I'm not ready.

I sniffle and turn away.

"Hey, what's wrong?"

"I'm just so happy."

She laughs. "So, you're crying?"

I open my mouth to tell her that I'm pregnant, but stop myself. It's her day, and I'm not going to take away from her. Plus, I want to get through the first trimester and out of the danger zone before telling everyone.

"Isn't that what we do when we're happy?" I ask.

Jessica kisses the top of Ember's head. "I guess it is."

Grayson enters the room, looking at us with a slightly terrified look in his eyes when he sees us whispering. "You okay?"

"I picked the name."

"You . . . picked the name?" he says carefully.

She nods. "Ember."

He lets out a sigh and then chuckles. "Delia liked it?"

"She did."

Jessica looks up at me. "So, I hear that Josh moved in?"

"Today is the day your daughter was born, we don't have to discuss that."

"Oh, I think we do," Jess says with her head tilting to the side. "Is there anything else you want to tell me?"

I shake my head. "No, nothing to say."

"Really?" she asks again. "Because, well, I'm not stupid, Deals."

"I never said you were."

Grayson gets up from the edge of her bed and backs toward the door.

"I know, but you and Josh . . . like, I'm pretty sure that you're a lot more than you're saying."

What, like, pregnant?

My heart stops for a second, and Grayson's feet stop moving. He looks back to me and then to Jessica.

"Jess . . . do not get involved in this," he warns.

"I agree with your husband."

She rolls her eyes. "I'm not getting involved. I'm worried about a friend, and I'm helping."

"There's nothing to help, Jess. I'm fine, and Josh moving in with me made sense because he's an overprotective ass."

"Jeremy did say these break-ins were something to be concerned over," Gray offers.

"Jeremy also believed there was a ghost under the bleachers that would grab your ankles at the football game."

Grayson has the decency to look ashamed. "It was a prank."

"He wore garlic around his neck for a whole school year to ward it off," I add on. "He's not all that bright."

Jess smiles and then shrugs. "Gray was very convincing."

"I'm just saying that Jeremy is the last person we should be taking advice from."

"Josh seems to think there's some validity. I know that we are setting our alarm again, and I'm a bit more vigilant," Grayson says as he moves to Jess's side. "There's nothing a man won't do to protect the things he loves."

I laugh once. "We all know that Josh doesn't love me. He's just . . ." He's just protecting me because I'm pregnant.

God, this is so damn hard to keep to myself. I want to scream and tell her everything. Jessica is my best friend, and I hate that I haven't told her yet. However, I need more time to wrap my head around it as well as I'm worried it won't stick. My mother has a history of miscarriages both before and then after me.

"He obviously cares about you enough to move in," Jess says.

"Because he's a stupid guy," I say with exasperation. "There were two possible break-ins, and suddenly, he's worried for my life."

Jessica laughs. "We all know that Josh is complicated. He always has been, but the one thing I will say is that he won't let the people he loves get hurt."

I force myself not to glare at her. I honestly don't want to hear it anymore. I let false hope take root. "Enough about me. Let's talk about your beautiful daughter and how perfect your life is."

"It's not perfect, but it's our family."

"It's perfect, Jess."

She shrugs. Both of our gazes move to Ember, and I force myself not to feel sad because my day won't come along with the same joys about being a family.

"Maybe a little."

I smile, my heart aching a little. "Yeah, maybe a little."

"Are you heading to bed?" Josh asks as I put the mug from my tea into the sink.

I lean against the counter and nod.

Josh shifts his weight from side to side. "Do you work tomorrow?"

"No, I'm off."

"Okay. Would you . . . like to watch television or something?"

He looks so cute when he's uncomfortable. "Sure. I was going to head to bed, but we can watch something."

We head into the living room and sit on the couch with at least two feet between us. Jesus, this is going to be a lot of fun.

"What do you want to watch?" I ask.

"You can pick."

"I don't really watch television. I usually read, but I'm sure we can find something."

After fifteen minutes, I give up, tossing the remote between us. Each thing I chose, he vetoed and vice versa. Do I look like I want to watch sports? I don't even understand half of what they're talking about.

Josh grabs the remote, muttering under his breath, and puts on one of the shows I was enthusiastic about. It sort of fit both of our wants, it's a love story, it's set in the 1800's England, and it's all about the game of what I think was rugby. It is perfect.

Episode one cues up, and we end up settling into the same position. Our hands are clasped in front of us, legs straight, and our postures so still it's as if we don't like each other.

It's like middle-school-dance level awkward.

"Josh?" I say softly.

"Yes?"

"Is there a reason we're being like this?"

He laughs, lifts one arm, and jerks his head. "Come here."

I don't wait, not just because I love the feel of his arms around me but also because today has been draining.

Jessica had her baby, Joshua moved into my house, and I took a stupid vow that we wouldn't have sex again.

I lie on his leg, and he pulls the blanket over me before resting his hand on my hip.

The show goes on, and it's really good. I mean, I could do without all the sports stuff, but then it wouldn't really make sense. I close my eyes, feeling warm and safe. Josh's hand moves up and down my back, and then his fingers graze my cheek.

My mind wanders between all sorts of nothing, and before I know it, I'm completely unaware of anything other than how content I feel. I can't remember the last time I was this comfortable with another person.

Eighteen

JOSHUA

This feels *too* right.

Too perfect.

Too easy.

And I've learned that there is nothing in life that stays that way.

I brush her hair back as she lets out a deep snore. That shouldn't make me smile, but it does. Moving in with her was a risk, but there was no way in hell I was going to let another woman be hurt if I could do something about it.

I will protect Delia.

I'll do everything for her because, while I will never allow myself to love her, I won't lose her either.

She shifts a little, and I pull the blanket up higher. I should wake her and put her to bed, but I don't. Instead, I pull her over a little so I can slide myself behind her, spooning her and holding her against my chest.

I tell myself that I'm not going to stay like this, but then my hand moves around her and rests on her stomach.

There's a child in there—our child. Something that was made because of us, and I'm still unsure of how to process it. If there is any woman in the world I would want to have a child with, it's her.

Delia has always been my weakness.

"You have no idea how much I hate that I'm not a better man," I whisper to her, knowing she's sound asleep and can't hear me. "I would give anything to go back in time and change things so that I was a better man who could not be so damaged. I just can't. I can't risk it, and you, Jesus, you would be the end of me." I may have lost someone I loved before, which was horrific and changed me irrevocably, but Delia is another stratosphere of feelings. "I worry just as much as you do," I confess. "Touching you, holding you, being with you is so effortless that I know I'll let my guard down."

She moves a little, sighing as she snuggles into my chest more. "Josh," she says, but her eyes don't flutter.

"And I'm undeserving of the reverence in your voice."

Her breathing is soft, and as much as I want to stay like this, I am smart enough to know it would be a mistake. I've made a lot of them, and I won't do anything else that will hurt her.

I push myself up, kiss her lips, and climb over her carefully. Once I'm in front of her, I pull her into my arms and carry her to bed. She mumbles something as I put her down and then tuck her in.

Using every ounce of restraint I have, I go into my room and stare at the ceiling, hating myself.

There is no sleep for me. All night, I thought of all the thousands of tiny decisions that brought me to this point. So many mistakes. So many things I should've done differently. In the end, none of it matters. I've decided the only way to make this situation work is to find a way for our friendship to survive. I get out of bed and get to work on phase one of our new living arrangements—breakfast.

The RV gave me zero chance to really cook. It was mostly heating up things and going to Jennie's when I was done with cereal or instant oatmeal.

Today, we're having the works. Eggs, bacon, waffles, and hash browns. Of course, I already went out and got her coffee, which should make her slightly more agreeable.

"What the—" Delia's voice causes me to turn. "Oh, God, you're one of *those*?"

"One of what?"

"People who like the morning and breakfast."

"Who doesn't like breakfast?" I ask, wondering because everyone likes breakfast.

"Umm, normal people."

"I think you have that backward," I tell her and then return to making the waffles.

"There's bacon, hash browns, and eggs over there."

Delia makes a noise, and I twist in time to see her hand fly to cover her mouth.

"Are you okay?"

She shudders and swallows a few times, getting only one word out. "Eggs."

"Yes, these are eggs," I say, mid-egg crack.

Her shoulders jerk a little and then she rushes from the room. "Crap," I mutter and then rush after her.

The bathroom door slams, and I hear her get sick. I didn't think about morning sickness.

I quickly clean up the kitchen, hiding any evidence of the eggs.

After another minute, the sink runs and then she opens the door.

Her coloring is pale, and she sighs deeply. "I can't look at eggs."

"Noted."

"That was embarrassing."

"You're pregnant, and I'm pretty sure food aversions are normal," I tell her, hoping to ease her anxiety.

She shrugs. "They are. I don't like mornings, and I like food in the morning even less."

"Then what do you like?"

"Coffee," Delia answers without pause.

I grin. "Well, that I have."

I lead her into the living room and away from the food or possible egg sightings before heading back into the kitchen to grab the coffee. She curls up against the arm of the couch, her legs beneath her as she sips from her cup.

"Thank you," Delia says as she seems to settle in.

"You're welcome."

"Sorry about your failed breakfast."

"I'll eat, don't worry."

She laughs. "Well, I appreciate it. I only used to eat breakfast when I worked nights because it was more like dinner."

"I see."

"I usually wake up with just enough time to get in the shower and get to work. So, yeah, mornings aren't my thing."

"Maybe you haven't had a reason to wake up before . . ."

"Oh, and are you that reason now?" she asks with her brow raised.

I lean in a little, unable to resist the allure of Delia. "Maybe."

"Maybe is an elusive answer."

I want to tell her the words she desires. To promise her that I could be more, give her more, but broken promises are all I can guarantee.

I go to open my mouth, when a knock on the door breaks the spell.

She blinks and then looks toward the front. "Who the hell?"

I shrug. "There's one way to find out . . ." I get up, going to the door. When I open it, a cake is thrust toward me.

"Oh, it's true!" A four-foot-eleven inches Mrs. Garner says. "I told you, Marivett! I said I heard that Joshua Parkerson moved in right next door, and you didn't believe me. But look, he's right here."

Mrs. Villafane, who stands a whole foot taller than her friend, smiles. "I heard you, Kristy, but I wasn't going to just take your word."

"Because I'm ever wrong?"

"Even a broken clock is right twice a day," she says with exasperation.

"Well, I was right this time. Look at you, you're all grown up and so big and strong. Isn't he big and strong, Delia?" Mrs. Garner asks, looking over my shoulder.

"Yes, he sure is," Delia replies with a laugh.

God help me. Mrs. Garner and Mrs. Villafane are complete

opposites in every way. From their personalities to their looks and the sounds of their voices. Mrs. Villafane is tall, skinny, and has darker features. Her voice is raspier, and her sarcasm can never be missed. And Mrs. Garner is tiny with a light complexion and an almost musical voice.

The two of them push their way into the house, and I honestly have no idea how it happened. "Come on in," I say even though they are already in the living room.

Mrs. Garner laughs softly. "That's so sweet of you. So, are you two a couple now? Bill says that you've been together quite a bit lately. I'm just taking a guess since you moved in here that there's something he's right about."

"Oh, please, Kristy," Mrs. Villafane breaks in. "We know better than to listen to that old goat." She turns to me. "But are you?"

"Uhh."

She continues. "I'd like to relay the correct information. Straight from the horse's mouth, so to speak."

I turn to Delia, hoping she'll offer some help, but she just grins. "We're friends," I offer an explanation that really doesn't give any information.

"And what kind of friends exactly? See, I was best friends with my husband."

"Before he became best friends with her neighbor," Mrs. Garner adds.

Mrs. Villafane slaps her arm. "You hush. Joshua would never do that to our Delia."

"No, of course not. He's nothing like his philandering father. We were so sorry to hear about your parents, but you see, we know that you're not like Mitchell. He always had wandering hands, but you boys, you're all good men." Mrs. Garner nods like the words are gospel.

I'm not sure what part of that to respond to. "Thanks, I think—"

"You're welcome, honey. Now, tell us. Are you a couple?"

"We're friends," I repeat, and I hear Delia snort. I turn to her, eyes wide, pleading for help, but she just shakes her head and shrugs.

The two older ladies share a look and then turn to me. "That tells me a lot."

"Me too," Delia agrees and then sips her coffee.

"So, you don't know what you are either?" Mrs. Garner asks Delia.

"Oh, no, we're friends."

Mrs. Villafane turns to me. "We'll just have to spend some time here today and help you guys figure it out. We're very good at problem solving. You know, just the other day, we were at Jennie's, and that Christopher Palmer boy was struggling with what to do about his feelings for Myra Prince. You know her?" I blink a few times, having no clue who she's talking about. "Anyway, he likes her and . . . are you listening, Joshua?"

"Of course."

Her lips purse. "Well, as I was saying we helped him out. Took a whole two hours to get him to finally see what we said in the beginning was right."

Delia grins. "That is so wonderful of you both. I'm sure that Christopher was so appreciative of that advice. And as much as I would just love to sit and chat with you, I have an appointment, and you'd just be doing me the biggest favor if you could help Josh out today."

"Help?" they both question in unison.

"Yes, help?" I ask.

Delia nods. "I was going to sit with him and talk about all the things that have been going on around here, you know, with the possible break-ins just down the road, but I have to go. Since you both are so knowledgeable about the situation, I was hoping you could help eat this beautiful breakfast that Joshua made and fill him in," Delia says, her voice rising with excitement. I'm in so much fucking trouble. "Come to think of it, he would probably love to listen to the scanner and learn all the gossip so he can protect us a bit better. Joshua is all about the protecting, and of course, if you happen to give him some advice, he could probably use that too," she adds on conspiratorially.

Oh, she's going to pay for this. So much.

"That's not really necessary," I say, not wanting to offend the two older women. "I have a lot of work to do."

Mrs. Garner rests her hand on my arm. "Nonsense. Delia is right, we should get you back into the thick of things, right, Marivett?"

"Oh, definitely. You've been away for a long time."

"I'm sure nothing has changed," I try to deflect.

"So much has!" Mrs. Garner says.

Delia creeps back toward the front door, and I give her a look that says we will be talking about her fictitious appointment at great length when she returns. Hopefully, by then, I haven't thrown myself off the cliff.

I clear my throat. "Delia, I think your appointment was cancelled."

She shakes her head. "Nope, it wasn't. I just got the reminder text. I have to get going or I'll be late."

Mrs. Villafane waves her hand. "You go on, darling, we'll

handle this."

The smile on Delia's lips is all mischief. "Deals . . ."

She clutches her hands to her chest. "I'm so, *so* sorry I can't stick around, but I appreciate you ladies helping our protector out here. He was extremely worried when he heard about the uptick in crime. So much so that he wanted to live here to make sure all of us were safe. He's the best friend anyone can ask for." I purse my lips and glare at her, but she doesn't seem phased. "I'll be back in a few hours. Bye!"

They wave to her as she exits—still wearing her freaking pajamas. When I finally drag my eyes from the closed door, both women's smiles tell me this is going to be a very, very long day.

Nineteen

DELIA

"I don't know whether to laugh or slap you upside your head," Ronyelle says as we're walking out to my car.

It seems that Mrs. Garner and Villafane have spread the gossip far and wide that the eldest Parkerson is living with me.

"I vote for laughing."

"You would."

I sigh deeply. "It honestly wasn't a choice. Things are really complicated, and . . . not that this uncomplicates anything, but it will at least give us a few months to get things right."

"What the hell do you need a few months . . ." Her brown eyes go wide. "No! No! Delia!"

I hush her, pulling her to the back of the parking lot. "Will you keep it down!"

"You're pregnant," she whispers, but she might as well

have yelled.

"Yes."

"I have no words, and I always have words. Lots of words. Words that come out in run-on sentences that no one wants to hear, but *you*—" She points her finger toward me. "*You* have rendered me speechless."

I would like to point out that her little tirade was filled with words, but I know better than to launch her into another tangent.

"I'm not full of words myself."

"Did you never hear of a condom? Or birth control? I swear, this town and the girls who find themselves pregnant . . . it's like no one paid attention in sex ed."

I let out a soft giggle. "It failed."

"The class? Yeah. I see that."

I huff. "No, the birth control *and* the condom. Trust me, we used both, and I'm here, a full-on statistic."

She blows out a breath and shakes her head. "So, what are you going to do? Other than let your baby daddy live with you."

"Can we never call him that again?"

She raises her dark brows. "What would you prefer? Stud? Stallion? Meat man?"

"Definitely not."

"Well . . ."

"I don't know what we're doing other than having a baby. The appointment for my ultrasound is tomorrow, and then we'll go from there. We haven't told anyone, so please keep this quiet."

"You know I don't gossip."

I nod. I think her iron clad rules about confidence and ethics is what makes her one of the best bosses at the factory.

"Stella is the only other person who knows."

Ronyelle leans against the car. "I don't know how you got yourself into this mess, but I can't say I'm shocked. You and Josh were bound to find a way to entangle yourselves together."

"That's not what happened."

She laughs once. "No? What do you call it? You're now tied to this man for the rest of your damn life. Birthdays? He'll be there. Christmas? Every year, sweetheart. That man may not want a family, but he's been bred to love the one he has. He will never turn that child away, and he'll want to be involved. Whatever man you decide to date, he'll be dating Joshua Parkerson too."

"Thanks for that stunning forecast of my life."

"You're welcome. On a serious note, are you okay?"

"I am," I assure her. "He took it really well, which was good. I thought he was going to freak out, but . . ."

"He may not want what he's about to get, but Josh has never run from responsibility."

"No," I agree. "I still wish it wasn't this way."

She sighs deeply, her head shaking at the same time. "Wishes are for fools."

I know that's true because I'm most definitely a fool considering how many times I wished for Josh.

"And I'm the biggest one."

She raises one brow. "You're something, my friend. Still, you know that whatever you need, we're all here for you."

"I appreciate that. I think it'll be okay. We've decided to go back to just being friends, so no more sex or kissing or cuddling."

Ronyelle's head jerks back. "Because you want to, what? Avoid pregnancy."

"Heartache," I reply immediately.

"I warned you about that after the first time."

She did, but I didn't listen. "I'm being smarter now."

"And you think that you're going to resist Mr. Sexy, who you can't seem to resist touching you, while he's living with you? Please. You're going to cave, and we both know it."

"No, I'm not. I'm being smart so that I don't end up hating him at the end of this."

Her arms cross over her chest, and she just looks at me. "I have my popcorn and the I-told-you-so poster ready."

"And I have mine because I'm not going there."

She nods with a grin. "We'll see."

"We will, and you'll eat your words."

My leg won't stop bouncing.

Around me, there are various women in different stages of their pregnancy. One is about to pop, her hands resting on her swollen belly, the other is maybe a few months along, just having the slightest bulge, and then there's the new mom, who looks . . . tired.

Josh grabs my hand, lacing his fingers with mine and placing it on my knee.

I turn to him, giving him a soft smile. "Sorry, I'm just nervous."

"That she'll tell us you're pregnant?"

"Yes," I say with a laugh. "It's just going to be weird. She said we'll hear the heartbeat and get the exact due date this time."

"It'll be fine, Delia," Josh reassures me.

I don't know that it will be. Everything feels so up in the air and confusing. I'm pregnant, and instead of Josh flipping his lid and calling me a whore, he's been really great. Other than the whole moving in with me thing, that is.

This morning, he woke me up with coffee and then ate his eggs, which he made with the windows open and a fan going, on the deck even though it was freaking freezing outside. While I probably deserved to puke after the day he had with Mrs. Garner and Villafane, he went out of his way to make sure I was comfortable.

Speaking of . . .

"Are you going over to check out Mrs. Garner's locks today?"

He gives me a side-eye glance. "Yes, after our appointment."

"It was very sweet of you to offer."

Josh snorts. "Offer? I think you mean got steamrolled into doing."

"Sort of sucks, huh?"

"What?"

I raise one brow. "Being steamrolled. This man I know, who is really hot and I hooked up with a few times, well, he did this same kind of thing to me."

Josh's lips twitch. "Did he?"

"Yup, one day, I made a comment, and the next thing I knew, he was moving in."

"Sounds like a caring guy."

"Oh, he cares like an overbearing brute."

Josh leans in. "Did you call me a brute?"

"Did you steamroll your way into my home?" I counter. As much as he did do exactly that, it's also more than any man has done to ensure my safety. It's kind of sweet, even if I have to sit on my hands to stop myself from mauling him.

"Maybe, but you're having my baby."

"And that means?"

He shrugs. "Nothing."

I huff and rest my head on the wall before cutting my eyes toward him. "Thank you."

"For?" he asks with confusion in his voice.

"Caring."

Josh's fingers tighten just a bit. "I've always cared about you, Delia. I've always . . . well, feeling and caring haven't been the problem for me."

No, it's been allowing himself to give me more.

"I know."

He'll love and care for our child, but we will just be friends. I fight back the emotions because, no matter how many times I draw that line between us or tell him that this is how it has to be between us, I hate it. I want more, and it's going to take me longer than a few days to find my footing in the idea that Josh will never shirk his responsibilities around our child, but that's as far as his love will extend.

The more I tell myself this, the easier it'll be.

When my name is called, Josh walks back with me. The nurse gives me instructions to pee in a cup and change into the paper gown so the ties are in the back before she lets us know that someone will be right in.

Josh goes to the chair, and I head into the bathroom.

Once I'm done, I hop up onto the table, draping the blanket over my legs. He sits there, looking extremely out of place, and I grin.

"What?" he asks, catching the look.

"Nothing."

"That smile isn't nothing."

"Just that you look like you're ready to bolt."

"What exactly is that?" He points to the ultrasound machine.

"Well, it's going to show us the baby."

"I know that, but what's that wand thing that looks sort of like . . ."

"It goes inside me," I explain.

He pales. "Seriously?"

"Yup." I laugh after he goes from pale to green. "It's fine. It's all safe, and it'll allow us to see the baby."

"How do you know all this?"

"Jess."

I went with her to an appointment before she told Grayson, and I got to see this part.

"Right."

There's a soft knock before the door opens. Josh gets to his feet as a very attractive male doctor enters. "Hi, Ms. Andrews. I'm Dr. Willbanks, an associate of Dr. Locke's. She's out today, so I'm filling in."

"Hi, this is my . . . the baby's father, Joshua."

Josh extends his hand, and they shake. "Aren't you a bit young to deliver babies?"

Dr. Willbanks laughs. "I assure you, I'm perfectly capable of handling Delia's care."

Josh doesn't look impressed.

"Steamroller?" I say softly, and he turns to me, rolling his eyes.

"Excuse me?" the doctor asks.

"Nothing," Josh replies. "I apologize, this is all new to me."

The doctor bows his head graciously. "I understand. It's a lot of information and very overwhelming." He opens the chart. "I see that you are already confirmed, which is great, and you're pretty clear on the conception date based on the situation. Your urine tested positive again, which we do each visit," he explains. "I see everything else looks good. Today we'll do an ultrasound, take a look at the progress, determine your due date, and hopefully, we'll hear the heartbeat."

I exhale deeply, looking to Josh with tears in my eyes. He moves toward me, taking my hand. I could pretend, for just a moment, that we're a couple and this is a joyous moment. That the two of us are a unit, bonded by love and happiness.

I could, but I won't.

Josh is a friend, a protector, and someone who is here because of duty, not love.

Don't fool yourself, Delia.

The doctor sets everything up and then explains what he'll do. "We'll try to do the ultrasound external first, and if we can't see clearly, we'll do transvaginal."

I nod, and Josh lets out a loud sigh of relief.

He's such a baby.

The cold gel goes around my lower belly, and then there's this sound. At first, it doesn't really sound like anything specific, but after the doctor moves the wand around a bit more, I hear it. This rapid whooshing sound.

Josh and I look to each other, and tears fill my eyes. "Oh my God," I say as it grows louder.

"It's so fast. Is this normal?" he asks.

The doctor looks at the screen, concentrating and almost ignoring us. Then his eyes meet ours. He smiles reassuringly. "The heartbeat is normal, plus, well, there is . . ."

"There's what?" I ask, feeling nervous that there's something wrong.

"Do you see this?" He points to something on the screen. "This is an amniotic sac, the placenta is here."

At first, I can't tell what the hell any of it is, but then he shifts the wand just a bit and there's no mistaking the shape on the screen. I blink a few times. "Are there supposed to be . . . two of each?"

Josh's hand falls away, and he shifts to get a closer look. "Two?"

The doctor nods, clicking a few buttons, and then smiles at us. "Based on the measurements here, you're about eleven weeks pregnant."

I shake my head. "That's great, but . . . that's two, right? There's an extra of everything in there."

Dr. Willbanks prints out the photo. "Yes. Congratulations. You're having twins."

Twenty

JOSHUA

Two. Twins. Two.

That goes around and around. I didn't even want one, and now I'm getting two.

"Josh?" Delia calls my attention as I'm walking in circles in the living room.

"Twins?"

"It would seem so. I mean, they do run in your family, don't they? Ugh. And they run in mine. Jesus!"

Right. Stella and Oliver are twins, so, yeah, I mean, it's possible. And now her family as well. I . . . two.

I run my fingers through my hair, wondering what the hell I'm supposed to say. Delia hasn't said much. We left the appointment in a daze. She took the photos from the doctor, who is probably still in training, nodded aimlessly as he asked if we were okay, and then drove back, not speaking.

Twins.

Two.

Dos niños.

Doubly screwed.

"I didn't think I would have them."

"I wasn't exactly anticipating this either, but here we are," Delia says, pulling the blanket around her.

I am being an asshole. I make my way to the couch and sit next to her. "You're right. I am just stunned."

"Same here."

"We're going to have twins, and we'll be fine."

She laughs once. "You're insane! We won't be fine! We aren't equipped to have one kid, let alone *two* of them! This is like some cosmic joke, Josh. Twins. Nothing is okay. I'm not okay. Are you okay? Because you don't seem so okay. You keep saying *two*, *twins*, and I don't know if you're aware that you're speaking. I'm freaking the fuck out. You don't love me, and now I have to have two of your babies? Do you keep one and I get the other?" Delia gets to her feet, starting to ramble and walk the same path I was pacing two minutes ago. "That seems insane, right? We don't split them, but then do you get one on one weekend, and I get the other? Again, that makes no sense. Now I have to wonder how to feed two babies, change two babies, clothe two babies. Not to mention, I am in my *prime*, Josh! My fucking prime, and now I'm going to have two kids. What man is going to want to date me? I'm going to be alone and fat and have saggy tits because two babies mean double everything. No one will want me!" Tears are streaming down her face, and she's throwing her hands up and down. "I am never going to find someone to love me." She turns, now shifting to anger. "And it's all your stupid fault!"

"My fault?" I ask, and I realize immediately that was a mistake.

She stalks toward me. "Yes. You had the condom that broke. You had to be nice to me that night and make me want to have hot, sweaty sex with you. It's. All. Your. Fault! Why do you have to be so damn irresistible?"

"I'm . . . sorry?" I say as more of a question, absolutely smart enough not to point out that she was who demanded I stay that night.

She groans and takes the blanket off the couch before tossing it in my face and then flopping down beside me.

I set the blanket aside and take her hands in mine. "No matter what you think, you are not going to be alone or fat."

"You don't know that."

"No, but I know that you could never be anything other than gorgeous." She shakes her head, but I continue, "I mean it. Any man who says otherwise is stupid and doesn't deserve to breathe the same air as you."

"That's sweet."

The saddest part is that I'm the stupid one. I know she's beautiful, funny, sweet, and everything a man should want. I also know that she loves me. So, here I am, letting this amazing woman walk around, believing I don't spend every hour of the day thinking about her, wishing I were a better man.

Delia sighs. The sound of defeat nearly breaks me. "What do we do now?"

I haven't a fucking clue. I will say that I'm smart enough not to say that to Delia. "We take a little time and figure it out."

"You know, we said we'd figure it out a few weeks ago, and you moved into my house."

"See how efficient I am? Now you don't have to worry

about having to take care of two babies alone because I'm here."

"Yeah. You are."

"Delia!" I call for the tenth time because she's still in her room getting ready. "We're going to be late."

"We're fine!" she yells back.

I look at my watch, the seconds hand taunting me with each tick. Stella will kill me if I'm not there on time. Four days ago, she called me, asking if I'd be the brother to walk her down the aisle because she decided not to invite our father to her wedding.

I can't imagine it was easy for her. As a kid, she spent way too many hours playing dress up for her imagined wedding. I can remember the one time in particular when she burst into our father's office with her white dress and requested their first dance.

It was one of the few times I saw him actually be a good father and oblige her.

That won't be the memory she makes today.

The minute hand moves. "Delia! Baby, we have to leave."

She opens the door and sighs. "I'm fat."

She is absolutely not fat. "You're beautiful."

Her eyes are brimming with tears. "I can barely get it to zip up. I wasn't supposed to start gaining weight yet, but . . . the cakes and the pregnancy and we're having twins," she rambles.

I walk to her, nudging her chin up so she can see my face when I say these words. "Delia, if there were a thousand women standing here right now, none of them would even compare to you."

She steps closer, her hands moving to my chest. I lean down and kiss her. It wasn't a thought. I just had to kiss her lips. She moves her hands up over my shoulders and into my hair, the two of us lost in the sensations. I press her back against the wall as I kiss her deeper, pouring everything I feel that I keep buried into it.

Too soon, she gasps and turns her head to the side. "We can't. I can't."

I step back, the loss of her immediate. "Shit. I shouldn't have . . ."

"It's not because I don't want to," Delia explains. "It's because I want to that we can't."

As convoluted as that sounds, I get it. "We're roommates, that's the agreement."

Her eyes shift to mine. "Right. Roommates."

I swallow and run my hands through my hair. "I'm sorry, Deals. I . . . well, I'm sorry."

"I really wish you'd stop apologizing."

"I wish I would stop doing things I need to apologize for. Anyway, I just wanted to say again that, clearly, I think you're stunning and I am going to struggle to keep my hands off you all night."

Delia bites her lower lip. "That is also the agreement. No touching and, you know what, Josh?"

"What?"

"I just decided this is going to be a lot of fun for me."

"Fun?" I ask, feeling a little uncomfortable.

"Yes. See, you want me. I know you want me."

"That has never been in question."

Delia takes a step closer, her finger runs down my chest. "Yes, that has never been our issue. The issue is that you have some reason that you keep this heart locked up. Until you find the key, there's no touching what you want, right?"

Oh, fucking shit. "This isn't a game."

"No," she says softly. "It's not. It's our lives. Our futures, and so, I've decided that I'm going to make this very hard for you. I'm going to show you all the things you're missing out on by choosing to keep me as your friend and roommate."

"Great."

She laughs softly. "I think it just might be—for me."

"You're insane. Do you know that?"

"I do. But so are you. Because I'm right here, Joshua." Her words break at that last part. "I'm here, waiting for you to get your head out of your ass."

I move closer, rubbing my thumb against her jaw. "I will only hurt you."

"One day, you're going to have to explain it because you keep saying you'll hurt me or fail me or whatever else, but you don't see."

"See what?" I ask, not really wanting the answer.

"That being like this, pretending that neither of us feel something more than this, is what's hurting us both."

"To the bride and groom!" Grayson lifts his glass, and we all follow the gesture.

I glance over at Delia, who is drinking sparkling cider from her champagne flute. She looks so happy and carefree. I hate that the only reason she's happy is because she's around everyone other than me. Delia and I were doing fine before today. I was keeping my head down, working on the renovations, and doing everything humanly possible not to think about my current mess of a life.

Stella and Jack head my way. My sister looks absolutely stunning with a smile showing her joy.

I extend my hand to my new brother. "Jack, really happy for you."

"Thanks, Josh. I'm a lucky man."

"That you are."

Stella shrugs. "I am a treasure."

"So you say."

We laugh, and he kisses her cheek. "I'm going to grab Kinsley and convince her to dance."

"Good luck," I tell him. All of her uncles have already tried to get her to dance, and she told each of us that she was keeping her options open. She's so her mother's daughter.

Jack heads off, and Stella grabs a drink from the bartender.

Sure enough, a minute later, Jack has his daughter on the dance floor, a wide smile on her face as her father spins her.

"He's a good dad," I say, wondering if that will be me one day.

"She makes it easy to be. I will never be able to express the joy she brings us."

"I'm glad, Stell. You deserve it."

She smiles and then lifts her hand to my cheek. "As do you, big brother."

"I'm getting there."

She rolls her eyes before turning her attention back to her husband and daughter. As the song ends, she turns back to me. "You look sad, Josh. I don't like seeing you this way."

"How could I look sad when I'm so happy for you and Jack?"

"That's not what I mean, and you know it. You keep looking over at Delia."

Like a moth to a flame, my eyes go there again. "I hurt her again."

She takes my hand in hers. "Then stop denying you're in love with her and that you're not worthy of love. Now, before you launch into some stupid excuse, I came over here for a reason."

"And what would that be?" I ask.

"Would you dance with me as my big brother who gave me away?"

"It would be my honor."

I know it was difficult for Stella not to have our father here. Regardless of the fact that he's a piece of shit, she loved him. We all did. My brothers and I did what we could to make the loss easier, which means anything she asked for, she got.

The DJ comes over the system, asking for everyone to please make their way to the dance floor as the bride is going to dance with her oldest brother.

"Why is he announcing this?"

Stella grins. "Because I don't have a father I want to dance with, so I picked my oldest brother, who has always taken care of me."

Now, I get another rite of passage, and I couldn't be more humbled by it.

I lean in, kissing her cheek. "You're very sweet."

"Don't let anyone know."

I pull my sister into my arms, and we sway. "Hero" by Mariah Carey plays, and she smiles up at me, singing the *words.* The words that are definitely not meant for me.

"I'm not a hero."

"You were always mine, Joshua."

"You were easy to save."

Stella's trust in me was infallible, but she also knows that any of her brothers would die before allowing anything to hurt her.

"When I was weak, you all protected me. You'll never know how much I love you guys."

I never thought we were doing something special, we just loved her. "It was just what you do for someone you love."

Her eyes move to her husband. "I know. I see that now."

"Jack is a lucky man."

She laughs. "He told me what you all said to *him* about needing luck being married to me."

"Tell me that you're an easy woman to live with," I challenge her.

Stella's smile broadens. "He really has no idea, does he?"

I spin her slowly. "Nope, and it's too late now."

"I'll go easy on him for a few months."

I shake my head and grin. "And this is why I'll never marry. It's never what we think, and we somehow fail the other person."

Stella's eyes fill with concern. "Josh . . ."

"No. Not today. It's your day."

My sister isn't one to let things drop, especially when she has the opportunity to give her opinion on one of our life choices, but I really just want to enjoy her reception.

"Fine, today you get a reprieve. It's nice that my wedding day won't have drama, unlike Grayson's."

I snort. "It's still early. Did you notice Alex being weird?"

She nods. "I think he's unhappy or something. I'm waiting for when he finally loses his shit. It should be funny."

"There's something wrong with you," I tell her.

"Oh, I know. But since Jack and I made a scene at Gray's wedding, I assume there's a plot to do something to mine. I figured it was you and Delia, but so far, you guys haven't given off a hint of the . . . you know."

The baby. Well, babies.

"Nope. We plan to tell everyone this week since she's out of the first trimester now."

Her lips part, and there's a warmth in her eyes. "Just love her, Josh. Love her because she's perfect for you." So much for not meddling. I go to speak, but Stella shakes her head, stopping me. "Don't say anything. I know what it's like to give up something you love. Jack and I endured an unimaginable hole in our hearts because we made that choice. When I handed her over to Samuel and Misty, I knew I was doing the right thing. It was the best choice for Kinsley to be raised in a loving home. Do you feel the same when you push Delia away? That she will be better off with someone else?"

"I'm living with her."

"Are you living with her or living in her house?"

I sigh. "I didn't realize there was a difference. Also, you really suck at this not getting involved thing."

Stella's smile is bright. "I think it's my right as your sister to step in when necessary. Now, shut up, let all of my brilliance sink into that thick skull of yours, and dance before . . ."

"Before what?"

A few seconds pass and the song cuts off.

I step back, and the mischievous smile on my sister's face says I'm in for something. Sure enough. That song—the song that she played every single freaking day—blares through the speakers.

"Everybody" by the Backstreet Boys begins, and when I start to back away from her, Stella grabs my hands.

"Oh no you don't, Joshua!"

"Stella."

She starts belting out the lyrics. "You know you love this song."

I don't know whether to laugh or cry because I really despise this song. All of us would beg her to stop, but she would just sing louder. My sister is many things, but a good singer isn't one.

Then, like the nightmare that was Stella's younger years, my brothers, Delia, Winnie, and Jessica line up beside her and start to dance as though they're recreating the video. Because, of course, she didn't just force us to hear the song. No, she made us watch the music video too. Over and over, blackmailing and browbeating us into learning the dance so we could entertain her.

Jack steps forward and starts to lip-sync the words to Stella, dropping down on his knees.

Then, because my only other option is to walk away, I line up, and pray that no one is recording this as I do the dance with my siblings while my sister laughs and smiles.

Twenty-One

DELIA

I can't remember the last time I had this much fun.

I've danced with all but one Parkerson brother, laughed, and enjoyed every moment.

In an hour, it'll end, and reality will creep back in, but for now, the problems in my life are on hold.

Jessica comes over with Ember in her arms. "Hey, you."

"Hey. How's she doing?"

"She's great. She slept through so much of it that I'm shocked. But I figure with Amelia's noise level, this probably is just a normal day to her."

I laugh. "Amelia is obsessed with her sister, huh?"

Jess's head moves side to side. "You have no idea, but she's wonderful with her. So loving and attentive. It's beautiful. Grayson and I are so very lucky to have two wonderful daughters."

Tears fill my eyes because, while Amelia isn't Jessica's biological daughter, she's never once viewed her differently. The two of them have loved each other from the minute Jess came into Melia's life as something more than just Grayson's friend, and I couldn't be happier.

I wish I could be happy.

I wish Josh was just a bit like Grayson and loved without fear.

"Why are you crying?" she asks with a laugh.

"You're such a good mom."

Jessica snorts. "I'm not sure why that makes you cry."

Suddenly, I have to tell her. I can't hold it in anymore. I am so drowning in this secret. It's too much.

"I'm pregnant," I whisper, and in the silence that follows, I wonder if she heard me.

But the way her eyes go wide and she stops moving tells me she did.

"You're sure?"

I nod. "I wanted to tell you, but . . ."

She grabs my hand, pulling me out of the tented area where we won't be heard. "You're pregnant?"

"Yes."

"It's Josh's, isn't it? That's why he moved in? That's why he's been so damn weird, and you guys were sneaking off all the time? Oh my God! You didn't tell me! You didn't tell me anything! *Delia!*"

"Will you lower your voice?" I ask through my teeth. "Yes, it's Josh's. Yes, it's part of why he moved in. The other part is because he says he's worried about the break-ins around my place. I don't really believe that though." I start to pace, my hand flying up and down as my emotions start to fray. "All of that is why, and it was my pregnancy test at Stella's spa day. I'm pregnant, Jess. I'm pregnant with Josh's baby, and that's not even the worst of it. We had our ultrasound the other day, and . . . we're having fucking *twins!*" I say the entire thing in one breath much louder than I planned.

Jess's eyes are like saucers. She clears her throat and then jerks her head to the side. It's quiet.

No music. No talking. Nothing but silence.

I turn slowly, coming face to face with the entire Parkerson clan.

Stella, Jack, Oliver, Grayson, Josh, and Alex are all there, staring at me with identical looks of utter shock.

Josh lifts his brows and then turns to them. "Well, I guess you all know now. Delia and I are having twins." He makes his way over to me, placing his hand on my back and whispers, "That was one way to do it."

"Twins?" Stella asks. "You're having *twins?*"

"Yeah, apparently they run in the family," Josh says sarcastically.

Josh's siblings rush forward, shaking his hand and offering us both a mix of skepticism and congratulations. Alex, however, doesn't move. He stands there, clenching and unclenching his jaw.

I go to him. "Alex?"

"I don't know what to say. Are you okay?"

I blink back the tears. Alex's concern is clear in every syllable. There's no censure, just worry. "I am."

"I just want you to be happy. You're one of my best friends, and he doesn't deserve you."

Josh does seem to have a way of constantly breaking my heart, but that's not his fault, it's mine for allowing myself the belief of *more*.

"Maybe not, but we're in this now."

His gaze turns to Josh as he walks up next to me, and while there was worry before, now there's something else. "You hurt her, and I'll never fucking forgive you. You'll be just like him."

I flinch, knowing the *him* he speaks of is their father. Alex will never forgive the things his father did. For so long, he thought he wanted to be like him, and when he learned how morally bankrupt that man really is, it broke him.

"Delia and I will handle this," Josh says, not rising to the bait. "You can offer your feelings later, which I'm sure you will."

"I'm sure too."

I reach out, taking Alex's hand. "I'm okay."

He gives me a sad smile. "If you say so."

Gray is the next one to offer his congratulations.

Then Oliver comes forward. "I don't know what the hell is going on in this town, but we've been back a few months, and it's like the water is tainted. People getting married, having babies, kids no one knew about. What the hell is next?"

"Maybe it's just all the Parkersons being around because, before this, we were all fine."

Oliver looks to Josh. "So . . . twins."

"Twins."

He laughs. "You're so fucked if they're anything like Stella and me."

"No shit," Josh agrees.

I'd been worried about the baby phase, but now I remember all the trouble Oliver and Stella caused when we were kids. If it wasn't one doing something, it was the other. They were hellions, egging each other on to do stupid things.

I look at Josh with fear. "They won't be like them, right?"

"I fucking hope not."

"I won't survive it."

He laughs. "We'll send them to visit their aunts and uncles as much as possible."

We sigh, and everyone starts to head off in different directions. Josh stands with me, his hand in mine. I feel bad, I should've been more careful about blurting it out. "I'm sorry I told everyone."

"Don't be."

"We had a plan," I remind him.

"Yes, but plans change. It's fine, Deals. No one cares, least of all Stella. I think she was ready to burst at the seams from having to keep this secret for so long."

I smile. "Maybe, but I still would've rather it happened another day."

Josh pulls me to his side, kissing the top of my head. My eyes close of their own accord, and I sink into his embrace.

God, it feels so nice to be held by him. Even after today, and the way I've felt each night when I'm not in his arms, but wishing I would be. I like this. I like him.

He lets out a low sigh. "Will you dance with me?" he asks.

He's the only one I haven't danced with. The only one I wished to dance with.

I gaze into those blue eyes, knowing I'll never tell him no, and smile. "I'd love to."

He pulls me to the dance floor. In his arms, I feel safe, which makes no sense because, of all the people I should be wary of, it's him. He's the dream. The wish. The never ever after. The man who will always be on the outside, not allowing himself in. I'll live in the memories of the times he allowed a moment of connection.

So tonight, during this dance, I commit every step, lyric, smell, and touch to my memory, knowing I'll be carrying it forever.

Twenty-Two

DELIA

We are officially out of the danger zone. I'm thirteen weeks pregnant, and I feel no better. Seriously, I thought I'd wake up this morning, feel like P-Diddy, and be raring to go. Instead, I'm lying on the couch—dying.

Well, not dying, but I want to do nothing.

Josh walks out, freshly showered, water still hanging from the tips of his hair, and I groan. Stupid, sexy, man.

"What?"

"Nothing," I grumble.

"I see you're in a good mood."

I shrug, my head lolling to the side as I push the air from my lungs. "I need sleep. Sleep brings good moods."

He comes over, lifts my feet, and then sits, pulling them on his lap. His touch sends tingles up my legs, and they settle where I really don't need tingles. One day, a casual touch by him won't be so bad. One day.

"What's the plan for today?" he asks.

"Not a thing. I'm going to just bake slowly today."

His brows crinkle. "Bake?"

I point to my stomach. "Buns are in the oven."

He smiles. "Good thing you're already preheated."

He has no idea just how hot I am—for him.

I brush that thought aside. "What are you doing for the day? House hunting, perhaps?" I hint. He was supposed to move in here to keep me safe. Since there hasn't been any other attempted break-ins for over a month, I think he should consider finding his place.

Josh smirks. "I'm good here for now."

"You know, this isn't forever."

"I know."

"Then you should probably start looking," I suggest.

"I will when I'm sure you're safe and after the babies come. You're going to want help with the twins, right?"

"I guess," I mutter and then huff. "You're currently sleeping in their room. This house isn't big enough for you to take up permanent residence. Where exactly will you sleep once they're born?"

Josh doesn't say anything at first. His eyes just study mine, and I swear he's reading my soul.

"We'll figure it out."

I raise one brow. "Right."

Instead of replying, he starts to run his thumb along the inside of my foot. And I moan. Oh, God how I moan. That feels heavenly. I can't remember the last time someone rubbed my feet, but this, this is amazing.

"Oh, sweet Lord," I say as he pushes along the muscle.

"Feel good?" His voice is low.

"So damn good."

I don't care that I'm completely embarrassing myself by moaning and arching my back. This is close-to-orgasm type good.

He moves his hand to the other foot, doing the same. My eyes close and sink into his touch.

"Josh?" I say as he massages in deep circles.

"Yes?"

"If you stop, I'll kick you in the nuts," I warn.

He chuckles. "Noted."

His fingers alternate pressure from light to harder. After a few minutes, he slows, and his voice breaks through the fog of pleasure.

"Let's do something together today."

I pry my eyelids open. "Like?"

"I don't know, isn't there fun baby shit we can do?"

I'll agree to whatever so long as he doesn't stop rubbing my foot. "I guess we could register."

"Register for what?"

I explain the entire process of registering for a baby shower. Jess claimed it was a lot of fun and gave her a really clear idea of the amount of shit she needed. Since we'll need two of everything, it couldn't hurt to get a small glimpse of things.

Josh's massage stops, and he rests his hands on my ankles. "We'll do that then."

"Go pick out baby things?"

"Yeah, it'll be fun."

"Fun?"

"Well, it'll be better than staring at the walls. Plus, Mrs.

Garner said something about stopping by—"

I sit up. "Let's go. Right now." I grab my coat and boots, and we head out the door a few minutes later. I love the winters in Willow Creek Valley, and there is always something magical about the first snowfall, but the part right before winter rears its head—sucks.

It's freezing, all the leaves on the trees are gone, and it's just gloomy.

What's not gloomy is Josh stopping at the coffee shop and getting me my favorite latte.

"You really know the way to my heart," I say as I sip the caffeinated goodness.

"You're not difficult."

I grin. "Coffee and new floors."

"And sex, let's not forget how much you like that."

I glare at him because we have not had sex since that day in my shower. In fact, I'm on a sex diet, which means cutting it out cold turkey.

I don't recommend it.

It sucks, and it does nothing but leave you irritated.

"I take it back," I say with a huff.

"Take what back?"

"That you know anything about my heart."

Josh laughs. "Do you suddenly hate sex?"

I put the coffee in the holder. "No. I don't hate sex. I hate pregnancy. And do you know why?"

"No, but I have a feeling you're going to tell me."

Oh, I so am. "First, it leads to unplanned pregnancy. Second, apparently, pregnancy makes you hornier than you usually are, which I'm not having. Third—"

"This list is long."

I continue as though he didn't speak. "*Third*, your body is invaded by other humans who make you hungry all the time while also making you incapable of eating most foods. Fourth, your friends who have had kids tell you every freaking awful story they can think of. I'm not sure what the goal of that is other than to terrify me."

"What stories?" Josh asks.

I shudder because, really, I don't think he wants to know. However, I shouldn't be the only one with these things haunting me, so I will edify him on the upcoming joys. "Things like, peeing your pants all the time. That you'll have extra skin, like a fucking kangaroo pouch because you're stretched like Gumby and it is wrinkly after. You get hemorrhoids that don't always go away after the baby is born. Oh, but the best is how you might shit during birth from pushing."

Josh's eyes widen, and he grips the wheel tighter. "Umm . . ."

"Oh, yeah, if that happens, I will die. I'm just warning you. You'll be a single father of two babies because I will have *died*, Joshua."

"I'll be sure to make sure no one ever lets you know."

"That would be wonderful," I say. "But, fun fact, there are fucking mirrors everywhere so the mother can see the joys of her vag being ripped open as a giant baby exits. Just imagine what I'll deal with because I'll get to see it twice. Like instant replay only it won't be a highlight."

He bursts out laughing. "Or it'll be beautiful because it's our children."

"Or that . . ." I say, feeling a bit contrite about him having to point that out.

Josh takes my hand. It seemed like such a natural gesture,

as if holding my hand as he drives, laughing about our babies coming into the world is somehow—right.

God, I need to see a shrink or have Ronyelle slap me upside the head.

He pulls our entwined hands into the center, resting them on the console. "Today, let's just forget about the horror stories that you've heard and have some fun."

I nod, not trusting my voice, as he parks the car outside the baby store.

"Deals, you good with that?"

My head turns, looking at his beautiful face, wondering why the hell my stupid heart doesn't listen to my very smart head.

"Sure. We'll have fun shopping for the twins." I smile and force myself to put all my worries away. This is the fun stuff.

We exit the car and head inside. After filling out the registry paperwork, they hand us one scanner gun and tell us to be practical.

Josh places his hand on the small of my back, leading me into the bottles and pacifier section.

When we got here, he was the practical, steadfast, and money conscious guy I'd known most of my life. And then . . . then Mary handed him this electronic that is almost like the gun from Duck Hunt, and the sensible Joshua Parkerson disappeared. Now, I have the lunatic who is on a power trip.

"Josh, we do not need that," I say as he scans some breast pump thing.

"What if we do? It's four hundred bucks, and I think my mother should buy it as part of her penance."

I blink. "You think your mother, who is now impoverished thanks to you and your siblings forcing your dad to come up with millions of dollars to buy out their shares of his company, is going to get us an expensive gift?" I ask, really wondering what universe he's living in.

"Okay, maybe not her, but someone. Oliver!" he yells and scans something behind him. "Oliver has no kids and money. He can buy us this overpriced thing you may need."

"Yes," I say with exasperation. "Ollie is totally the breast-pump-buying guy. Let's be real, he's going to get some stupid thing you're scanning that doesn't have a purpose. Gimme the gun. You're cut off."

He pulls it away as though he's three. "No. You should have gotten your own. Mary gave it to me."

"And you're messing up the process."

"Don't rain on my parade, Delia. I'm helping."

I shake my head quickly, taking it from him. "No, you're not. You're registering us for stupid things. We need two car seats, two cribs, two of these swing things." I scan them before I forget. "And you've gone scanner gun crazy."

He snorts. "You're just jealous that I'm better at scanning than you."

"Yes." I drag the word out, making sure the sarcasm is thick. "That's exactly it. It has nothing to do with my wanting us to register for stuff we might actually need."

"Semantics." Josh moves around me pulling the gun back out of my hand and heads to the car seats. "There. Car seats." He scans one without really looking. "You can thank me now."

"Those aren't the ones we need." I sigh. "That's a booster seat, which is what Amelia sits in. We need different ones."

He scratches his head. "It's a car seat."

I roll my eyes and point to the infant one. "Yes, but this is the one for babies and it snaps in and out and . . ." I groan.

"Just . . . stop scanning."

"But Mary at the front said it was very important for the father to be involved in this," he says with a smirk.

Oh, that smirk totally turns me on. Damn him and his smirky mouth.

"It's going to take me hours to clean up this list."

"What do you mean?"

I raise my brow with my own grin now. "It means that when we get home, I'll log on and erase all your stupid scans."

"You wouldn't," he says, his voice low and playful.

"Oh, I would."

He moves toward me quickly, wrapping me in his arms, and I giggle, trying to escape. "If you do, I'll come back here once a week and scan more."

"You wouldn't," I repeat his words.

"Oh, darling, I think we both know I would."

His gaze drops to my lips.

He's going to kiss me. He wants to, and I want him to so much. I am desperate for him and how his lips feel on mine.

"Are you both doing okay?" Mary, the not-so-helpful woman from the registry department, asks.

Josh flashes her a smile. "We're great."

"Oh, good, because it can be a bit overwhelming."

He nods. "Especially with twins."

"Oh, how wonderful. How far along are you?"

"We're still early on, but we wanted to get a jump on things," Josh explains. "Twins need a lot of stuff."

"Yes, they definitely do. Your wife didn't mention twins earlier or I would've given you a different items sheet. She just said you guys needed to register."

If a person could choke on air, Josh would be doing it.

"We're not . . ."

I finish so the words are mine, and I can save myself some smidgen of pride. "We aren't married. He has commitment issues and decided that knocking me up was an easier choice than dating me."

Her eyes widen. "Oh, I see. I didn't . . . I see, it's not that you have to be married. You both just looked so happy, and I assumed."

"It's fine," I assure her. "Josh and I were supposed to just be a fun night, and it kind of spiraled out of control. And now, here we are."

"Delia," he says with a warning.

I turn to him, batting my eyelashes. "What? I'm not lying to her."

He smiles at Mary but talks through his teeth. "She doesn't need all that information."

I shrug.

"I should be going." Mary slowly backs away. "I hear . . . someone . . . calling me."

"You do? I don't hear anyone," I say, wondering what she heard.

She nods and smiles. "Yes, I do, it's probably God or something."

I hold in my laugh, and as soon as she's gone, which is really quite fast, Josh and I burst into laughter.

"That was mean," Josh admonishes after his fit of laughter passes.

"Oh, whatever. It was all true, and it'll teach her not to assume that just because someone is knocked up it also means she's married," I say flippantly, even though I feel anything but.

My heart hurts because, while I joke about it, it's all I want.

And doing things like this. The laughing, playful, fun things where we hold hands and almost kiss as we pick out things for our babies . . . makes me crave more.

"All right," he says, flipping his scanner in the air and catching it. "Let's get to work and get registered."

I let out a breath and force a smile. "Okay, since we don't know the sex of the babies, we can't do crib stuff."

"Why not? We can do gender neutral."

I scrunch my face. "I have a design *idea*, Joshua, and if we have two girls then it's easy and we do all pinks and yellows. If we have boys, we'd do blues and greens."

"I thought yellow and green were the neutral colors."

"Yes, but I want them in a certain pattern. And I will probably change my mind a hundred times."

"I see," he says, but it sounds like he really doesn't see.

"Whatever, it doesn't matter. Until we have the ultrasound again in a few weeks, it's not . . ." Josh, being the child he is, starts to scan a bedding that is yellow and green with bears. "I don't want bears."

He takes my hands in his, pulling me down the aisle a little. "What about this one?"

I shake my head and smile. "Josh, we have to wait."

"Why?"

"Because it doesn't make sense to decorate until we know."

He scans it anyway, and I groan.

"Listen, at your place, you can decorate how you want, but at my house, I want bears and these weird things."

My lips part, and it feels as though I've been punched. "What?" I ask, barely a whisper.

"When the twins are with me, they'll need bedding, right?"

Yeah, they will. Because we're not together, and they'll stay at his house sometimes because I wouldn't keep them from him and just said earlier how he should be looking for a place.

"Right."

He squeezes my hand. "Good. Then maybe we should register for four of everything."

"Four."

"That way, we both have a set for each kid. I'd rather we both be prepared."

I swallow back the tears. "Yeah. Okay."

"Delia?" I look up at him, forcing my emotions to stay down. "Are you okay?"

"Just . . . the nausea is back."

His hand moves to the small of my back, and he leads me toward the rocking chairs. "Here, sit."

Don't leave, Josh. Don't go. Just love me and stay.

He presses his lips to my forehead. "You okay?"

No.

"Yes."

"I'll finish scanning a few things I saw while you rest. I'll be right back. I want to get that stroller for both of us."

I bite my tongue and nod, the tears pooling in my eyes.

Two *sets* of everything . . . including two homes because Josh won't ever stay.

Twenty-Three

JOSHUA

The last three weeks have been calm. Delia is working, I'm working on the house, and once a week, Mrs. Garner and Mrs. Villafane bring over some kind of baked good to thank me for keeping the neighborhood safe. Of course, I haven't done a damn thing, but I won't turn away their cake since it makes Delia smile.

Today, I'm hoping she'll smile because I finally finished the floors.

I hear her car pull up, and I'm at the door before she gets there. "Hey."

"Hey," she says with a weary smile as her hands move to rub her belly. It hasn't been until this last week that it seemed as if she were actually pregnant. I know she was before, but now she has the bump, and I swear, the woman is glowing. "What's up?" Delia asks as she comes to a stop in front of me.

I shake my head before taking her hand. "I have a surprise for you."

"Is it cake?"

"No."

Delia's lips turn down. "I like cake."

"I think you'll like this too."

I walk her inside and to the living room. The furniture, which had been shifted to the dining room, is back to where she had it. Except now, the floors are shiny, all new, and perfect.

"Wow!" she says, looking around. "It's gorgeous, Josh. Thank you!"

"You're welcome."

"No, really. Thank you. This is amazing, and you got it done—free, too."

She's smiling as if I just won the world for her. She looks so happy, and it's what I wish I did for her daily.

"Next, I think we work on the nursery."

Delia turns quickly, losing her balance, and I catch her. Her hands are against my chest, and I can't fucking breathe. For weeks, I've fought against the urge to hold her, touch her, kiss her all-too-perfect lips.

I almost lost that battle when we went shopping, and had we not been interrupted, I might have. When that woman said Delia was my wife, it was as though I got woken up from the dream.

Since then, I've been keeping my distance. I make sure that I don't touch her or hold her hand like I did that day. None of that because we're just friends who are going to co-parent.

But now, my hand is splayed against her spine, and she shivers in my arms while I wait for her to push me away. Instead, her pupils dilate, and when her tongue slides along her lips, I know.

She wants this.

I want this.

But . . .

Before I can think too much, she comes closer and she kisses me.

My hand moves up her back, holding her to me, losing myself in her. She tilts her head to the left, and I slide my tongue against hers. I drink in the slow moan that comes from her throat, and savor the taste of mint.

Delia and I clutch each other, holding on as the last few months of restraint crumble around us.

Holding on to her hip, my grip tightens, afraid she'll pull away. I want this. I want her. I need everything and yet know I won't give it to her.

As if she can feel me distancing myself, she turns her head to the side, both of us gasping for air.

"No." The single word comes out like a bullet from the gun. "No. No."

I lift my gaze to hers. "I know."

"I think you living here is a mistake, Josh."

"Why? I said I was going to be here to help you. I fucked up just now. I realize that, but if we're going to be technical, you kissed me," I say with a laugh, hoping to ease the tension.

Her lips purse.

"Okay, then technically, I didn't ask or really want you to move in here. You did it for my safety, and we can all see that's no longer an issue."

"Maybe that was why in the beginning, but it's changed. We're friends, and . . . I want to be here for you and the babies."

"Right," she says before wiping her tears. "Okay, well, *friend*, here's why I can't handle this. Because it's too hard to stop myself from wanting to kiss you. I keep wishing that you'll fall madly in love with me. For you to see that, all this time, it's been you for me. That's never going to happen, is it?"

"Delia, I'm . . . I don't want to hurt you."

I want to make her happy. I want to give her all the things she's asking for, but what about what I want? What about the fact that I didn't want kids or a family or to live with someone else? I didn't ask for this, but I'm doing the best I can to give us both what we need.

"You are hurting me! You're hurting me, and I don't get it. You danced with me, stare at me, you hold my hand, and I think: here it is. He's finally going to let me in. And then you don't."

"I have always been honest about where this goes. Not once have I said differently."

The one damn thing I have prided myself on is that. I've tried not to lie to her about the desire for more. I want it. I want it so fucking bad that I ache for it, but I don't tell her.

She takes a step back. "No, you haven't said it, but I feel it, Josh. So why won't you even try?"

"Because I know the ending of this."

"But that's where you're wrong. You don't know the ending. I appreciate that you want to be here for the babies. They are going to need you, and I know that you're going to be an amazing father, but I am losing my mind with you here. I get these glimpses of hope and then it's gone. Why do you do these things that make me feel like there's a chance for something when there isn't? Please, just tell me what has you so sure that we can't work. Is it me? Do you not want to be with me? If that's the case, then why are you in my home? Just find your place so we can just co-parent."

"It's not that simple. It's not that I want to be away from you."

She shakes her head. "Then what? Because if it's not that you don't love me or can't, then I don't get it."

I have been halfway in love with Delia Andrews for a long time, but saying it aloud would leave her open to hope. Giving her that would be the cruelest thing I could do to her because I've seen what that does to women I love.

I fail them.

I lose them.

I hurt them.

I shake my head. "You are too good for me."

"That's not the truth. I'm not perfect. I'm not too good. What I am is here." She steps closer, placing her hand on my heart. "Right here. In front of you with my heart in my hand, asking you to take it or at least tell me why you won't meet me halfway and try. Help me understand why you're so against all of this."

I shift away, feeling the ache of the past that I've buried gaining strength. I should tell her so she can see that she's wasting her love on me, but there's a selfish part of me that craves her love.

"Because I can't protect you! I can't assure you that I won't be what hurts you!"

Delia's eyes widen. "What are you talking about? I don't need you to protect me. I just need you to love me. To be here. To want me and not . . . not do this!"

"Do what?"

She pushes her arms to the side. "This! How do you do it? Because, God, I really want to be able to just shut the emotions off. I want to just go on like I did before, not knowing how good it feels to be with you. How do I close my heart off from you? Each time I look at you, I remember, wish, and want more. I want it to be easy for me too."

I close my eyes and see someone else's face. A woman I loved. A woman I lost because I was so selfish. "You think this is easy? You think I want to be like this?"

"No, I think you're too scared to be anything else, but I see you, Josh. I see the way you look at me. I see you reach for me and then deny yourself."

I shake my head. "And I see how much I'll hurt you."

"Then you have to leave."

"Delia . . ."

She lifts her hand, wiping away her tears. "I can't get over you. I can't get over what we could be when you're here, living with me, doing things for me, giving me these . . . moments . . . where all I want to do is kiss you. When you make me feel like I am special, and I swear you love me."

I do love her. God, that's the damn issue. I have always loved her. Then I caved. I let myself have a taste of her, and now look where we are. The idea of me leaving has me ready to fall to my knees and confess it all.

Maybe that's exactly what I need to do.

"Love is a lie."

"No, Josh, the lie is that you don't care."

"I care. I never said I didn't. I care so fucking much that it's why I push you away. I see what love does to people. The trust that's there right before everything falls apart and then you're left broken."

Delia steps closer, tears filling those brown eyes. "Who hurt you?"

There's the rub. No one hurt me. I'm the destroyer.

"What if I'm the breaker of hearts?"

"So, that means you'll break your own to stop from hurting me?" she asks, the truth in every word.

"That's exactly what I'll do."

Her lower lip trembles as she tries to smile, and then a lone tear falls. "Well, you're failing, Josh. You're breaking my heart right now."

The need to comfort her and make things better overrides my desire to keep her away. "Delia . . ."

She moves away from me. Her hands going up. "Tell me why."

She pushes, and I know there's no getting out of this. I have two choices and neither works for me. I tell her the truth of my past, let her see everything, and then don't stop her when she walks away. Or I don't answer her and be the one who walks out the door.

The issue is that I don't think I'm strong enough to leave her.

It's no surprise this is where we are. That she's pregnant, in love with me, and I'm desperate for her.

Delia is my biggest hope and my greatest fear.

So, I'll do it now. I'll break both our hearts and tell her the truth.

"You want to know?"

She nods.

"You're sure, because there's no going back. I'm going to break your heart more than you think I am now."

Delia wipes at the wet rivers running down her cheeks.

"Tell me so that I can understand."

"Fine."

Although none of this is fine. Nothing about that day is fine. Nothing about telling her is fine. In fact, it's going to destroy me.

"What happened, Josh?" Her question is soft and filled with understanding that I don't deserve.

I steel myself. Allowing the past to become the future. I see the face of the woman I loved. The trust that I didn't deserve in her eyes. The sound of her voice, the musical notes of her laugh, and the ending that neither of us anticipated.

"I killed her."

Twenty-Four

DELIA

My lips part, and I hear my own intake of breath. "What do you mean?"

Josh is many things, but a murderer is not one.

"You asked for the reason, Delia. Here it is. I killed the woman I loved."

"You're not making sense."

"Of course I am!" He practically roars. "I failed her. I was . . . I was selfish, and she paid the price for it."

A part of me breaks as I hear the pain in his voice. I move closer, slowly as to make sure he doesn't retreat. "Who did?"

His blue eyes move to mine, and the agony that fills his gaze makes my heart crack. Josh looks haunted, and I want to take it all from him, but I don't move. He's finally talking about what happened, and even though he isn't making any sense, I won't do anything that will destroy whatever progress he's making.

"Her name was Morgan. She was . . . well, she was beautiful and smart, and I loved her."

I try not to hurt, not to allow the words that I've craved and wished he'd say about me enter into this because this isn't about us, it's about him.

Josh's gaze doesn't waver. "It's my fault she's dead."

The certainty in his voice makes me pause. "How?"

"Do you remember the hurricane ten years ago?"

"Of course," I say quickly. The hurricane barreled through New Orleans. The destruction was . . . unspeakable. So many lives lost, homes gone, and it was catastrophic. I remember that word because it was said over and over again on the news. Alex was a mess, and no one could get in touch with Josh. The phone lines were down. Cell phones were barely working. It was days before we knew he was safe, and I swear, I died a thousand deaths while we waited.

"I'll never forget it. The sounds of a hurricane of that force coming through, it was . . . terrifying. My job was to make sure the guests at the inn were safe. I did everything I could from boarding windows to making sure we had water, gas for the generators, and food stored. I worked for four days—no sleeping, no stopping—to do anything possible." I try to take his hand, but Josh pulls away. "Don't comfort me, Delia. I don't deserve it."

"I don't believe that."

He gets to his feet, moving around the room. "If it hadn't been for me, she would have evacuated. Morgan would have been safe."

"You just said that you did everything possible."

The laugh that comes from his mouth is full of self-loathing. "Not for her. No, for her, I was thoughtless. I worried about the inn. I wanted to make sure my property and the people staying there were safe. But who cared about her? Who's responsible for her death? Me. I told her what to do. I was the one . . ."

I get up, refusing to let him push me away. Not this time. I approach him, standing closer than I know he wants, but not giving a damn. "The one who what?"

"She was so scared. She lived closer to the water, and we knew that she needed to get out of there. So, I told her to go to my house. My apartment was on the third floor and in a better location. The surrounding area would flood, but at least the house wouldn't."

"Sounds very reasonable."

"I told her I'd come get her because she didn't want to drive. She was afraid because there was already flooding where she lived." Josh runs his hands through his hair. "I told her to wait ten minutes. I told her I would come as soon as I finished one thing, but the storm picked up speed and started moving in faster. I was so focused on my job that I didn't leave when I said I would. It wasn't ten minutes, it was an hour."

I watch the memories flash across his face. His lashes fall and that single movement says everything about the pain he feels. Josh has always cared about the people in his life. He is protective, caring, loyal, and this is breaking him.

"That's not your fault. It was a storm."

"Yes, but I said I would go to her. I promised her that it would be fine and I would come get her. It was over an hour I was late. Too late to get to her and help her."

"Josh, that's not . . ."

"It is, Delia. It's my fault. I should've left when she needed me. Who cared about boarding up the fucking pavilion? I did. I cared about that more than her. She got in that car. She didn't wait because, when she tried to text and call me to find out where I was, I didn't hear my phone. I was busy, and she was fucking terrified. So, she left her house as the winds and rain raged."

My heart races, already able to guess how this story ends. "I'm so sorry."

"When I called her back, she was panicking. She pulled over, and I told her to just stay put and I'd come to her. The rains, you couldn't see. I couldn't . . . I couldn't see anything. I drove to where she said she was while the panic in her voice got worse." Josh's hands start to shake, and I take them in mine, lending him whatever strength I have. "The flooding came so fast. Between the surge and the rain, it just was . . . there was nothing I could do. I couldn't get to her. I tried so fucking hard. There were others there, we made a chain, and tried, but the current took the car and . . . I found out . . . I found out after that she was pregnant."

My breath stops. "Josh . . ."

"She was going to have a baby, and I let her and that baby die. I was right there. I was so close, and I watched her go."

I grip his hand harder, trying to ignore the idea that he very well could have died that day too. The selfish part of me is glad he's here, and then guilt weighs on me, reminding me that this event took something from him. It took a part of him, washing away and leaving him broken.

"Josh, you didn't kill her. *You* didn't. The storm did."

"I wasn't there for them."

"You were there. You were there, and she knew that because you tried to save her."

His eyes meet mine, and the shame and sadness is too much. "You didn't hear her scream for me or watch it happen."

"You tried, Josh."

"And I fucking failed!" He releases my hands and starts to walk. "I was there, Delia. I was right there, and I didn't reach her. Had I left five minutes earlier. Had I done a hundred different things different. Had I said fuck the goddamn inn and gone to the person who mattered, she and that baby would be here."

"But you wouldn't," I say the words, my voice even. Whatever he hears in it causes him to stop and stare at me. "You wouldn't be here, Josh. You wouldn't be in Willow Creek Valley. We wouldn't be standing here, having this conversation. It doesn't mean that what you've been through hasn't changed you." I step to him, and he stands ramrod still. "It doesn't mean that what you endured wasn't incredibly sad and painful. I'm sorry. Truly sorry that Morgan and that child are gone. If you loved her, she had to be special and wonderful. Their loss, it's tragic and awful.

"You're here, though. You're alive and here, and I am standing before you with my heart in my hands, giving it to you without fear. We aren't replacing all you've lost, but we're a second chance. I love you, Josh. I have loved you my entire life, and I don't care that you think you're undeserving because you're wrong. You do deserve to be happy."

I move again, and the tears in his eyes slash through my already battered heart. "Don't."

"It's too late. It was too late when I was fifteen, and it's definitely too late now." While he may not want it, my heart is his, and I'm going to push him to accept it or push him out the door. Those are the only options for me. I can't live this half existence with him. "Tell me this, did you try?"

He blinks, shaking his head. "Try to what?"

"After the current took her car, did you try to go after her?" I already know the answer. I didn't have to be there to see it or have him tell me. Joshua Parkerson doesn't give up on people he loves. He fights. There isn't a single doubt in my mind that, even as that car drifted, he was moving after it. That every person who made that human chain had to hold him back from going after her.

"I couldn't get to her . . ."

"Someone stopped you," I guess, but it's said as a fact.

"I would've drowned for her."

My hand lifts, resting it on his cheek and willing him to see that I love him and I'm glad he didn't die that day. His fingers wrap around my wrist, and the two of us don't say anything.

We don't need to.

I pour everything into this moment with him. The feelings I held back in the hopes that maybe they'd lessen over time, but never did. I give him all my love. I open myself to him, wanting him to see that while he's lost, he has a chance to have love again. We won't ever replace all that was taken, but it doesn't have to rob him of anything more.

"Delia." His voice is a whisper.

"Kiss me, Josh. Kiss me and see that I'm right here. I'm not going anywhere."

JOSHUA

I'm not able to stop myself.

My head lowers as Delia lifts up onto her toes. Our lips touch in the softest, most perfect kiss that any two people have shared.

Her tongue meets mine, and I'm pressing her to me, needing her, needing this. I have to forget, and she's the only thing that can help.

I'm raw, feeling as if I'm back in that water, helpless as I watch everything drift away.

But I have her. She's in my arms, touching me, holding me, kissing me like I'm giving her life.

"Delia." Her name is a prayer that falls from my lips.

The hushed moan that escapes her is swallowed as we kiss again. Her fingers grip my shirt, holding on as though I have any intention of letting her go.

She molds herself closer, and then we're moving to the couch. I pull her onto my lap, and her legs settle on either side of me as her hair falls around us.

"Josh, I need you," she confesses. "I need you, and I love you."

I take her face in my hands, pulling her mouth back to mine before I say something. I want to tell her that I need her. I want her. I am fucking losing my mind being in this house and not touching her. I ache for her and the closeness we had before. She makes me feel like I'm not a monster, and it's terrifying.

Delia grinds her hips down, rubbing against my straining cock. "Take what you want," I say, allowing her to have whatever she needs. "Take everything because I can't lose you."

I say too much, but maybe this is what we both need.

"You," she breathes the word.

"What do you want? Tell me, and you can have it."

Her deep brown eyes meet mine. "Make me feel good again. Make me feel beautiful. Make me yours."

Jesus Christ. She's the most beautiful woman there has ever been. I lift my hands, sliding them through her blonde hair. "You have no idea how perfect you are. How being around you makes me insane." Her eyes flutter, and I move my fingers down her throat. "Your skin, so fucking soft." I lean up but pull her hips toward me, kissing the skin where my hands were. Delia sighs deeply. "I want to kiss every inch of you, worship you."

"Yes."

"Yes? Is that what you want?"

She nods. "Yes. You, only you, Josh. You're what I need."

If this is happening, it's going to be done right. Not another fuck session. I'm going to do exactly what I promised.

I lift her, and her arms wind around my neck as I carry her to the bedroom. When I reach her bed, I lie her down, staring at the gorgeous woman before me.

"Say something," she implores.

"I can't. I can't because you're so goddamn beautiful, and I can't . . ."

She's here, and she's looking at me like I'm the sun. I am not good enough to be with her, but I'm not strong enough to leave.

"Then kiss me."

I move to her, taking her face in my hands and pressing my lips against hers. It feels like ages since I breathed, and now I know why. It's her.

She's been a weakness, but she's also my strength. I don't know what to do, how to fight it anymore.

Her love makes me think there's hope, and that's something I haven't experienced in years. Everything seems possible when I look at her.

Maybe we can be happy.

Maybe I've been battling the wrong war.

Maybe Delia is right, and had I not loved and lost Morgan, I might not be here right now, in this moment. I wouldn't be looking at the woman who I've always loved but was too afraid to give my heart to.

It's why I took the New Orleans inn. This woman. This wonderful woman has terrified me since the first time I saw her. She was fifteen, smiling with Alex as they watched some stupid movie. I was transfixed, sure that there was no way this girl was real.

She was so beautiful, and when she smiled, my breath was

gone.

I was already in college, and she was too young for me, so I stayed away from her until the night of her graduation. We were at the diner and both exited the bathrooms at the same time. I don't know what happened. It was instantaneous. Neither of us spoke before we came together in a crash, and I kissed her.

Maybe we could have it all now.

"What are you thinking?" she asks softly as her hand runs through my hair.

"Maybe," I answer. "I just keep thinking that word. Maybe."

I don't tell her more. Mostly because it's terrifying. The idea of allowing myself a chance at something more.

Her smile is soft as her fingers move down, brushing the scruff on my face. "Maybe is hope. Maybe is possible. Maybe is a start."

The words flow around us like a shell to protect the hope that is born from that statement.

I lean down and press my lips to hers. It goes on until I don't know where one stops and the next begins. We kiss for the past, the present, and the future. I lose myself in her touch, and small broken parts of my heart are put back together. I will never lose the scars, but in her touch, I can heal a little.

She pushes me onto my back and then shifts to straddle me. Her shirt is lifted over her head and then her bra follows.

I lift up, cupping each breast, which are just a little bigger than the last time I saw them. "You're gorgeous," I say as I move my hand down to her belly. The ache in my chest grows as I touch where our children are. "Delia." There are tears in her eyes, and I pull her into my arms. "Why are you crying, love?"

"I want this. I have wanted this, and . . ."

"You're afraid." I finish her thought.

She nods. "I want you. I have always wanted you, and now you're here. I want you to always be here."

I wipe the tears from under her eyes. She doesn't see that leaving her is the last thing I want to do. It's why I pushed my way into her home, saying it was just for her safety. It's why I couldn't even bring myself to call a realtor or find a new place to live. She's what I want. She's the part of my heart that has been missing and searching for this.

Her.

"What if you get sick of me?" I ask her, resting my cheek in her palm.

"Never."

The promise slays me in so many ways. "You say that now, love."

Delia lifts her other hand, taking my face in her grasp. "I love you, Josh, and I think you love me too."

Her brown eyes shine with all the promises of a future. "I do," I admit.

"You love me?" she asks, the tears pooling again.

"I think I always have, but I can't say it . . . I can't trust myself."

Delia leans in, her lips touch mine, and I'm fucking done. The emotions overwhelm me, and my need for her crashes like a wave on the shore. I can't stop it. I can't do anything but hold her as I get lost in the current. My fingers tangle in her long hair, guiding her mouth to fit better against mine.

"Josh," she moans, and I swallow it.

Carefully, I move her so she's on her back, close my lips

around her nipple, and suck. She gasps and makes soft noises as I move to the other. "God, yes," she says as I bite gently.

My hand moves down her torso, stopping just briefly over her swollen belly. I love that she's growing heavy with our children. That something I thought I never wanted is happening, and it's happening with her. My God, I'm a lucky fucking bastard.

I keep moving, wanting to touch another part of her. To make her feel the passion she brings out in me. The hope she rekindled.

"I want you so much," I tell her as I lift my head from her breast. "I want to make you come so hard that you pass out after. I am going to take you higher and higher until the fall makes you afraid, and I'm going to push you over it." She arches her back, and my finger slides under the seam of her panties. I touch there, knowing that she's aching for it. "Do you want that, Delia?" I ask. "Do you want me to make you come?"

"Yes."

I increase the pressure, just barely, and she lets out a deep throaty sound. "Does that feel good?"

"So good. You always feel good."

I smile. "Do you want more?"

"Please."

"So polite," I murmur as I kiss her belly on my way to where I want her most. "So beautiful." I kiss her lower and then pull her pants off. She lies there like a goddamn goddess before me. Her blonde hair spread out around her, eyes gleaming with passion, and her trust on full display. Delia doesn't move as she allows me to look at her, see her, take her. "So fucking perfect."

She shakes her head. "No, not perfect."

"To me, you are. To me, you're everything." I kiss her thigh and then move up, running my tongue along her clit.

"Josh." She sighs, and I do it again. I flick, lick, and suck. I want her shaking and desperate for me to take her to the peak. I need to be that man today. To do for her, give her, show her just how much she's ruined me.

I will never be the same again. Not after this time. When we had sex before, there was a part of me that I held back. I wasn't able to let myself love, not really. Now, she owns everything that I am, even the marred pieces of my soul that drowned that day.

My tongue swipes hard, moving fast, flicking her clit as she grips the sheets. I don't stop or let up. I want to hear her scream my name. To know that I'm the one. The only one who can make her crazy this way.

"God. Josh. Please!" she yells, and I slip a finger into her, pumping in and out as I suck harder. "Josh. Oh, God. I'm going to come."

I keep it up, and then I feel her muscles contract as she cries out. After the last of the spasms fade, I lift up, staring at her all flushed and sated.

Her eyes meet mine, and she smiles. "I need you, Joshua. I need you to make love to me."

I need it more than she can ever know. "This time will be different."

"I know."

"I won't be able to let you go."

"I never wanted to be anything else but yours." She leans up and pushes my pants down. As I kick them off my ankles, Delia runs her fingers up my arms and then along my jaw.

"Make love to me, Josh."

I move my hips, feeling her heat beckoning me. "Condom?"

She smiles. "It's a little late for that."

I push closer, my cock just at her entrance. She trusts me, and I don't know that I deserve it. I know I don't deserve her. This woman with a heart the size of Texas and the strength of Atlas.

As though she can read my mind, she lifts her hips slightly, pushing me deeper into her.

The warmth envelopes me, and I close my eyes.

"Take me, Josh. Take me because I have always been yours."

I open them, seeing the truth in her gaze. Without another thought, my hips move forward and I make love to her.

Twenty-Six

DELIA

Waking up in Josh's arms is new and dreamlike. A part of me, the one that has had this particular fantasy a billion times, is waiting for the weight of his arm to disappear and the sound of his heartbeat to be an alarm clock.

But the steady strum keeps it's beat beneath my ear. His arm doesn't disappear, in fact, it tightens around me.

I lift my eyelid, peeking up to see him looking at me with a lazy grin. "Good morning."

"Morning."

His hand rubs up and down my spine. "I don't remember the last time I slept past six."

I glance at the clock and gasp. "Holy shit! It's eleven!"

Josh chuckles. "It is. Seems we were both a little worn out."

The ache between my legs agrees. Last night was amazingly slow and perfect. The two of us giving ourselves to everything in the past and . . . well, I'll never forget it.

The next two times. Yeah, that was fun. Sweaty, messy, sex that made me thankful for the extra blood flow from the pregnancy. Wow.

"I could do with being worn out from that," I tell him, resting my chin on my hand.

"Same."

"We didn't get to sleep until four, so it doesn't shock me we slept half the day away."

He pushes the hair back behind my ear. "Are you okay?"

I hear the fear in his voice, and it causes my stomach to drop. "Do you still want to be here with me?"

"Yes."

"Then I'm fine."

He smiles. "We just aired out a lot of shit last night."

I sit up a bit, pulling the sheet around me. "We did, but I think it needed to be done."

Josh releases a long breath through his nose. "I guess. I haven't told anyone about Morgan. My siblings don't know. Honestly, I just couldn't talk about it."

"No one knew you were together?"

Josh pushes himself up, resting his back on the headboard. "I didn't want anyone to know things about me. My father used whatever he could to manipulate people in his life. I watched him break my mother down, bit by bit. When I was eight, he took me with him to meet his mistress. He figured my mother wouldn't think that was what he was doing if he brought his kid. So, I learned to keep my personal life far away from him. Look at what he did to Stella and Jack and to Grayson and Jessica. Hell, do you remember the girl Alex liked when he was in high school? All my mother and father cared about was appearances, and Morgan was funny, sweet, and would've been eaten alive by them."

"I'm sorry."

"It sucked, but it was better that way. I didn't tell my brothers or Stella in the beginning because we were so new, plus, they're a lot younger than me. We were only together a year before the hurricane and when I was going to finally tell them, I lost her."

"But they could've been there for you."

His eyes meet mine. "I hated myself. I didn't want comfort. I still don't want comfort."

"Well, too bad," I say with defiance. He may not want it, but I'm going to give it.

He smiles. "This won't be easy. It's been ten years, and I still haven't forgiven myself."

I shift so I'm resting against his strong chest. "I don't expect easy. Nothing is easy. I understand grief. My mother is still dealing with the unexpected loss of my dad. She punishes herself, whether she believes it or not because he had been showing signs of heart problems, but they pushed them aside since he was young. Losing him destroyed the hope of love for her. It doesn't always make sense, but I think losing someone like that changes you."

The low sound in his chest says more than the words do. "It does."

I know this. My father's death was hard on us all, but my mother took it to another level. She refused to even think about another man and would say her heart died when he did. Thankfully, she loved me as well and fought the despair and then she got cancer.

I can remember times during her chemo when it seemed like she wanted to die. Not because she didn't want to live but because she missed him so much. It's just recently that I think she's truly healing and seeing that it's finally time to stop mourning him.

While I don't think it's the same for Josh, seeing how he says he loves me, I think he still very much needs to deal with the trauma of having to watch Morgan die like that.

"The first step to fixing anything is admitting there's a problem, right?"

He kisses the top of my head. "You think I can be fixed?"

I lift my head, looking into his gorgeous blue eyes. "Not you, but the way you're thinking about it all. You need to forgive and allow yourself to be happy."

His thumb grazes my cheek. "I want to be happy with you."

"Then we just have to try."

"There is no one else I would be able to do this for."

I shake my head, holding his wrist. "No, I don't want you to do this for me, Josh. I want you to do it for you. You deserve happiness. You deserve love. You deserve to have all the things you want. So, don't do it for me, do it for you so that you and I have a chance."

He moves toward me at the same time I go to him. The kiss we share is soft, sweet, and tinted with hope that I'm going to hold on to with both hands.

Josh and I stand outside my mother's door, our hands clasped together while I gather the courage to go inside. While she and

I have the best relationship, there's a lot of apprehension about telling her that we're pregnant.

I don't know if I can ever recall us ever being angry with each other, but she has very firm beliefs on marriage and the order in which children come. So, I'm slightly afraid our first fight is going to be when I tell her that I'm unmarried and pregnant and living in sin.

Yeah, not really excited about this.

We talked every week while she's been away, but I never found the balls to tell her. It's probably a conversation best had in person anyway.

Well, if I ever go inside.

"Are we going to stand out here all day?" Josh asks.

"Maybe."

"Your mother is amazing, Deals. I don't know why you're nervous."

I look up at him and sigh. "We should tell her we're engaged."

Josh's eyes widen, and he sputters. "What?"

"If we do that, then maybe she won't be upset."

"Or we don't do that because we're not, and we tell her the truth."

I let out a half laugh. "Oh, yes, that sounds like a brilliant plan. Let's tell her that I'm unable to keep my legs closed and we were going at it so rough the condom broke."

"I don't think she needs details, but it's better than lying about being engaged."

I close my eyes, feeling a hundred times a fool. He's right. "I'm sorry. I just . . . I love her and don't want to upset her."

"I don't think it'll be bad."

"We'll see," I say and then finally open the door. "Ma? You

here?"

"Delia?"

"Do you have other children I don't know about?" I ask with a laugh.

She comes rushing down the stairs, a smile wide across her face. "I didn't know you were coming by! I just got home an hour ago and was going to come see you!"

"I saved you the trip."

I knew she was home because I heard it on the scanner app, which is actually pretty freaking cool. Josh and I keep it on when we're doing things around the house because it's amazing what people put out on there. Strange cars or bikers taking up too much space on the road, and the other night, there was a really interesting tidbit about a certain woman going into a certain man's home that was not that certain woman's husband. I get why Mrs. Garner and Villafane are always listening.

She doesn't break stride as she reaches me, pulling me into her arms. I close my eyes, sinking into her touch. There is nothing quite like my mother's hugs.

"I missed you so much!"

"I missed you too. How was your trip?"

She smiles. "It was wonderful! I can't wait to go on my next adventure." Mom turns to Josh. "Well, Joshua! Hello!" Her eyes meet mine, and I see the questions.

"Hello, Mrs. Andrews."

She walks over to him, pulling him in for a hug. "It's so nice to see you."

"You too."

She turns back to me again, her lips parted but eyes bright. "And why are you here—the both of you—together?"

"Well, Josh and I are dating, and we—well, we're living together also."

The brightness in her expression dims just a bit. "Living together?"

Josh jumps in. "Oliver needed my RV, and with the break-in that happened down the road from her house, I felt more comfortable knowing she wasn't alone."

Mom nods slowly. "I see. And you're dating too?"

Oh, yeah, here comes the fun.

"We are, and there's more, Mom." I pause and then decide it's just better to spit it out and let the chips fall where they may. "I'm pregnant . . . with twins."

She stands there, watching me, and then she bursts out laughing. She laughs, and Josh and I share a look as she cackles on and on. After a minute, she's gasping for air and trying to speak. "Oh. Delia. Funny."

"I'm not . . ."

Her hand covers her mouth for a second. "You were always so good at tricking me."

"I'm not tricking you, Mom."

"You can tell me the truth now. You've had your fun."

Not sure about that part, but I can see why she'd think it was a joke. "I swear, Josh and I are together, and we're having twins. I found out the week you left, but I didn't want to tell you over the phone."

She steps back and hits the couch, which is far better than her passing out and hitting the floor. "Oh."

"I know. I just wanted to tell you as soon as you got home."

"Oh," Mom says again. Her eyes move to my stomach where you can see the bump if you look for it. Tears fall down her cheeks, and she rests her hand on my belly. "You're pregnant."

"I am."

She looks up at me, both our gazes watery. "You're going to be a mommy." I nod, and she smiles again. "I'm going to be a Granny."

"You are."

Her hands move to my face, and she holds me still as she kisses my nose. "My baby is going to have babies."

"Two of them."

"Oh, what a . . . wow." She laughs. "I don't know what to say. I'm happy, and at the same time, I have so many things to ask."

I break in quickly. "We're not getting married."

Her hands fall away, and she looks to Josh. "Is there some reason?"

He clears his throat. "For one, we are in no hurry."

She raises her brow and looks to my stomach. "I would beg to differ. You have two reasons right there, and they have a clock going."

"Mom, we don't need to get married. Josh and I just started even being a couple two days ago. I'd like to . . . you know, take this one day at a time."

Her hands move to her cheeks, and she just keeps shaking her head. "You're four months pregnant, Delia, not two days. So, this isn't new, and I don't understand the problem with wanting to see you married."

"People can have babies without getting married."

"I know that happens, but I never thought you'd be one of those people."

I let out a long sigh. "I'm sure you'll survive once the twins are here."

"Twins," she says wistfully.

Then she looks at Josh. "You are a lucky man, you know this?"

His eyes meet mine. "I do."

And just like that, he wins her over and leaves me feeling weightless.

Twenty-Seven

JOSHUA

Oliver, Alex, and I are doing a walk-through of the layout.

"I like this change, but I think this part should be bigger," Alex notes.

"I'll see if Odette can do it." Ollie writes something down, and we keep moving.

"What about this section?" I ask.

Alex looks around, turning side to side. "This is the sitting area, and I wouldn't adjust anything here. With the way the flow of the room goes, if we change this wall, it cuts off the view to the door, which then messes up the front desk area."

I nod, I never would've seen that. "You know, you were always so good at this."

"I would've been great at it if I were allowed to actually do what I went to school for."

Oliver huffs. "No shit. We all have degrees in things Dad thought would help him."

"Yeah, but Alex is the only one who actually loved what he studied."

I got stuck with a business degree and hospitality. It was always clear that I would be running the family business. Grayson followed my path, but took more finance interests, but Alex was dead set on being able to draw up plans. Dad wanted to expand, so I imagine he saw it as a great opportunity to get free designs.

"A lot of good it does me," Alex says while moving around the room. "I had the chance of a lifetime, and I had to walk away."

"What do you mean?" Ollie asks.

"Nothing."

"It's clearly not nothing," I push him.

Alex sighs. "My mentor called about a week ago with an offer to go to Egypt to run the new office out there as a lead architect. Obviously, I said no because we're doing this, but it would have been incredible."

Oliver looks to me and then at Alex. "You wanted to take it?"

"Of course I did. It was like being asked to play in the Superbowl of the architecture world. I would've been working on a design that defied rules, and the building is going to be incredible. It would've been a dream, but this is family."

He starts to walk away, but no way am I letting him leave it at that. Part of what this family had to deal with was our father controlling our lives and forcing us to give up our dreams to further his. That's not what this resort is supposed to be about.

It's about a chance to do something for ourselves.

It's about having what we've always wanted but thought we couldn't have.

If Alex has dreams, he should chase them.

"Wait," I say, moving toward him. "Look, I'm going to speak for the family when I say this, but if you want to take that job, do it. We've all given up so much, and for what? To suffer more?"

"I'm part owner."

"And you'll be part owner wherever you live. It's not as if we don't have enough of us to handle this shit or won't be able to reach you if we need something."

Oliver nods. "You're really not all that useful anyway. Once the walls are up, you're pretty much done."

"Gee, thanks," Alex says with an eyeroll.

"He's right." I shrug. I know Alex well enough to know that he needs this push. My siblings would never want him to stay here if that's not what he wants. "You've done your part, Alex. We needed you to be involved with Odette during the drawings and layout. Now that it's done, we can all handle the rest."

"You're acting like I can just move away on a dime."

"That's exactly what he's saying," Oliver explains. "You live in an RV, you helped us when we needed you to, and I don't think a single one of us would be okay with you passing up this chance because you felt like you didn't have a choice. What do you have to stay for?"

Alex's face scrunches. "Oh, I don't know. He's having twins. Stella just got married. Grayson just had another baby. Not to mention Amelia . . ."

"You can have all the quality time with Amelia you want, just stay there for a week," Ollie says with a shudder. "That life . . . so not for me."

"My point is that things are happening here, and my running off to Egypt doesn't make sense."

"Do they no longer have planes in Egypt?" I ask. "Or the internet?"

Alex throws his hands up and then starts to pace. We're making sense, and he doesn't want that.

"Delia is my best friend, and she's going to have a baby."

"I'm fully aware."

"And you're an asshole who will fuck this up somehow," Alex tacks on.

Oliver nods. "He has a point there."

I flip them both off. "You're reaching here. We're doing just fine. Delia having babies or my hypothetical fuckup, which isn't going to happen, doesn't mean you shouldn't do what you want."

"I don't even know if this is what I want."

"That's a lie." Oliver smirks. "You know you want this or you wouldn't have brought it up. Dude, just take the job. If it sucks, you own a resort that your *much* smarter and better-looking siblings will have started. And if it's Stella you're afraid of, I'll handle her."

Alex laughs. "She's terrifying."

"She is, but she's manageable. Plus, we have Jack now."

I raise a brow. "How does that give us an edge?"

"He has to listen to it, not us. He married her, and now . . . he should have to suffer the consequences."

Alex and I chuckle. "I won't tell you what to do," I say. "But life is short, and we don't get many chances to do something we want."

He looks to Oliver and points at me with his thumb. "Do

you hear this shit? The guy who has had one of the best women I've ever met be in love with him for over a decade and has passed every chance with her is now telling me I shouldn't let this go."

Oliver nods slowly. "The man has a point, Josh. You're not exactly following your own advice."

"Delia and I are together now."

Oliver laughs. "When did this happen?"

"A few days ago."

"Took you long enough."

"Has anyone ever told you that you're a pain in the ass?" I ask Oliver.

"Daily."

"We should say it more then," I mutter under my breath and turn to Alex. "This isn't about me. It's about you and following your dreams. Delia and I are doing good, Oliver is an idiot, Stella is happy, Gray just had the baby, and Amelia will love you on video chat—just like she did when we were all living around the country."

I can see the indecision building in him. He shifts his weight and then grips the back of his neck. "I don't know."

"What's holding you back?"

Oliver steps forward with his mischievous grin. "Is it a woman?"

"Is *what* a woman?"

"Your mentor."

Alex shoves him. "Shut up."

"It is! I knew it. That's why you don't want to go. You're hard up for her, and she knows you're a total loser who lives in an RV and is now broke."

Alex rolls his eyes. "He's a forty-year-old dude who was a

few years ahead of me in school. There's no woman."

Oliver nods. "I see, you still have no game."

I laugh.

"Fuck off," Alex says to both of us.

"Think about it, Alex," I say seriously. "We've all given up our dreams, if this isn't yours, then don't waste time living it. This was meant for us to get out from under Dad's thumb. It wasn't meant to put us under another."

Oliver nods. "What he said."

"I'll think about it."

"You do that, and while you think, let's discuss our big brother and his girlfriend," Ollie tacks on, and I know this conversation is going to become an interrogation, but I'm ready for it. I'll deal with it all because, at the end, I get to go home to Delia.

Dr. Willbanks enters, his hair pushed to the side, looking like he just walked out of a damn cologne ad. What the hell is with this guy? Shouldn't doctors be old and ugly? Also, why is he here again?

Delia shifts a little, and I grumble under my breath.

"Hello, Delia and Josh. It's good to see you again. Dr. Locke is at the hospital for a delivery, so you get me again today. Hope that's all right."

"No worries. It's great to see you too," Delia says. Since I don't feel the same, I just grunt. Which earns me a nasty look from Delia.

"How are you feeling?"

She rests her hands on her stomach. "Good. You were

right, the second trimester is much better. I have more energy, and I haven't had any more morning sickness."

"Wonderful. Have you felt the babies move at all?"

I look to her, wondering if she has because she hasn't said anything to me about it. She shrugs. "I don't know what I feel. Jessica says it's the babies, but then . . . wouldn't I know? Like, a mother would know it's the baby moving and not bubble guts."

He smiles warmly, flashing his perfect white teeth. "A lot of women don't think it's movement, but if you feel something like soda bubbles, that's probably the babies. You're at eighteen weeks now, so it's safe to say you'll start to feel stronger shifts sometime soon."

She looks to me, her eyes filled with hope, and my chest aches. God, she's so damn perfect. "It'll happen," I assure her.

Delia nods quickly. "So, today we get to see them and find out the sex, right?"

Dr. Willbanks nods. "Yes, we're going to check on the twins, see how they're growing, and then, if they cooperate, I'll check to see if we can find out their sexes."

"You both cooperate!" she says to her stomach.

Someone knocks on the door and a girl enters. The doctor explains that Sara is the ultrasound tech and he's here to narrate and observe. Great.

"Do you want to see the screen?" he asks me. "If so, go ahead and stand up there."

I move to the spot he pointed to before taking her hand in mine, bringing it to my lips. "You ready?"

"So much. Then we can go register again."

I laugh. "We have a lot of things we need to remove when we go back."

Her eyes fill with joy. "We do?"

"Yes, baby, we do."

Like the two sets of everything. We can have one set and see where our relationship goes. While I may not be ready for marriage, I know I want to be with her. I want to wake up with her beside me, and I want to be able to raise our children together. If things change, then we'll handle it. I'm taking this one step at a time.

The technician spreads some gooey stuff on Delia's stomach, and then smiles. "All right, here we go."

Once again, the sounds of the heartbeats fill the room. Delia's hand tightens in mine, and we watch each other as the moment hits us again. These are our children.

"Josh . . ."

"I know."

Tears fill her eyes, and she wipes them away. "I hope that never gets old."

I lean down, kissing her lips. "I doubt it will."

The tech and the doctor talk a little and then he points to the screen. "This is baby A and this is baby B. Since you have fraternal twins, you can see that they each have their own amniotic sac as well as a placenta."

Her hand tightens a little. "That's good, but are they okay?"

"Baby B is a little smaller, but that's normal with twins. We're going to look at each one now and check their organs," the tech explains.

Delia and I watch the screen as the tech works, my eyes wide and this feeling of contentment flowing over me. I can't believe this is where my life is. I'm watching my children, our children, growing. The doctor and the tech explain things as we move along. Both of their hearts are developing beautifully, and so far, things look great.

"Would you like to know the sex?" the technician asks.

Delia's head lifts. "Yes!"

She laughs, and we learn what colors we need to go shopping for.

Twenty-Eight

DELIA

"Pink! I want that one there!" I tell Josh, who once again has absconded the scanner gun. He gets that one on our registry, and I search for one for the boy. "Do you like this?"

He looks at me with a brow raised. "I really don't care. Pick whichever one you like."

"I picked the one for the girl. Don't you want to pick for the boy?"

"An hour ago, I would've said yes. Now, I'd just like to get the hell out of the store."

I refuse to let him piss in my cereal today. I'm too happy. We're having a boy and a girl. It's like I won the lottery because, no matter what happens with my relationship with Josh, I will have a piece of him.

"This is important."

"Bedding?" he asks incredulously.

"Yes. I mean, this will be what our children see each morning and night. These colors will be their comfort."

"Delia, you're insane. They are sheets."

I huff. "It's their first sheets."

He shakes his head. "I have no words."

"Well, have an opinion and help me pick."

For the girl, it was really easy. I love dragonflies, and they had the most beautiful pink quilt set with yellow dragonflies and white polka dots. The lace trim around the top made it perfect. For the boy, I'm sort of lost. I don't want trains or cars, but there's not a lot of options other than that.

He walks down the aisle farther. "What about this one?"

I look at it with lips pursed. It's actually adorable and will match perfectly in the room. It's quiltlike with navy-blue, white, and teal patches. There are anchors on the navy-blue patches, arrows on the teal ones, and blue, teal, and gray mountains on the white ones. I love it.

"It's perfect."

He smiles. "I'm getting them both now."

"What?"

"The bedding. We're buying it."

"But we're registering."

"No, I want to buy this for our kids. Now. I want to start to put their room together." I want to protest, but there's something in his eyes that tells me not to. Josh takes a step to me, pulling me in his arms. "I've spent so much of my life waiting for something. For someone. For something to make me want to live again. I was waiting for you, for them, for . . . God, I don't know. I'm tired of waiting. I've seen the other side, and I don't want to do that."

I lift up on my toes, pressing our lips together. "I don't want that either."

"Good."

"Good."

He lets me go, and I smile as he loads both into the cart. It all feels so real now that we know we are having a boy and a girl. He's also moving out of the second bedroom tonight, not that he hasn't been sleeping in my bed the last week, but we're making plans. Josh is going to stay with me, and we're going to be a couple, raising our children together.

My mother is close to having a coronary from the thought of it, but we're taking it as it comes.

I'm in no rush to get married. I'm honestly happy just knowing he wants to be with me. Maybe that makes me a total idiot, but it's how I feel.

We head home with a few bags of baby things, and when I walk into my house, I look around at how much this place has changed. The floors are beautiful, and the kitchen is just about done now too.

When Josh, Jack, and Grayson were working on it yesterday, they found a cabinet that had some rot, so what was meant to be an easy painting job has turned into much more. I tried to argue that we didn't need to do it, but they gave me identical looks of incredulity as they ripped the cabinet off the wall so I had no option but to replace it.

They rebuilt that section, and I love it.

I head in there while Josh puts the baby gear in the spare room.

Feeling hungry and a little tired, I make us each a sandwich. As I'm putting the mayo on the bread, I feel Josh come up behind me, hands resting on my belly. "Do you know how beautiful you are?"

I smile, leaning back into his touch. "No, feel free to tell me."

He chuckles against my neck. "You are the most beautiful woman who has ever drawn breath."

"Ever?"

"Ever."

I turn my head so I can get a glimpse of him. "You're not so bad yourself."

"Not bad?" Josh asks with a smirk.

"I mean, I've seen better."

"Yeah?"

I giggle when he tickles my sides. "I'm totally lying, I don't know that I've ever had eyes for anyone other than you."

Fate is a funny thing.

He brings his lips to mine, and I sink into his touch. Each time we kiss, it's like a surreal experience, and I never want it to end.

When we break apart, he runs his finger down my cheek. "What's wrong?" I ask.

"I keep waiting for everything to change," he confesses.

"What do you mean?"

"This happiness. I'm just waiting for it to stop."

"Why would it?" I ask.

"It always does."

"It doesn't have to."

"No, I guess it doesn't, but I feel like it could, and it might."

Josh and I are new, and I'm scared of losing him as well. Of losing what is suddenly right in front of me. What if tomorrow, he wakes up and is like, "I'm out"? Then what? I am alone with two babies and a broken heart.

"Look, it will only end if we let it. I have no plans of letting you go, do you?"

"I'm not going anywhere, Delia," he says with conviction. "Trust me."

I want to believe him so much, but I too have insecurities. "I do trust you, but we both have fears and have to rely on each other to get us through it. I also know that life isn't perfect."

He nods. "It's not, and I'm just as scared as you are, Deals," Josh confesses. "I've had my fair share of disappointments too. I worry that you'll wake up and be done with me or that something is going to happen to you and then what?"

He's insane. I have never been able to deny my feelings for this man. "I'm fine. I'll be fine. Why would I ever leave you, though?"

"Because I could screw it all up. I have before. I've failed and lost and broken things that were precious. You could walk out that door and then what?"

It won't ever happen, but I understand fear. It's not rational, and it feeds into the very worst of us, just like it's doing to me now. We are both on unsteady ground, waiting for it to fall out from beneath us. I have to remember that.

"Nothing is guaranteed. I know this as much as you do. My parents were so in love and my mother thought they had a lifetime to love, but he died, and we had to go on. You have to stop living as though the other shoe will drop because, at some point, it always does. We have now, Josh. We have each other and the babies, and we have to live for now."

He rests his forehead against mine with eyes closed. "I don't want to think about losing you."

"You won't," I promise.

It's going to take time for him to believe that. For both of us to believe that. It's been a long time coming, and all of it has happened so fast that it will take us time to really trust it.

Josh raises his head, and his blue eyes are filled with emotion. "I don't want to hurt you."

"Then be happy. Smile, laugh, and love the fact that you're going to be a father and that you have a pretty amazing girlfriend."

"I have the most amazing girlfriend. You're all I need."

He kisses me as though there is nothing else he can do. As though my kiss can heal him as thoroughly as I want it to. I want to be his salvation and hope, but it scares me. What if I'm not enough?

I shake the thought loose and let it float away because I need to take my own advice and enjoy the now. Josh is here, he loves me, and that's more than I ever thought I'd have.

Twenty-Nine

JOSHUA

"Where are you taking me?" Delia asks with a laugh as I walk her forward, covering her eyes.

"Just keep going. Three more steps." She sighs and does as I ask. "Okay, stop."

I drop my hands, and she gasps. The cabin we're at is just down the road from Delia's cabin, but it's beautiful. The roof's peak is incredible with floor-to-ceiling windows and the white holiday lights line it. There are smaller, softer peaks to the right and left of the center one, and a wraparound porch hugs the whole exterior. It's a house that we all grew up admiring.

"Do you remember this place?" she asks with hesitation.

"I remember everything regarding you." Her eyes widen, and then she looks back at the house. I come from behind her, taking both her hands in mine. "I met my brother's friend here when I was twenty. My brother had been drinking and had passed out on the deck, and she called me to help move him."

"She was probably pretty nervous to do that seeing as you were so much older than she was."

I laugh. "She probably was, but she was brave enough to reach out."

"I doubt your brother thought that. I seem to remember him not talking to her for a week because he had to do extra chores as punishment for waking his brother up in the middle of the night."

"You're ruining my story," I scold her.

"Sorry. I'll be quiet. Do go on about this brave girl and her selfless acts of heroism."

I lean in and kiss her neck, causing her to giggle. "Anyway, she called me, I came and got him loaded into the car. When I turned to find out where she had gone, I found her standing in this very spot, staring at this house."

"This very one?"

"This very one. She told me how she dreamed, that one day, she'd own a house with three roofs and windows that looked out at the world. She said she'd meet a man who would love her, give her a home filled with happiness and love."

Delia turns her head. "She had big dreams and a big mouth."

"I happened to think her mouth was perfect, and I wanted to kiss her that night."

"Dirty old man you were, lusting after a fifteen-year-old."

I burst out laughing, pull her to me, and spin us so we're both turned to the side, the house silhouetting us. "Do you remember what else you said?"

"I told you that this place was magical and was somewhere

that people could forget their troubles if they let themselves."

"You did. You also said that you met someone who stole your heart."

"Did you know I meant you?"

I shake my head. "I thought you meant Alex."

"I didn't."

"I know that now, beautiful. I think you stole my heart that day. We stood here, with you looking at that house and the snow all around you, and I thought: God, that girl is special."

Her hand lifts, pushing my hair back. "And I thought: God, I'd really like him to kiss me."

I wanted to. So damn bad, but she was young, and I was in college. It felt wrong to think of her that way, so I held back. I gave Delia every indication that she was too young, too immature for me, even though I wanted her more than anything.

But I can kiss her now, so I do. I kiss her with everything inside me. "Sorry I'm a little late on that kiss," I say as I pull back and press my forehead to hers.

"I forgive you. But if you loved this fantastic girl so much, why didn't you ever come back for her?"

"Because I was an idiot. I left town, did my best to forget this one magical kiss I had with her, and tried to give her a chance at love."

"There was no love, Josh," Delia says with a little bit of sadness.

"No, but I wasn't ready for you. I knew you'd own me, Delia. I knew that if I let myself near you, I would stay in this town and become what my father wanted. I couldn't do that. So, I went back to New Orleans after that day in the diner."

Her lips turn down and she sighs softly. "That kiss is why I never could get over you."

"I'm sorry."

She shakes her head. "Don't be, tell me more about this fantastic girl who you knew would own your heart and soul. She sounds like a keeper."

I chuckle, and we turn our heads to see the house. "She and I talked for an hour while Alex was passed out in the car. She told me about losing her dad, how she wanted to go to college but was afraid to leave her mom alone, and she made me forget about our age difference." I take a pause, remembering it all. "You scared the hell out of me that night."

"Me?" she asks, her voice going up a notch. "What the hell did I do?"

"I wanted you, but I was so much older, and it felt wrong."

"Is that why you always made me feel like a little girl after that night?"

I nod. "If I put you in that category, I thought it would help."

Delia smirks. "Guess that didn't work out for you."

"I'm glad it didn't."

"Me too. And I can't believe that you remembered that night," Delia says with a smile.

"I told you I did."

The snow is falling around us, and the lights from the beautiful house she loves shine on the unmarred white ground. She is so beautiful that I know this moment will be in my heart forever. When I'm old, I'll recall the time that I stood in the snow with the most breathtaking woman who looked at me like I was her entire world.

"Why are we here?" she asks.

"Because I rented this house for the weekend."

She turns her head, studying me. "We live right down the

road."

"We do, but I think we deserve a little magic, don't you?" Delia's hand moves to my face, she rests it on my cheek. "I think you're the magic, Josh."

"And here I thought I was just charming."

"You're that too, when you're not an ass."

I lift her into my arms, twirling us in the snow. "I want to make you happy. The things that I would do if we were dating are different because we live together. While I can't give you the house with three roofs to live in, we can borrow it."

The owners of this place are good friends with my mother and have been renting the house out in the winter while they go to Florida to get away from the winters here. I called them, and they were all too happy to let me take it for a few nights.

Her eyes fill with unshed tears. "I am really glad I was never over you."

I grin. "Me too. Come on, let's go inside."

Delia takes my hand, and we walk up the stairs and into the house she dreamed of. The house is unbelievable. The entire back wall is nothing but windows up to the peak. The only obstruction there is the floor-to-ceiling rock fireplace.

"Wow, inside is even better than I remember."

"They've done a lot of work to the house."

She turns, taking everything in. I know Delia loves her home, but if things work out for us, I'd like to move her into something like this. To give her and the twins the life she wanted.

"I still am in shock," she says with a laugh. "You rented the dream house."

"For you."

Delia walks toward me, her eyes full of warmth. Her arms

loop around my neck. "And all I was hoping for is that you'd make love to me."

Now that I can do.

I take her hand in mine without a word. Her trust in me so absolute that she doesn't question it. She just follows me. I may not have said the words to her, but I hope she feels it in my touch or the way I look at her.

I love her.

I think I have since that night I first laid eyes on her, but I forced it away.

Now, there's nothing stopping me from having it. We aren't kids anymore and there's no one in our way.

I push open the door to the bedroom, and she gasps. "Josh?"

I came here earlier and did everything I could to make this special. The room is swathed in candlelight. Hundreds of flames flicker all around.

She steps in, looking around. "This is beautiful."

"You're beautiful."

Nothing else but her matters. I want her more than anything else in the world. I was so stupid for so long, and I don't want to waste another second with her.

"You did all this for me?"

I move to her, needing to touch her and feel her skin. "I would do anything for you."

"Anything?"

My fingers slide along her jaw and then I cup her cheek. "Ask me for what you want and find out."

She starts to speak but then stops herself. I want this to be perfect for her. I want tonight to be what should've been from the start. Where she feels desired, worshiped, and . . . loved.

That word has been a weapon I've feared, but looking at

Delia, open and trusting, suddenly it isn't so scary.

My thumb moves against her silky skin. "I love you, Delia. I should've seen it before, but I was a damn fool."

Tears track down her cheeks. "You don't have to say it."

"No, I do because I mean it."

"It's . . ."

"It's what I feel."

Her lips turn into a tentative smile. "Do you know how long I've prayed for you to love me?"

"Probably as long as I've fought it."

She closes her eyes, and I brush the tears aside. "No tears, baby."

"It's just too much, being here with you in this house and having you tell me you love me. You love me, and we're together. I don't feel like this is real."

I lift her face, forcing her gaze to stay locked on me. "Everything about this moment is real. It's you and me, and I am so fucking sorry I fought against it. I am so sorry that I made you question everything. I never want to hurt you, and I can't deny that you're all I think about."

"I love you. I will always love you."

I smile. "I'm going to kiss you, and I don't plan on stopping until I've erased every doubt from your mind."

Her hands frame my face, and she pulls me to her. "I'm going to need a lot of convincing."

"Then it's a good thing we have all weekend."

I pull her to me, crushing our lips together in the sweetest kiss. The last few months I've had Delia in many ways. We've had sex, fucked, and everything in between. A few weeks ago, I would've sworn that it was making love. It was sweet, slow, and I poured myself into every touch.

This is otherworldly.

There is nothing between us. The barriers of the past are gone, and all I feel is hope for more—for her.

Delia is the future. She's always been here, waiting, and I am not going to waste another second.

Our tongues glide against one another as we kiss languidly because there's nothing else in the world but this. We have time stretched out before us, and there's no hurry to have this stop.

I tilt her head to the side, giving me better access, and drink in her moan.

"Josh," she says between shallow breaths as I move my lips to her neck, kissing the soft skin there.

"I am going to kiss every inch of you," I promise. "I'm going to strip you down and worship you like the goddess you are."

I push the sweater off her shoulders, and return my lips to the skin there, moving down along her collarbone.

"Don't stop."

"I don't plan to."

I lead her toward the bed, loving how her skin looks in the candlelight, how the warm glow moves around her. For so long, I've been cold. I've shut out heat and passion, but tonight, I'm going to burn for her.

When we reach the mattress, I peel her clothes off, watching the fabric fall to the floor as she stands before me—bare. I wish she knew how it was me that felt exposed. How giving her those words, giving her my heart felt natural, but also terrifying.

In the back of my mind, I worry I'll fail her.

I worry I'll cause her pain or she'll face the same fate that

Morgan did.

I let her down.

I let her fall, but the love I have for Delia is a hundred times greater. It will kill me if I lose her.

Her long lashes flutter as my hands move down her body, feeling each curve. I lower myself to my knees, and her fingers slide through my hair.

I press my lips to her stomach, to where our future grows, and pray I can do right by her.

Thirty

DELIA

He's so gentle. So caring that it causes my heart to ache.

This entire night has been overwhelming and incredible. This house has been a part of me in so many ways. I've often wondered about the people who lived here, imagining a love and life that I didn't think possible.

Josh looks up at me after kissing my belly, and my world pivots. I sink down in front of him, wanting us to be equals, and he presses our mouths together. It's hungrier than before, but no less tender.

"I love you," I tell him.

"I love you."

My throat gets tight because those words from him mean everything to me. We kiss deeper, breaking when I lift his shirt. I want to feel his skin against mine. I remove his pants, pushing them down, and then he helps me to my feet.

Our mouths don't stop tasting, and our hands don't stop caressing as he guides me back onto the mattress. I squirm.

"I will never be good enough for you, Delia, but God help me, I'm going to try."

"Don't place me on a pedestal. Don't make me out to be something I'm not because you don't think you're good enough. Look at this," I say, my eyes going around the room. "You did this for me because you love me. If you weren't good for me, you wouldn't care."

Josh parts my knees, and his lips graze my thigh. "I care. I care about you more than my own life. I want you to feel good."

"I do. I always do with you."

He kisses lower. "I'm going to make you come on my tongue. I'm going to love you so hard that you never question how I feel about you."

My eyes roll into the back of my head, and before I can say anything, his mouth is there. Josh does exactly as he promised. I climb higher and higher with each swipe of his tongue. He moves at a steady place while his hands hold my legs down so I can't move. I'm completely at his mercy, and what a damn place it is. I start to shake as my climax grows nearer.

"I'm so close," I whimper.

Josh doesn't relent. He adds more pressure, then pulls back a little, toying with me over and over. I can't breathe or think or speak.

It's too much.

I'm too close and too emotional to hold back.

I cry out, yelling his name as I arch up. I'm weightless and heavy at the same time as I fall apart. He continues to touch me, drawing out every drop of pleasure my body can give.

Then he's over me, his arms on each side of my head. Josh's eyes are hazy as he stares down at me.

"What's wrong?" I ask.

"Nothing. Nothing at all."

My hands move up his arms, gripping his shoulders. "I want you inside me." My legs wrap around his hips, and he settles himself there.

I feel the pressure as he just barely enters me. It's so intense, the feelings that we are both experiencing, and tears begin to fall. "I love you," I say, watching him through watery eyes.

"Say it again," he asks as he pushes deeper.

"I love you, Josh."

He moves forward again. "Don't stop."

"I love you. I love you. I need you." I repeat the words over and over.

Josh thrusts forward, burying himself inside me, and the tears fall from being so overcome with love as he drives me to another orgasm.

Wrapped in a blanket on the floor, Josh feeds me cheese and bread. We've been like this for an hour, still finding ways to be touching. Making love was everything, but this is even better. Intimacy.

"Have you thought about what you're going to do with work?" he asks as I lean against his chest.

"I'm going to keep doing it if that's what you mean."

He laughs. "I'm saying are you going to take some time

off?"

I shrug. "I'd like to."

"I think you should. You spend a lot of time on your feet at work."

"That's the truth. Still, with the house payments and the other stuff, it's going to be hard to take that much time off."

I have some vacation saved, and I'll get a few weeks for maternity, but it still doesn't feel like enough time. Thankfully, childcare is completely taken care of. Josh's family and my mother have already offered—demanded—that I let them help. Mom will be the primary person, and if there's a reason she can't, Jess said I better call her.

Still, she has an infant, and I'll have two. I'd like that to be a last resort.

"You know that I have money saved, right?"

"Yes, and that's yours."

His arm tightens. "I want to take care of you, Delia."

I lift my head to look at him. "And you have. You do. Look at the work you've done to the house that you refuse to take any money for."

"You let me live with you, that's my rent."

"If I recall, I didn't *let* you do anything."

He grins. "Look how it worked out."

Mollified, I let it go and put my head back down. "Josh?"

"Yeah?"

"I think you should move in with me," I say with a grin.

"I thought I already had."

I sit back up. "You have, but I want the reason to be different. Not because of some bullshit about a break-in but because we want to do this. To start a chapter in our lives where we are a couple and are having kids."

He slides his thumb against my lips. "I'd like that."

"Good."

It may seem small to someone else, but this is a huge deal. He didn't flinch or shy away from taking that step. It's a more permanent step in our relationship, and I couldn't be happier about it.

"You know this means I'm not leaving once the babies are born?"

I nod. "Did you really have any intention to do it in the first place?"

He grins. "No."

"I didn't think so."

The tone in his voice grows serious. "I couldn't imagine leaving you. I couldn't picture a morning where I wasn't getting up to get you coffee or seeing you in those tight shorts you call pajamas. I don't ever want to."

I lean in, giving him a kiss. "Now you don't have to."

Thirty-One

DELIA

"This place is amazing!" I say as Josh leads me around the bare bones of the resort.

"It will be. Right now, I don't know how you can picture anything."

I grin. "I have imagination. More than that, I know you guys never do anything half-assed. I have no doubt that this will be the number-one destination in North Carolina."

"Your lips to God's ears. We invested everything we have, so it needs to be."

"Have faith, Josh. You'll see."

The Parkersons don't fail. They're like some weird anomaly, and I know they'll do exactly what they hope.

Josh walks me through the original building first, which has been torn down to the studs. "All the actual bedrooms will be in the old house. Grayson and Stella felt really strongly about it having the most character. We salvaged whatever we could during the demo, and Odette plans to reuse most of it when they start putting it back together."

"That'll be really cool. The old meets the new."

"Exactly."

"What's this going to be?" I ask as we move to the new construction. They expanded the original structure by almost three times, putting additions on each side and the back.

"That'll be the recreation room, and through there is the piano bar. Alex really wanted to set up the place so the families can enjoy their vacation."

Alex has always been impressive when it comes to these things. Between him and Stella, I'm pretty sure they could've run the world. They are driven and see problems as more of obstacles they have to find a way around. It's not at all surprising that he was very involved in the planning of this place.

"It's really great."

"I think so too. I'm really pleased with the design and how authentic the additions are. We want it to be like this place has always been here, just hidden away from the world."

I like that. It's romantic in some weird way.

"And what about you, what are you working on?" I ask.

"Mostly, playing referee between Alex and Odette for now," he says with a hint of frustration.

This isn't the first time I'm hearing about their feud. "Why? What's going on with them?"

"Apparently, they slept together a long time ago, and it ended badly. Honestly, I think he wants to take that job in Egypt."

"He told you?"

Josh grins. "He did, and it seems like he really wants to

go."

"I think you guys need to push him. You know how he is. He wants to be like you, the protector, and do what's right for the family."

"He has to find his own way."

"Yeah, but I don't think he'll take those steps if he thinks it will be detrimental to what you guys have going on here. I don't think he'll ever admit that this town isn't where he wants to put down roots."

There is a slight disappointment in his eyes. "I don't either. I hoped we would all do this together, but I think he'll be miserable."

I nod, feeling a bit sad about it too. However, I would be even sadder if he stayed and ended up unhappy.

Josh shakes his head. "I'll talk to him, and if that doesn't work, I'll get Stella involved."

I grin. "I think your sister should run for office, she's scary and gets shit done."

"She definitely does."

"Maybe she and I can get through to him."

Josh lets out a long sigh. "Don't get involved, baby."

Yeah, like that's going to happen. He should know better by now. "I make no promises."

He groans. "Enough about Alex, let me show you the rest so we can get home."

Home. That word. It's shared between us, and I get a rush from it. I love that we have a home—together.

He takes my hand and pulls me deeper in. All the walls aren't up yet, but orange, blue, and red spray paint make lines all over. Josh explains each section, explaining more about the building and their hopes for the resort.

"It's so much bigger than I . . ." I start to say when I feel something, causing my words to stop. My hands fly to my stomach and Josh moves quickly.

"What is it?"

My eyes meet his and I grin. "I can feel it."

"Feel what? Delia, what's wrong?"

I shake my head, struggling to speak. "No. It's the baby. Or both. One of them just moved."

His hand covers mine. "You felt the baby kick?"

I nod. "Maybe. It was so strong. It wasn't flutters it was—" There it is again. I take Josh's hand, placing it on the spot. "Do you feel that?" I ask.

Neither of us says a word as we wait. After what feels like forever, the baby moves again, and Josh's eyes go wide. "Holy shit."

"You felt it?"

His smile is so bright it could blind someone. "I did. That's the baby?"

"One of them."

He laughs, and then squats in front of me so he can press both hands to my stomach. "Hi, kids." My fingers tangle in his light brown hair as he waits.

My hand sits at the top of the swell, waiting and willing them to do it again. After a bit, I feel it again. Josh's smile tells me he did as well, and I feel like things in my life couldn't be any better.

Today we are having a girls' brunch. I love how my friends think they're so sly. My birthday is in two days, and they're not fooling me on why we're doing this.

"Why are you smiling like that?" Ronyelle asks.

"Because life is a beautiful thing, my friend."

While I go to brunch with Jessica, Stella, Ronyelle, Winnie, and Kinsley, Josh and his brothers will be painting and assembling furniture. My mother, in all her impatience, went and bought an entire bedroom set for the babies.

We had no idea until the boxes started showing up at the house.

"And why is that?"

"Because I am happy, having babies, and my boyfriend loves me. Which neither of us ever thought was possible."

She rolls her eyes. "That man has fried your brain."

"He has."

"I am so glad you can't drink, if love impairs your judgment this much, imagine what some booze would do."

I stick my tongue out at her.

"Where are we going to eat?"

"Stella found some place a town over. She swears the food is great."

"I can't wait until the Firefly is open. Josh was telling me about the two restaurant options they'll have."

Ronyelle nods. "And with Stella deciding things, you know the food is going to be good."

"And the drinks even better."

On the ride over, we talk about work and how busy our production schedule is. There have been rumors that Ronyelle will be promoted again and additional rumors that I will get her position. A few months ago, I would be praying for that to happen because not only is it more money but also much better hours. Gone would be the shifts and rotating schedule.

Now, though, I don't know if I want that added stress. My life is about to be stressful enough.

"It's not going to happen," she says again.

"You don't know that."

"Come on, we both know that I am never going to get the job because they've never once had a woman in that position."

She's right. The owners are dicks that way, but Ronyelle is the most qualified.

"It's unlikely, but it's possible."

She gives me a side-eye look. "Stop it."

"Fine, fine, but if it does happen, don't put my name in to fill your spot."

"What?" she yells. "Are you insane?"

"I know, but . . . I don't know if I want to take over all that work with two newborns. Plus, Josh is busy with the resort and while I have no intention of working there when it opens, Josh will probably be putting in a ton of hours and our lives are going to be on overload."

Ronyelle blinks a few times. "You've always wanted that position."

"No, I always wanted someone other than Ray in that spot. He was horrible and rude. I couldn't stand it."

"He was definitely a shitty boss. Still, I'm surprised you wouldn't want it. It would be a good raise."

"Maybe. I don't know."

We park at what looks like an old warehouse that has been renovated. "If it happens, I'm going to suggest you," Ronyelle says softly. "If you choose not to take it, then that's one thing, but my not putting your name in isn't the right decision."

I reach over, taking her hand in mine. "You're a good friend."

"Oh, I know."

We both laugh. "So, brunch?"

"Let's brunch."

We get inside where the girls are already seated. Everyone gives hugs and fawns over Ember, who is asleep in her mother's arms. Throughout brunch, we laugh, talk about the current insanity of our lives, and then the topic turns to me.

"So, how are things with Josh?" Winnie asks.

"Fine."

"Just fine?" Stella questions.

"No, we're good. We're really good."

"I heard that Josh made a rather grand gesture the other day," Jess says conspiratorially.

Stella gasps, grabbing for my hand, which I pull out of her reach. "He didn't propose! We've been together a few weeks."

"Months," Ronyelle corrects. "You've been screwing each other's—"

"Ears!" Stella says as she nudges her head toward Kinsley.

Kinsley shakes her head. "Like I don't know what the end of that was going to be?"

Stella places her mimosa down. "You're twelve. You shouldn't."

"I've had sex ed."

"At *twelve*?" Stella's voice goes up an octave.

Jess laughs. "Would you rather her not know?"

"Yes. Yes, I would."

"Well, I know about the birds and the bees. Also, three girls in my class have their periods already. I'm not that young."

Stella's eyes widen, and it looks like she's going to cry. "I'm not ready for this."

"Do you remember what you were doing at twelve?" Winnie unhelpfully adds.

Now Stella turns green before turning to her daughter. "You are not allowed to talk to boys. Look at boys. Even thinking about boys is a bad idea. Do you know how I know this?"

"You had a baby at eighteen out of wedlock and hid it?" Kinsley asks, and I have to bite my tongue to stop from laughing.

However, two people around us aren't able to control themselves and do laugh.

"Well, yes, but that was my first time, and . . . we are not having this conversation other than to say that you should avoid boys. They are really horrible creatures."

"You love Jack," Jess says with a smirk.

"Jack is different."

"How is he different?" I ask, enjoying her discomfort far too much.

"He just is!" Stella hisses.

Kinsley picks apart her bread before popping a piece into her mouth. "I wonder if Braydon is different."

"Who is Braydon?" I ask.

"Yes, Kinsley. Who is Braydon?" Winnie follows up with a smile.

"He's just a guy in school. He's really nice to me."

Stella blinks a few times, moving her gaze to each of us before snapping out of it. "No, he's not nice. He has a penis, which makes him completely not nice. Boys only want one thing. I know this because I grew up with four of them who . . . only wanted one thing."

"What did they want?" Kinsley asks, and I am ready to fall off my chair. She is her mother's daughter, and I am here for it.

Stella opens her mouth and closes it. "You know."

Kinsley bursts out laughing. "I totally do, but this was a lot of fun."

Jessica laughs, and then Ember starts to fuss. "Crap. Can you hold her while I get her bottle?" she asks me, already moving the baby into my arms.

I take her just as she starts to fuss, so I pat her butt, cooing and trying to calm her. I have not had a lot of experience with babies. None of my other friends have kids, and I'm an only child.

"How is the pregnancy going?"

"It's fine."

Jess smiles. "That good?"

"Umm, is it normal?"

"Is what normal?"

I lean in. "This is so embarrassing, but I have really bad gas. All the time. No matter what I eat it's just bad, but then I can't . . . you know . . . go."

She snorts. "Oh, you don't even know what you have ahead of you. It's all normal and just part of the joy of bringing a baby into the world."

I drop my head back. "That's what I was worried about."

"How's Josh about the babies—and gas?" Jess asks as she puts some powder in water.

"He doesn't mention the farts, thank God. It's all still surreal."

"That you're pregnant with twins?"

I snort. "That, and that we're together."

Jess shakes the bottle and her brows knit. "Why is that so surprising?"

I'm not sure what part of it confuses her. "Maybe because I've loved this guy forever and I never thought he'd ever choose me."

"You're gorgeous, funny, and have a heart of gold. If Josh didn't pick you, then he'd be stupid."

I know it's stupid, but sometimes, I still feel like that fifteen-year-old girl.

"I'm being silly. I know."

"Yes, you are because it's very clear to everyone that Josh cares about you and the babies. He's a totally different guy since being with you. The fact that he fails to mention your new flatulence is proof of that."

"I regret telling you about the gas."

"I'm sure, but just wait until you start pissing yourself. Also, fun fact, I don't have a seven pound baby dancing on my bladder and I still pee myself. Forget sneezing or laughing, it's a done deal."

This is the stuff that the baby book fails to mention, and I wish I never knew about.

"Great, just great, Jess."

Her hand moves to my arm. "You'll be fine and you'll have two beautiful kids at the end. That is the good stuff. Anyway, I get what you're feeling about Josh and you. I was the same with Grayson. It's probably different for you since you've pined for the man . . ."

"Forever."

She laughs. "You said it." Ember's fussing turns to more of a wail. I look to Jess with panic and she hands me the bottle. "Here, feed her for me, I have to pee."

"Jess!"

"It'll be good practice," she says, getting up. "I told you this is the fun stuff."

I put the tip into her mouth, and she begins to drink, thank

God. After about two minutes, Stella reaches out, pressing her hand to my forearm. "Burp her now so she doesn't get too gassy."

Right. I should do that. I should also know this. I lift the bottle, which causes Ember to fuss again, but I move her up, patting her back until a loud belch comes out of her.

Dear God. For something so tiny, she sure can let it rip.

Jess returns to the table, but she doesn't take Ember back, so I keep going. Once her bottle is done and she's been burped again, I keep her in the crook of my arm, looking down at her as she starts to drift off again.

When her eyes close and her mouth is a little "o," I look up at Jess. "I did okay?"

"You did great," she assures me.

One of the twins kicks as though they agree, and I smile softly. I don't give Ember back until we're ready to leave, thinking of little else other than the moment I'll get to hold my own babies.

Thirty-Two

JOSHUA

My brothers and I busted our asses to finish the nursery in one day, and I can't wait for Delia to see it.

"She's going to love this," Alex says.

"Yeah, I think she will."

Grayson sits on the couch with a grin. "I am a genius."

"You?"

Oliver snorts. "You're far from that."

He ignores us. "I'm the one who told you to do this, and she's going to be over the moon."

"You didn't tell me to do this, Gray. I called you and asked you to come help while the girls were at brunch."

"Whatever." Gray leans his head back. "I like my version better."

Oliver turns to Alex. "So, are you going to tell everyone now?"

"Tell everyone what?"

"That he took the job in Egypt and leaves in two days."

I blink a few times, waiting for him to say something, and Alex slaps Oliver's chest. "Asshole. You can't keep your mouth shut."

"Two days?" I ask.

"What job?" Grayson cuts me off. "You have a job, in case you forgot, we're opening a resort."

"I'm aware of that, Gray."

"Two days?" I ask again.

Alex shoots daggers at Oliver. "I wanted to tell you, but it all happened very fast. I got offered a permanent position as the lead architect for a building overseas. It's a huge opportunity, but I wasn't going to take it because I didn't want to leave you guys hanging with the resort. But Stella found out about it and called me to basically demand I do it."

"Did she?" he asks leaning forward.

"I did too," I speak up, knowing that Grayson will back off a little.

Alex raises an eyebrow at me because I didn't push him, but I would've.

"You knew?"

I nod. "I think everyone but you knew he'd been offered the spot. We just didn't know he accepted it or that he'd be leaving so soon."

Gray stands and starts to pace. "How are you going to leave while we're building the Firefly?"

"Because he doesn't need to be here for us to do this." I place my hand on Alex's shoulder. "He helped, and we're able to take it from here. This is your dream, and it's ours now as well, but Alex has the right to follow his, and we know it's not here in Willow Creek."

His head drops, and he lets out a long sigh. "I didn't know. You didn't tell me that you didn't want this."

Alex moves toward him. "I didn't know I didn't. I still don't. I want to take this project. I want to leave here and see what life is like doing what I love."

Grayson might be stunned, but we're family, and we all want each other to be happy. "Then you should go. You shouldn't be stuck here if there's something else you want. This resort was never meant to be a prison."

I smile. "I agree. We can handle things, and besides, it's not like Oliver is doing anything. He can take on more work."

"Right, I'm just living on the property and making sure things run smoothly. And . . . booked our first wedding. You're welcome."

"You booked a wedding? We don't even have floors in!" I groan. I swear, sometimes he just doesn't think.

"It's for a year out. Calm your tits. I explained we're new and offered her a great deal."

"You offered her . . ." I trail off as I get control of my anger.

Grayson laughs. "So, you booked a wedding before we're even open with a bride who was okay booking a venue sight unseen?"

"She's an old friend from college, and she remembered I'm in the hospitality business. It seemed perfect. We'll be fully booked with her wedding, and it gives us someone who isn't going to expect perfection. It'll be a great test run."

I bite back a scoff. What bride doesn't expect perfection at her wedding?

"I might come back just for this." Alex laughs.

Grayson glares at them both. "I swear, you're both pains

in the asses."

"This is true," Ollie says, kicking his feet up on the coffee table. "But you're stuck with us. Oh, and, Josh?"

"Yeah?"

"Stella was on board, so this is what life is like with twins."

That's what I am worried about.

Double the trouble.

After her brunch, she ran some errands and did some shopping with her mom, which allowed Stella to come over and actually decorate the nursery. I'm anxiously waiting for her to get home. An hour passes, and I see her car pull up the driveway. I head out to help with the bags.

"Hey."

"Hey," Delia says, not sounding like herself.

"What's wrong?"

"Nothing. I'm tired, and I think I ate too much. My stomach is tight, and the babies are kicking and moving a lot. I don't know, it's just been a long day."

"You were gone all day."

She nods. "We got a lot done, but I'm just . . . blah. I'm getting bigger, feeling more bloated too. I'm sure it's all par for the course and will only get worse."

"Maybe the doctor will have some suggestions."

Delia shrugs. "Maybe. I'll ask Dr. Locke when I go in for my next appointment."

This will be the first appointment that I miss. I'm really not happy about it, but I can't miss the meeting with the bank. "You're sure you'll be fine without me?"

"Yes, I am sure. It's just a routine monthly check. I promise, I'll be fine."

"I can ask to reschedule with the bank."

"No, you can't," Delia says with exasperation. "You're not going to change a meeting that you *have* to be at."

"I don't like not being there."

"And I appreciate that, but it's an appointment, not the birth. I promise that it'll be fine, and I'll call you once it's done and tell you what they said."

"Fine," I relent and grab the bags from the trunk, holding them in one hand, and press my palm to her back. "Why don't you put your feet up when we get inside?"

"I want to see the nursery first," she says with a little perk to her voice.

As much as I'd like to argue with her, I know better. There's nothing that will stop her from appeasing her curiosity. "Then you'll relax?"

She grins. "Yes. Then I'll go lie down and let you take care of me."

I kiss her temple. "Good."

We walk to the door of the nursery, and I push it open, feeling a wave of nerves. I think she'll like it, but I don't know.

Delia's gasp tells me all I need to know. We did all right.

The room is painted light gray and the cribs are positioned with the window between them. On the right will be our son's side. The bedding is all set up and looks far better than I could have done it. Stella found rustic antlers, which she had made into the shape of a P, and we hung that above his crib. I was really not sure we should since Delia may want the babies to have her last name, but Stella insisted, saying that if that were the case, it would be easy enough to change it.

It's very hard to argue with her when she uses logic.

It really is perfect though. His side is masculine but not so much so that it's obnoxious. The furniture that Mrs. Andrews bought is a dark gray wood and finishes off that side.

Opposite of that is our daughter's side. Here is where my sister went ridiculous. Her furniture is a whitewashed wood that has gray undertones that are feminine. Above her bed is a white canopy that makes the space soft. She had paper flowers made that go above the crib, and she said we'll add an initial once we know her name.

"This is . . . this is incredible," Delia says before taking a step inside. "I can't believe how perfect it is."

"I'm glad," I say with a smile. "I was a little worried."

"Why?"

"I just was. You didn't really give us any direction."

"I didn't really know how to do it, but this is better than I could've imagined." She kisses me. "Thank you."

"You're welcome."

Lovingly, she runs her hand along the bedding that's hanging over the edge of the crib. She's in front of the antlers staring up at the letter above our son's side. "For Parkerson?"

My chest tightens. "Stella had it made. I really didn't know what you'd want, but we can always take it down."

Delia's eyes turn soft. "We haven't really talked about it."

"No, we haven't, and I don't need to."

She sits in the rocking chair and her hands move to her belly. "We should."

I release a deep breath, steeling myself against whatever decision she is going to make. We're not married. This wasn't planned, and if she doesn't want the twins to be Parkersons, well, I can't say I would blame her. My family name isn't something we're all very proud of at the moment.

"We can wait," I assure her. When she's really ready to talk, we can.

"Josh, I want the babies to have your last name."

I look up, surprised she said that. "You're sure?"

"Of course, I'm sure."

"But we're not married."

"That's true, but it feels right."

"I love you," I say as I take her face in my hands. "So fucking much."

"I'm glad."

I smile and then kiss her lips. "So, you like the room?"

"I love it."

"Now that we have last names, we should start thinking of first names."

She grins. "I agree. Do you have any favorites?"

I hadn't really thought too much about it. The babies have been sort of abstract for me. I know they're in there, but until I felt them move, it was hard to think of them as real. Now, it's all becoming very real. We have furniture, decorations, and some clothes. We're five and a half months into this, and her baby shower is in a little over a month.

"I really don't. You?"

She purses her lips. "I'd be lying if I said I didn't."

"Okay, what are your choices, maybe I'll like them."

"Yeah right." She scoffs. "You are never that easy. Let's remember the bedding . . ."

"That was you."

"I knew what I wanted."

"You also wouldn't pick. I was fine with anything," I remind her.

I would've picked pink for the boy if it meant we were done.

Delia wraps her arms around my middle. "Fine. It's a bit weird, but for a girl, I like the name Gina. My father's name was Gene, and it felt like a good compromise for using a part of his name. And then for a boy I like Everett."

I let them sink in, and honestly, I really like them. Everett sounds like a strong name, and I can picture a little girl named Gina with blonde hair swaying as she runs around the house.

"I'm not just saying this, but I think they might just be perfect."

"Really?" Delia asks, her eyes wide.

"Yeah. I really like Everett. And I know how much you love your dad, and I also know your mother would probably love having your father's name honored that way."

"If you hadn't liked Gina, my second choice was Brynlee. I know they're a bit different, but that was just my idea."

"Let's put that as our backup."

Her smile is bright enough to light up the night sky. "Okay. Do you have anything you like?"

"I'll think about it and let you know, but for now, we'll create a list."

She rests her head on my chest as we stand in the nursery where our babies will sleep. I never imagined my life would be here. That I'd be holding the woman who I love and naming our children. It's different, amazing, and I am eternally grateful that things turned out this way.

Delia changed everything, and I'll never be able to give her the things she's given me, but I'll never stop trying.

Thirty-Three

DELIA

I'm sitting at the edge of the exam table, waiting for the nurse to come in. I've already gotten two text messages from Josh, requesting I text him as soon as I'm out of the appointment so he knows I'm fine. He's so crazy, but I love him for it.

Today is a big day for him. The family had enough money to get the build done, but they decided to take out a loan in order to keep some cash on hand. Josh has been working so hard to get a deal closed because, while the siblings may have a lot of knowledge, they don't have anything proving their experience to the bank. Everything was done through their father's name before, and they're a risk to loan money to.

But Jack worked up the numbers to show they are worth the investment. I have faith.

The nurse enters with a warm smile. "Hi, Delia. I'm Aly,

and I'm going to do your vitals and see if we can hear the heartbeats before Dr. Locke comes in."

"Great."

She takes my vitals and asks me a series of questions. "How is your sleep?"

"It's fine. I feel them a lot more at night."

"I have two, and I remember trying to fall asleep and they'd be doing somersaults."

I nod. "The last two days they've been a little less active."

"Yeah?"

"Last night especially. That's normal, right?"

Aly grabs the doppler. "You'll definitely have times when they're more active than not. Let's see if we can hear them."

She sets it up, and we hear something almost right away. I smile at the sound. It's still mesmerizing, and I can understand why Josh wants to be here, it's really special. "That's one of them, I'm going to press around to see if we can get the other to let us hear."

Her hands push around, shifting things, and I feel one of them push back. "Seems he or she isn't happy."

"Definitely." She moves it around more, focusing. "Twins are so hard some days. I'm going to grab the ultrasound machine to get a peek. One will often hide behind the other, and the doppler isn't always the best way."

"Is everything okay?" I ask, my nerves spiking.

Aly's hand rests on my shoulder. "I promise, this is totally normal with multiples. I'll grab Sara, our ultrasound tech, and be right back."

I release a heavy sigh. "Okay."

She heads out of the room, and I do everything I can to relax. She returns quickly with the tech and the ultrasound machine.

"All right, I'm going to take a peek, and then we'll get Dr. Locke in here," Sara says.

"Sounds great."

When she presses the wand to my stomach, I don't see much on the screen, just a lot of blurry objects as Sara clicks buttons. The sound of one of the twins' heartbeats keeps a steady rhythm, and after a few minutes, she sets the transducer down and smiles. "All done. I'm going to grab the doctor and let her know you're ready to see her."

"Was everything okay?" I ask Aly.

"I'm sure it is. We'll have Dr. Locke look it over and then someone will be in."

"Okay, thank you."

Aly smiles. "Of course. Sit tight." She exits the room, and I grab my phone, sending a text off to Jessica.

Me: How many ultrasounds did you have?

Jess: A lot because we were worried about Ember from the fire.

That's right. I'd forgotten about that.

Me: They just did another one, and I'm just wondering if it's normal.

Jess: I'm sure it's fine. They once had an issue finding the heartbeat and did an ultrasound.

Me: Gah! That's what we're doing now. So, I shouldn't worry?

I bite my thumbnail and try to calm myself. No one seems

worried about anything. The technician said this is really common with twins.

Jess: No, don't worry. Is Josh there?

Me: He has the bank meeting, and I didn't want to re-schedule since I have meetings the rest of the week.

Jess: Shit. I forgot that's today. Grayson has been slammed and working so much that I can't keep up.

There's a knock at the door, and Dr. Locke peeks her head in.

Me: Doctor is here. I'll text you later.

Jess: Love you.

I put my phone under my leg as she enters. "Hi, Delia."

"Dr. Locke. It's good to see you."

"You too. Is Josh here with you?"

I shake my head. "No, he's at work."

Her blue eyes watch me as she sits in the chair. "I see. Is anyone here with you today?"

"Nope."

"Okay, I just reviewed the videos from your ultrasound." Her voice takes a different tone, and she moves closer to take my hand in hers. "I am so sorry to tell you this, but one of the twins doesn't have a heartbeat."

I shake my head, staring at her. "What?"

Her eyes turn soft. "I'm sorry, but we can't find a heartbeat and there's no movement."

She's wrong. She's wrong and she's lying. I start to shake and my chest aches. "No! No. That's not possible. They were fine."

Dr. Locke clears her throat. "This happens sometimes, usually much earlier in the pregnancy, but it does happen. I'm so sorry, but I personally reviewed it from several angles, and there is no heartbeat on the girl."

My daughter. My little girl with the blonde hair and Josh's eyes . . . gone.

I lost her.

Tears fill my vision, and I start to tremble. "I don't understand. I'm not bleeding. I did everything right. Maybe it's wrong. Maybe the machine just didn't see it. She's in there, and she's alive."

"I know this is hard, and you didn't do anything wrong. Things sometimes look great and then suddenly they're not. I really wish that it was different news I was telling you, but it's not."

I can't stop shaking my head as the tears fall. "But I felt the baby kick. I felt it move. It was fine. You're wrong. Please, you have to check again. We have a plan, and we're going to have a little girl and a boy. We have names and a nursery."

The doctor shifts the ultrasound machine closer and pulls up the recording Sara took. She moves the mouse around as my tears fall relentlessly. This isn't possible. I can't lose her. I can't do this. How do I go through the rest of my pregnancy like this?

Dr. Locke opens the screen. "See that?"

There's a steady flutter. "Yes."

"That's baby A, which is the boy. His heartbeat is regular, and you can see him moving around." She moves the screen to a different image. "This is baby B, which was the girl. There's nothing here."

My eyes are riveted on the monitor, watching, waiting, and searching for anything. A tiny blip or a flinch, but there is nothing. No kick. No heartbeat. Nothing.

The tears fall, and I clutch my arms around my stomach, wanting to protect myself and the babies—baby in there. God, I lost one.

How did I do this? How could I lose one of them?

"Delia," Dr. Locke says with compassion. "You didn't do anything wrong. There are a hundred reasons this could have happened, and sometimes, there's just no explaining it. I am so sorry."

The sound that escapes my chest is painful to my own ears. I lost a baby. I lost one of our babies. I don't know how to feel, what to feel. One of the two is gone, and I feel lost and broken.

"I don't know what to say," I admit.

She takes my hand. "I know, I want to send you to the hospital for some bloodwork and monitoring. My biggest concern is a possible infection. I'd like to get you started on some antibiotics as a precaution."

I know she's speaking, but it's little more than white noise against the pain. All I can do is imagine the little girl we dreamed of and how that will never be.

"Delia?" Dr. Locke calls my name.

"I'm not even bleeding," I say again.

"You won't bleed. The fetal demise will stay in since you're not experiencing labor. It's the best course for baby A. We want to keep you and him as healthy as we can."

I try to hold on to the fact that I still have one. "Will he be okay?"

"There is nothing on the ultrasound that suggests he is in trouble, but you're going to be high risk, and we're going to monitor things very, very closely. If I see anything that concerns me, we'll come up with a plan. Do you need to call anyone?"

Josh.

His face flashes before me, and I can't breathe. I will never be able to tell him this. All the progress we've made and it's all going to fall apart here. He will inevitably blame himself when he is the last person who is at fault. He'll focus on how he wasn't here when, even if he were, it wouldn't have changed the outcome.

I shake my head, my hand resting against my throat as I struggle to speak. "No."

"You should have someone drive you, Delia."

There's only one person I can think of, and it's not him. Not yet. I need to think of how I'll ever be able to explain this to him.

"Okay. Yeah, I will."

The doctor leaves the room so I can make the call. I reach for my phone, and she answers on the second ring. "Jess," I say quickly. "I need you. Something's wrong."

"I'm on my way." The response comes without hesitation, and I curl up on the table, crying harder than I ever have before.

JOSHUA

While today's meeting was great, it was draining. We secured the loan we needed by impressing the bank with the progress we've made with the budget we have now. I'm walking the property with Odette, addressing some changes made that weren't approved by me or Stella.

"Who asked for that?" I gesture to one of the walls that has been pushed forward.

"That was Oliver," she says pulling out the change form. Sure enough, there is his signature with a note on the bottom that says: I wanted this. I don't care that I didn't ask. Vote me off the island for all I care.

"He's an asshole," I mutter.

"I think he was right," Odette says. "By pushing it back, it gives you more space here, which will help when you're dealing with the events."

"He's not often right."

"That's not the discussion," she says smoothly.

"You know, you do a good job managing us Parkersons," I note.

"Do I? After squabbling with Alex during the plans, I would think not."

"What happened with you two?"

She waves off the question. "It was nothing. I'm really happy for him. I think he'll do great work on that project."

"Me too, even if it means he's now across the world."

"That part is unfortunate, but if I got the offer he did, I would go too." Odette smiles. "What about you and Delia? How is she?"

Her name makes my lips turn up without even thinking about it. "She's great. We're doing good, ready for the twins."

"I don't know how you're going to handle twins and this place. It's going to be crazy."

I think back to how this all started, and it's crazy. One moment changed everything, which is what it's been for me and Delia too. A split second altered our lives.

My father's decision that caused the riff between him and Grayson. He chose to sleep with his ex, force Grayson to make a decision, and think the rest of us would fall in line. As insane as it is, I'm glad it happened this way. I've missed my siblings, and had I not come back to Willow Creek Valley, I wouldn't have Delia.

"I think we'll manage. We've dealt with worse."

"I have complete faith in you all." Before I can respond, Samuel walks over, hand raised, and Odette turns to me. "Excuse me."

"Of course."

Samuel has been a great help to Odette, and I know that Jack and Stella are more than pleased he and Kinsley moved here. It means their daughter might stay in Willow Creek permanently and they get to spend more time with her.

I let them talk and head out to the back deck area. We're going to have this connect to the restaurant, but we're also going to build another extension off the front that will have a cozier feel. Somewhere you can read a book or sit and talk.

I walk around, inspecting and measuring the side when my sister appears. "Really, Josh?"

I blink. "What?"

"What are you doing?"

"I'm doing what I need to. Working."

Stella lets out a deep sigh and shakes her head. "When Grayson said you were here, I thought . . . no. No way would he be working. Not my brother. Not my oldest and most amazing brother."

"Stella, I own this place too, in case you forgot."

My sister scowls. "Are we back to this?"

I'm getting a fucking headache. "To what?"

"Where work is all that matters? What about the people who need you, Josh? You're not this guy."

"I'm clearly this guy, and when the hell have I said work is all that matters? I think my actions have proven otherwise." My voice is clipped.

She throws her hands up in the air. "Then why the fuck are you here? Why, Josh? Why would you abandon her? Why would you be walking around the goddamn inn that's not even built yet instead of being at her side?"

"Whose side?" I yell.

Stella blinks and looks at me as though I'm a fool. "Delia."

I take a step toward her. "What about Delia?"

I watch as my sister seems to piece together that I have no idea what she's talking about. "She . . . she called . . . didn't she call you?"

My phone is in my hand, and there's nothing. "No. She hasn't called because she's at her appointment."

"Josh, I—" Stella pauses and then inhales deeply. "I thought you knew and weren't going. She called Jessica, and I was with Grayson when Jessica called him, telling him he needed to come home. He said he had to go but not why and was gone before I could ask. So, I called Jessica, who said it was Delia. They're taking her to the hospital, something is wrong. That's all I know."

I don't respond or think. I just run. I'm moving toward my car, my sister screaming my name, but I keep going. Something is wrong, and I am going to be too late. Again. I will fail her like I knew I would. I pull my door open, and Stella is there, pulling open the passenger side. "Josh, stop!"

"I have to go."

"You have to calm down. You can't go in there like this."

"I don't even fucking know what this is!"

Stella scrambles into the car. "I'm going with you."

I don't care. I just start the car and throw it in reverse. I feel as though I'm reliving ten years ago, racing to get the girl I love, needing to save her before it's too late.

"Josh, you have to slow down," Stella warns. "She's okay. Jessica is with her."

"I should be with her!"

My sister grips my wrist. "Calm down. You're going to be no good to her if you're a raging lunatic. I know you're worried, but she's with the doctors."

"I fucking did it again, Stella! Don't you see? I should've fucking been there. I should've been with her today, but instead, I was here because work was too important. I didn't leave after the goddamn meeting, I stayed and walked the property. She didn't call me! She didn't even call me because she knew!"

Stella watches me as I move through the streets, each mile feels like it takes an hour to cover.

"She knew what?" Her voice is soft and full of concern.

"That I'd be too late. That I wouldn't make it to her, and I'd hurt her."

"You're not making any sense."

I'm making perfect sense. I'm the guy who doesn't get there. I'm the one who allows the people I love to get hurt because I don't make the right choices. "This isn't the first time I've loved a girl and she died."

When we stop at a red light, my hands tighten against the wheel, and the sense of dread grows.

Stella's hand is still wrapped around my wrist, but when she speaks, her voice is soft and cautious. "Joshua, what are you talking about with a girl dying?"

This is the longest red light in history.

I turn to her, my body feeling tight and my heart racing. I never told my siblings because I couldn't handle disappointing them. I've tried my entire life to be almost a father to them. To give them what our own father never did. The idea of them seeing me even the slightest bit like him—selfish—is too much.

However, there's no stopping it now. My sister will see me for the man that I am, and I have to accept it.

I tell her a very short version about Morgan and the baby I

lost, and her fingers tighten.

"Oh, Josh, why did you never tell me?"

The light finally turns green, but I can't seem to move my foot off the brake. "How could I?"

"Because I'm your sister."

"Just like you told me about Kinsley?" I toss back, not to hurt her but to show her that we're all guilty of it.

"I was wrong, and so were you. We all keep these secrets, and it eats us alive. We judge ourselves harder than we would judge each other. I don't know why we're this way, but we have to stop. I should've told you about Kinsley when it was happening. I can blame the ignorance of youth and the fear of what you'd all think about me, but at least I had Jack through it all. Who did you have?"

My heart is pounding against my chest. "I couldn't talk about it."

"I understand, but this isn't the same."

It sure as hell feels like it. Once again, I'm at work when the woman I love needs me. Only, this time, Delia didn't call me. She didn't beg me to come because she knew I wouldn't make it. That I'd be at work and unable to get to her.

"I can't lose her, Stella."

"We don't even know what it is. Let's get to the hospital so we can find out, but you didn't fail her, and I refuse to let you think it. Drive, Josh, and get to her so she knows she isn't alone."

I race to her, desperate to reach her before it's too late.

Jessica is pacing the hallway when I get to the labor and delivery. "Josh . . . I . . . she asked me not to call. I'm sorry that I didn't, but I . . ."

I lift my hand, not wanting her to feel guilty. "I understand. Just tell me she's okay."

Stella called Jessica who explained she promised not to tell me. After that, I wasn't sure I should come, but Stella, the voice of reason, pushed me. So, here I am, where she doesn't want me and felt strong enough to keep it from me. She doesn't trust me, and right now, I'm fucking broken.

Jessica steps to me. "She's alive, and she's okay, to a point. I really think you need to hear all of it from her, but she's not in any life-threatening danger."

I let out a sigh of relief. "The babies?"

Her lower lip trembles. "I begged her to call you. She's just so afraid, Josh. She's afraid that you're going to hate her."

"Why the hell would I hate her?"

"I don't know, and she can't answer me."

"Tell me what happened."

Jessica shakes her head as her hand grips my shoulder. "You should go in there and talk to her. She needs you, but she's got herself so worked up about this being the end of you both. Just, I'm warning you. In all the years I've known her, I've never seen her this broken." Jessica tells me the room number and how to get there. Each step is slow, as though my feet have lead bricks on the bottoms. I don't know what I'm walking into, but no matter what, I vow that I won't fail her. Whatever she needs, I'll give it.

I get to the door and pause before knocking softly in case she's asleep. When she doesn't answer, I push the door open and walk in.

Delia is lying on her side, facing away from me. Her long

blonde hair falls down her back, shifting with her quiet sobs.

The sound of her crying takes what was left of my shriveled heart and destroys it.

"Delia?" I say quietly, and she flips around to face me. Rivers of tears flow down her cheeks, and her nose is red.

"No! No, I am not ready. I am not ready to lose you too!" She cries harder.

"Lose me?"

Her shoulders shake as tears come harder. "*I* lost her this time, Josh. I did, and now you're going to leave me too. I needed more time. I needed to prepare to go back to a life where I didn't have you."

I move quickly, gathering her into my arms as she sobs. "Talk to me. I don't know what the hell is going on, and I'm not going to leave you."

She lifts her head, sniffling hard. "I lost our little girl. There's no heartbeat . . . she's gone. I lost her. I lost one of the babies. Again, you lost a baby."

I pull Delia tighter to me, holding her because it's the only thing keeping me together. The little girl we spoke of, named, and gave a space to will never be. The loss of a child we never even knew slicing through me so hard I feel as though I'm losing everything.

But I hold it in because, right now, Delia needs me more than anything.

"You didn't lose her."

She sobs, clutching at me. "She's gone."

"It's okay, Delia. You didn't lose her."

Delia's brown eyes are filled with so much pain. "It was my job to keep her safe, and I didn't."

"That's not the truth."

She didn't do it. I did. It was me allowing myself to think I could love something and not lose it, but I don't say it.

"It's how I feel. The doctor said sometimes this just happens, but I don't get it. We were out of the danger zone. I felt fine. Tired, but fine. I didn't bleed or have contractions. She just . . . she stopped being alive, and I'm fucking lost. How do I do this?"

I brush back the hair that's stuck to her wet cheek. "You are strong. You are brave. You are an amazing woman, and you did nothing wrong."

Her tears fall. "You have lost so much already, and I . . ."

I've felt pain before, loss of something I loved, but this is a hundred times worse. Losing my daughter is devastating, but seeing Delia fall apart because of it is unbearable.

"Please, baby, don't," I beg. "I know that you're sad, but you didn't do this."

"I should've called you, Josh. I wanted to, but I was scared," she admits, her hand moving to my cheek. "I was so angry at myself and at life. We were happy. We gave her a crib with pink flowers over it. I just . . . I am so sorry."

My hands cup her face, hating the tears that continue to flow. "I'm sorry. I'm sorry I wasn't there today. That you did this alone and I wasn't here for you." Just like last time.

"I just didn't want it to be true."

I bring my lips to hers, tasting the salty tears. "I wish I could make it that way. What happens now?"

She sniffles and then pulls away, lying back in the bed. "They're making sure I don't develop an infection on what they keep calling a fetal demise. That word . . . it's just so . . . hard, and I can't hear it. She's not a fetal demise, she was our baby girl. She was going to be a person."

I hold her hand, unsure of what to say but offering her the comfort that I can give. "She was."

"She's not now. They're doing some tests to make sure the other baby is okay. I have to stop working because now I'm high risk and will be until I deliver—if I don't lose him too."

"Whatever we have to do, we'll figure it out."

She turns her head. "I can't . . . I just . . . can you hold me?"

She shifts over, and I climb onto the bed with her. My arms shelter her, and I wish I could shield her from the pain she's feeling, but I can't. All I'm able to do is try to hold her together. We stay like this, staring out the window as people come in, changing IV bags and talking, but neither of us pay attention. We just lie together, feeling the loss of a child, and I pray we can find our way through it all before I cost her anything else.

Thirty-Five

DELIA

My mother used to say that when the sun rises the day after heartbreak, the light clears away the pain. She is a liar.

As the brightness from the sunrise fills the hospital room, I feel no better. I feel like I lost a baby, which I did. I try to find solace in the fact that I am still having at least one baby, but it hurts. It hurts because there was still a loss, and I have to carry her because it's better for our son than if I deliver.

I use every bit of strength I have, which isn't much at all, not to start crying again. Josh's arm tightens around me. "You awake?"

"I am."

He shifts and then stretches. "Did you sleep at all?"

"Off and on," I say, keeping my back to him.

He was wonderful last night. He stayed in this incredibly

uncomfortable bed, holding me all night long. I needed him, more than I can say, and I am so worried that, once this all sinks in, we're going to fall apart. Josh has felt loss so deeply that he's still recovering from it ten years later, and now to go through it again . . . I'm scared.

He moves his hand up my back, rubbing the tight muscles. "The doctor said she'd be in this morning to talk about everything."

"She did say that."

He sighs and then gets out of the bed. "Yeah, I know it doesn't feel like it, but you're going to be okay."

I move to my back so I can look at him. "No, it doesn't feel that way. It feels worse. It feels like I'm pregnant and like I lost a baby. The life we envisioned has been ripped away, and I don't understand why. I have no answers."

Josh takes my hand. "Because that's what it is. We've lost a child, but we still have one, and we have no explanations other than it happens. I'm not really sure what the hell to feel either."

"I just keep trying to wrap my head around how what should've been a good appointment turned into this."

"Some of us just seem to be destined to suffer."

My eyes widen. "What does that mean?"

"Nothing. It means nothing." Only it doesn't feel like nothing.

"This isn't your fault, you know that, right?"

Josh lets go of my hand. "Yeah, I know that."

"Do you? Because if you're telling me this isn't my fault, and I'm the one who is pregnant, then it sure as fuck isn't yours either."

Something in my stomach clenches because I can see

something in his gaze. The way his eyes aren't meeting mine. Then he comes back to me. His hand brushes my hair back, and he gives me a sad smile. "I love you, and you're hurting, and I can't fix it. I can't help you feel better because I don't have any fucking way to change things."

I wrap my fingers around his wrist. "We're going to be okay."

He nods. "Eventually, we will. We'll move on because that's what happens after loss. We just . . . keep going forward." Josh leans in, his lips touch my forehead. "I'm going to grab coffee, want some?"

I shake my head, feeling unsettled. "No."

"No?" Josh asks.

"I'm not . . . I don't want it."

He's quiet for a beat, and I turn to see if he's still there. He watches me, concern etched on his beautiful face. "*You* don't want coffee?"

His tone causes me to wonder if I just imagined that exchange. Maybe he's fine, and I'm reading into everything. God, I'm such a mess. I'm so sad and angry that I can't think straight. Josh has been wonderful. He's been by my side the entire time, holding me as I cried and never once pulled away. I'm just such a riot of emotions right now. I can't unravel where one feeling starts and another begins. Each time I think I'm okay, I start sobbing again.

I shake my head and let the truth slip out. "Not even coffee can soothe my broken heart today. Nothing can. I think I'm going to be a mess for a while."

The defeat in his eyes is heavy. "All right. Want me to send someone in to sit with you?"

The last thing I want is another person consoling me. They

have nothing to say that I want to hear. "No, I'll be fine, I'm not a child."

"Well, I hope I'm excluded from that since you are my child," my mother says from the doorway. I turn, instantly feeling the urge to cry again.

"Mom."

She enters and rubs Josh's arm. "I'm so sorry for you both. I came as soon as I heard."

Mom was visiting her friend in Charlotte, and we got in touch with her late last night. Josh pulls my mother in for a hug. "Thank you. We're both . . . trying."

"That's all you can do."

He looks to me and then at her. "I'm going to grab coffee. I'll give you both some time together."

Mom nods once and then sits in the chair beside my bed. She doesn't say anything, but she doesn't have to. My mother has always been able to test my mood and then do whatever I've needed.

Her beautiful green eyes are filled with love and under-standing. She has felt the pain I'm in. She was pregnant and lost that baby four weeks after my father died. "We gave her a name. The day before my appointment. We sort of agreed on what to name her. How stupid were we? So hopeful and think-ing it would all be okay."

"And what name did you agree on?"

"Gina."

My mother's lip trembles and a tear falls, but she brushes it away quickly. "For your dad?"

"Yes."

The warmth of my mother's hand slides around my cold one. "I'm sure she would've been beautiful, like you."

"I don't know how to feel," I confess.

"I know."

"I'm still pregnant and yet I'm not."

"I know."

I close my eyes. "I just want to cry."

Mom's hand squeezes a little. "Then cry."

The permission that comes is freeing, but the tears don't follow. I want them to come, to let myself drown in them. "I don't have anything left."

I am struggling to come to terms with the reality of my life. How can I be both happy and utterly broken at the same time? It doesn't make sense. My son kicks at that moment and I move my other hand there.

"Your son still needs you, Delia," my mother says, pulling my attention. "He is still in there, needing his momma to take care of things. You can be sad. You can be angry, but you still have a son who's growing. I can't imagine what you're feeling. I know the devastation of losing a baby, but not when I was still pregnant like you are. I lost your father and that child within a few weeks. I was . . . well, devastated doesn't begin to describe how I felt, but I had you. I had to get myself up and dressed to make sure you were cared for."

"You're stronger than I am."

"Oh, sweet girl, I am definitely not. *You* saved me, Delia. *You* gave me a reason to go on with my life after feeling so lost. You're in pain and things look bleak, but there is always light. Tomorrow, the sun will rise again, the birds will chirp, and you aren't alone. You have Josh."

"He didn't even want this. He didn't want a family."

She shrugs. "He's here."

"For now."

She sighs and then shifts a little. "Do you want him to stay?"

I turn quickly. "Of course I do."

"Then don't push him away. Lean on each other and let love heal you both."

That's it, I've decided . . . no more tears. No more crying because my mother is right. I'm going to have a baby still, and I need to be strong. While it hurts and I'm sad, I have to grieve and prepare for the life that's still growing inside me.

I open my eyes to see Josh sitting in the chair. His head is down, resting in his hands, and it's as if the weight of the world is on his shoulders. The last two days we've been quiet, both dealing with the loss in different ways but trying to be there for the other.

He lifts his head and blinks a few times. "Hey."

"Hey."

"Did you sleep okay?"

I shrug. "I guess. It'll be nice to be back in my bed."

He sighs deeply. "I think we should ask the doctor to let you stay a few more days."

"Why?"

"Because what if you need something?"

"Then I'll call her. I can't stay here until I have the baby."

"I'm not saying for that long, but at least another week."

I shake my head. "I really want to be home. I'm tired, and I want to start moving on."

"What about the baby? You're still pregnant."

"And I will still be pregnant at the house," I say carefully because who knows if that's true. I lost one baby already.

Josh gets up, his hand gripping the back of his neck. "I just think, until we know about how this is going, that you should be here, where someone can monitor you at all times."

I move, sitting up straighter. "The doctor said last night that everything looks good and it would be better if I was home resting."

"That's great, but I don't see how. If we're here, then we have a team ready to fix things. Here, we know that the baby is okay because that machine tells us it is."

My lip trembles, and I bite down, trying to get control of my emotions. I'm just as scared as he is, but I am trying to keep my cool. Once I feel like I can speak again, I try. "I don't feel comfortable either, but we can't stay here."

"I think we should ask again."

A few minutes later Dr. Locke enters.

"Hi, Delia, I just went over your morning bloodwork and things are right where we want. No signs of infection or complications. We'll continue to monitor you and the baby closely for the remainder of the pregnancy, but based on what I'm seeing, you'll get to go home today."

"Why not just keep her?" Josh asks.

"Keep her here?"

"Yes, at least then she's on the monitors."

Dr. Locke's smile is full of understanding. "We can't do that because she doesn't require that level of care. There's no medical reason to keep her. She will do much better when she's at home and can be comfortable."

"How will I know if something is wrong with her?" His voice is clipped.

"I understand the concerns you're having. I can assure you

that if I thought she or the baby were in any danger, we would have her stay here." She turns back to me. "Your white blood cell counts are normal, and everything looks good. Going forward, we'll be monitoring you weekly, and I want you on bed rest for at least a week," Dr. Locke explains again.

Josh starts to pace. "You're asking us to go home and, what? Hope? How do we know if there's an issue? We won't. We're just going to have to wait for things to happen and then hope to God we get help in time."

My chest tightens as I listen to him go on about what's coming.

Dr. Locke speaks before I can. "You're nervous, and that's okay, but we did another ultrasound yesterday, and the baby looks good. We can go over the things to watch for. My office is ten minutes from you and either me or Dr. Willbanks are always on call."

My hands are shaking as my heart begins to race. "I just . . . I can't do this. I can't be freaked out, and I'm trying not to be."

Josh clears his throat, and when he speaks, this time, his voice is calm. "I just want to protect her."

And I want him to relax because he's freaking me the fuck out. "You can't protect me, Josh. You can't do anything to save this baby, just like I can't. We have to be vigilant, but I can't be afraid."

"You have both gone through a loss, and uncertainty is normal. I would be concerned if you weren't at least a bit worried." She heads over to Josh. "There are things you can watch out for. If she feels sick, vomiting, bleeding, decreased baby movement, we want you to call. Also, they make fetal heart monitors that you use at home. I want to warn you they aren't always accurate, but if it brings you both some comfort, it could be worth the investment." Josh pulls out his phone, and I would bet my ass he's ordering one. She turns to me. "Being on bed rest is just a precaution, and after this week, we'll evaluate if it's still necessary. You'll come in weekly so we can do bloodwork. I know you're nervous, but your health and the baby's health are my concern. If I believed either were in danger, you'd be staying here."

A shaky breath leaves my lungs. "Okay. Josh, please get the car so we can go home."

I can see that he's reluctant, but he doesn't fight me. He kisses the top of my head and then he and the doctor talk a little more, going over my discharge papers. When he leaves to get the car, I feel so alone and confused. All of this is too much for my heart.

The fears he has are everything I'm not saying. Now, I'm worried that this will ruin him, us, and whatever is left of my heart.

Thirty-Six

JOSHUA

We pull up to the house after a very quiet car ride. I'm not sure what to say to her because I have no idea how to explain feelings that are completely irrational.

Everything I worried about has become true. Delia is suffering because of me. Once again, I failed someone I was supposed to love and protect.

One day, she'll see it, and then, I'll be left with nothing.

"Josh?" she asks after a minute of me staring out the window.

"Yeah?"

"Are you okay? Are we okay?"

I look at her, finding her brown eyes filled with tears and uncertainty. "I should be asking you that."

"You seem distant."

"I'm just thinking about everything."

She sighs. "Me too. I keep thinking this wasn't real. That we didn't just go through all this, but the loss of her is . . . it's just . . ." Her voice cracks, and she starts to cry again. "I don't know how I feel. We have him, and he needs us. But it's not them or they anymore. I keep thinking about the twins, but now it's just one. It's crazy, right? I shouldn't feel this way because it feels selfish. I'm at least still going to have a baby, but Celeste won't."

Celeste was the woman in the room next to us. During Delia's stay, we met her and her husband, who had told us this was her third loss.

"You're not selfish."

She cries harder. "God, I'm a mess!"

I exit the car, moving around to her door and opening it. I pull her in my arms, holding her tight. She's not a mess, she's in pain. I don't have the right words to say or anything to make this pain go away. All I can do is be here for her until she sees that it was me who caused this.

"A mess or not, you're still beautiful," I tell her as I lean back.

She shakes her head. "Don't lie to me."

"I'm not."

"Well, I'm glad you think that, even if it's not true." Delia's gaze moves to the front door. "I'm not ready to go inside."

"Why?"

Her watery eyes find mine. "She had a home, Josh. She had a place for her."

The words slash against my soul, making everything ache. I should've thought about the nursery. The place where she was going to sleep next to her brother as the four of us built a life. A life that will never be.

"I'm sorry. I'm sorry I failed you."

Delia wipes the tears away. "How did you fail me?"

I love you. I love you and those babies, and I fucked it all up. Had I stayed away, allowed you to have a life free of me, it would've been different.

"I just did."

Her hand slides against my cheek. "You didn't fail me, Josh. You have been the only thing keeping me together."

I push against the words, the lie she's clinging to because seeing the truth is too hard.

"You are much stronger than that."

She laughs once, her head dropping. "I don't feel that way. I want to scream and cry and throw things. I want this all to be a lie, but it's not."

"No, it's not."

"So, now we move forward and try to find a way to get through the next few months."

I'm not sure that's possible, but the hope in her voice makes me keep my mouth shut. Grief is an unending thing. People think you get through the stages, and then, at the end, you just move past it.

That's not how it works.

It lives inside you always. A song, a scent, the whisper of the wind can bring it all back. In an instant, I'm there on that road, watching her drift away with the current. It creeps up on me, forcing me to see that moment over and over again. It may happen less often as the years have passed, but it still is there, waiting for the moment my guard is down.

Like now.

Losing our little girl was God's way of telling me that I am unworthy of the life I was forging.

I stand, extending my hand to her. "Then we go inside, and we begin finding a new future. One that isn't what we thought it would be a few days ago."

Her hand moves to her belly, and a wobbly smile pulls on her lips. "He just kicked in agreement."

"Glad he agrees."

Delia places her hand in mine, and I help her out of the car. We get to the front door to find baskets and coolers stacked up.

"What is all this?" she asks.

I grab the card, read it, and hand it to her.

I lift the cooler and laugh softly. Mrs. Villafane and Mrs. Garner have cooked for the last three days. There's food, cakes, breads, and pastries.

"Those two women are the sweetest things," Delia says as she peeks in the other basket. "I don't think we have to cook for a month."

"And you have cake."

Delia smiles. "Come on, babe. Let's go inside and eat cake on the couch and pretend that we aren't breaking."

"That I can do." I've perfected the art of pretending everything is okay when, clearly, it's not.

She may want to scream and cry, but I want to rage at the injustice of it all. I find love again, only to lose it.

Thirty-Seven

DELIA

I'm standing outside the nursery.

My hand on the doorknob, trying to decide if I'm ready to go in. It's still dark out, the morning sun hasn't awoken yet, but I can't sleep. My mind is racing, and fear has kept me restless.

Josh is asleep, and since we got home six days ago, neither of us have had the desire to look at this room, but at some point, I need to do it. Today we go back to the doctor, and I know that the lie I've been living is about to end. We won't be able to just act as though nothing is going on. I'll have an ultrasound or hear the heartbeat of just one.

Slowly, I turn the knob, push the door open, and walk in. Everything is just as we left it. Her bedding is hanging over the edge of the crib, and the pink flowers are still on the wall, waiting for her initial.

I walk over to the crib, touching the soft cotton bumper.

I don't know how long I stand here, but it's long enough that eventually I notice the sunlight starting to filter through the blinds.

It's there that Josh finds me.

His hand starts at the small of my back and then moves up to my shoulder. "How long have you been awake?"

I close my eyes, the orange light the only thing I see. My heart is pounding, and everything in me feels as though it's about to explode. But this is the first time since we got home that I've felt like he's here with me, even though he hasn't left my side.

"A while."

"I was going to take this all down." Josh's voice sounds strained. "I kept planning to do it, but I couldn't."

"We weren't ready to face it," I say, still not looking at him or anything really. "I don't know I am now either."

He lets out a long breath, and then I feel his lips on the back of my head. "We have to leave soon. I'll make sure this gets done."

The explosion I felt building slowly detonates. I whirl around, anger flowing through my veins. "Don't touch this!"

"What?"

"She was someone to me! This is where she should be, and she's not. Don't take her away!"

Josh blinks a few times and steps back. "I don't know what to do here."

"You can't just erase her. I still have her with me, and I can't . . . I can't fucking pretend anymore. I have to carry her around, knowing that she's not a baby anymore."

"I know, and I hate it."

"I do too. Now she's just a demise. How can I love something I never met? How do I feel the loss of her when I've never seen her, touched her, felt her in my arms? I don't understand why this hurts so damn much. We won't get to hold her, Josh. We won't get to see her and say goodbye to her. Instead, I have to carry her until the end and then she'll just disappear. Taking all her stuff away will do the same!"

The words come out of me as the tears do. Days of pretending haven't lessened the pain. It's all here inside me, and I can't hold it in anymore. No one can understand how this feels. To know that inside me is a child that isn't alive. They said she won't resemble a baby when she's born. I will never get to say goodbye to her, not really.

"That's not what I'm doing. I'm trying to make it easier for you. I don't want you to come in here and have it hurt."

"Do you think removing her crib will make it hurt less? That I won't remember that her crib was once here every time I walk into this room? I will. I'll always look at this room that will be our son's and remember he should have a sister."

"And do you think I don't feel that way? That this is easy for me?"

"You make it look easy!"

I'm not being fair. I'm not, but I'm so far past the point of reason that I can't stop. He hasn't mentioned her. He hasn't talked about anything other than asking me a million times if I'm okay.

"How do I make this look easy? I'm fucking broken, Delia. I'm trying to hold my shit together and be strong for you."

"Well, maybe I don't want you to be strong. Maybe I need you to break down so I know that I'm not the only one hurting. You haven't cried. You haven't said anything about it other than to ask if I'll lose our son."

He looks down at my belly and then to my eyes. "When did I say that?"

I throw my hands up and start to pace. "All you do is ask me over and over if I feel him kick? Do I feel sick? Do I need to call the doctor?"

"So, my being concerned for you is a bad thing?"

"Yes! Yes, because I can't stop it! I can't stop it," I say as I feel myself sink to the floor. Josh is there in an instant, pulling me into his arms, holding me as we both sit. I clutch him, needing his strength that I was so resentful of just a moment ago. "I can't stop it because I don't even know how it happened."

He and I stay like this, gripping one another as I cry in his arms, no longer able to keep my feelings inside. I repeat those words, over and over, until no more sounds come out.

"How are you doing?" Dr. Locke asks.

"We're okay."

She looks to Josh and then to me. "I am here if you have questions, I know this is a very difficult thing to come to terms with."

I nod, still too raw from this morning to talk about it.

Josh clears his throat. "How does everything look so far?"

Dr. Locke looks down at the papers. "Bloodwork looks good. The antibiotics we gave you as a precaution did well. We're going to have to keep a close watch on things, make sure that we don't have any signs of that. I think you're okay to return to work as long as you're not on your feet too much."

"I already requested that, and my boss said it was fine."

"You what?" Josh asks quickly.

"What?"

"You should stay home, off your feet, where you can rest." I clear my throat, doing my best not to snap at him again. He's lost his damn mind if he thinks he's going to dictate this to me. All I do is sit and think. I need some fucking normal again. I am falling apart and can't lose my job and my house too. "No, I need to work and pay my bills, so . . . if the doctor says I'm okay, then I am going to work."

His back goes straight, and I can see the frustration in the lines of his mouth. This is so not going to be fun. However, Josh surprises me by not saying anything more.

Dr. Locke, probably wishing she were in any room but ours, turns back to me. "I think you're safe to do that, but if you have any concerns, you come in right away. You're still considered high risk, but if you take it easy, it may be good for you to have some sense of normalcy."

"I agree." I raise my brows, looking at Josh.

"Sure," he replies.

"Okay, I'd like to do an ultrasound to check on the baby and listen to the heartbeat."

I lie back on the table, a sense of dread filling my chest. What if there's something wrong again? What if she can't find his heartbeat? What if, in the last seven minutes since I felt him move, something has gone wrong?

My shirt lifts, and the warm gel hits my skin before the monitor presses against me. I don't look. I don't watch because, if this happens again, I won't be able to handle it. Instead, I watch Josh's eyes, which are studying the monitor.

And then a thought that has no right to be here enters.

What if they were wrong about her? What if she's really okay?

No. I know it's not possible. I saw the ultrasound and know the truth. We lost her, and she'll never come back.

I fight back the tears because I've cried so damn much.

Josh turns to me, his blue eyes find mine, and I reach for him, needing him to touch me, tell me I'm okay, and that we're okay. It's been a rough week, and I hate the distance that's spreading between us.

His fingers tangle with mine as the doctor speaks. "See this here?" She points to an area. "That's the baby's heartbeat, and everything looks great. He's moving around in there like he should be."

The two of us exhale, and then Josh leans down and kisses my lips. "Thank God."

"You're sure?" I ask Dr. Locke.

"As far as I can see, you're doing well and so is the baby." She wipes my stomach. "I'll have you come in each week so we can keep checking on him, but he looks healthy."

Josh's hand tightens. "I'm glad Delia and the baby are okay."

She nods once. "I'll see you next week."

"Thank you."

He helps me up, and I brace myself for whatever fight is going to come from my wanting to go back to work. He may have let it drop in front of the doctor, but I know better.

He doesn't understand that I can't afford not to have an income, and Josh forgets that he is living on his savings until the resort is up and running.

Josh keeps quiet on the ride home. The tension in the car is palpable. When we get inside, he finally says something.

"I don't want you to go back to work."

At least I was prepared. "Why?"

"Because there are too many variables."

"Do you like having a roof over our heads?"

His head jerks back. "What?"

"I have to work. I have to pay for this house, my bills, and all that. I know you're helping, and it's been great, but you're not exactly in the financial position you were before. I'm working so that we don't end up having to move in with my mother."

He runs his hands through his hair. "I have plenty of savings."

"That doesn't change things. I want to make sure that I have vacation time once the babies—baby comes. I'd like to stay home with him for a bit. Not taking all my saved time now will allow for that."

"I just worry," he says, his voice thick with emotion.

"I wouldn't do anything to put us at risk."

Josh lets out a deep sigh. "I know. Can you at least take a few more days? Just let me feel a little more comfortable."

I catch my lower lip between my teeth and think about it. He's not asking for a lot, but the longer I stay cooped up here, the less normal I feel. I've always worked, and while many people don't enjoy it, since my promotion, I do. But he's not asking for me to never work again, just take another few days.

"I can do that. I'll take three more days, and then I'll go back."

"Okay."

Thirty-Eight

JOSHUA

"We brought you a casserole," Mrs. Villafane says. "Kristy baked Delia a cake too."

I smile, forcing my lips into the foreign state. I can't remember when the last time I truly smiled. Probably before we lost our daughter. "Thank you."

Delia comes up behind me. "Is that a cake?"

"It is. Oh, you sweet girl, how are you?" Mrs. Garner asks.

"I'm doing okay. One day at a time."

I open the door fully, letting them inside because it seems they were doing that anyway.

Mrs. Garner presses her hand to Delia's cheek. "I'm sorry, honey. I lost two babies before my last son was born. It's such a hard thing to grieve."

"Thank you. Cake makes everything a little easier, right?" Delia tries to sound light, but I hear the sadness in her voice.

"Cake is a magical thing," she agrees.

Mrs. Villafane points to the door. "Joshua, out in the car is a basket with more food. Be a dear and grab it for me."

I catch Delia's grin as I do as she asks. When I get back in, the women have sliced the cake and are dishing it.

"Now, I know this is a hard time, but if you need anything, we are always here."

"We appreciate it."

"Even if you just need someone to check in every few hours," Mrs. Garner offers.

A piece of cake falls from Delia's lips. "No, no. That's not necessary. Josh has been home with me."

"Yes, and it's been great because I heard Jeremy caught those kids that tried breaking into the house."

"Which kids?" she asks.

"Oh, just some teenagers."

Delia looks at me. "Told you it was nothing to be worried about."

"Better safe than sorry," I toss back. And it goes for more than that.

"I'm glad to hear that, Mrs. Garner."

"Me too, but as I was saying, I'll come by every day and we can just sit together if you need some company."

She shakes her head. "That's not necessary, I go back to work tomorrow."

Their eyes bulge, and they look to me. "You're letting her go back to work? What if she falls? What if something happens to her?"

"I tried to stop her," I add in. "I wanted her to stay home."

I'm beginning to like these women a bit more. They brought food, dessert, *and* they're on my side in this.

"I'll be fine," Delia says quickly. "Josh and I have discussed it, and my doctor thinks it's fine."

Mrs. Villafane waves her hand dismissively. "Please. Those hacks don't know the first thing about babies."

"Considering she delivers them every day, I trust she does," Delia says quietly.

"Well, I could deliver them too, you know. I had five, and by the last one, I don't even think I was needed there. The baby does the work, and the doctor is just there to catch it. Clearly, Josh doesn't agree with the doctor either," Mrs. Garner helpfully points out.

"I don't."

Delia crosses her arms against her chest. "It's a good thing that I have my own mind and can decide for myself."

I wait for my new best friends to say something to sway her.

Instead, it's mutiny.

Mrs. Garner pats her arm. "Don't be upset, honey. We all just love you. If you think you're okay to do this, then you should."

Delia nods once. "Thank you."

"I still think it's a bad idea."

She huffs. "You also don't want me to walk to the bathroom or go outside because of tripping hazards."

"Because I don't want to see you get hurt," I defend myself.

"I appreciate that, babe, but I can't be in a bubble."

I'd really fucking prefer that.

We let it drop as the two ladies continue to chatter on, offering the newest pieces of gossip.

Apparently, Bill and Fred have decided on a name for the

baby, William Frederick . . . how original. And then Mrs. Garner tells me that she saw my mother.

"Have you talked to her much?"

Delia looks to me expectantly.

"I haven't."

"Why not? She's trying."

"I didn't realize you knew her well."

"We don't, she was always a bit too uppity for me, but I've
seen her spending time working at the youth center. It's nice to
see her making an effort, unlike your father who is still causing the gossips, not us, though, to talk."

I cringe internally. My father is a piece of shit. "Not really
my concern anymore."

Mrs. Garner taps my arm. "Of course not. You're nothing
like him. You're a good man who loves the woman he's with.
You'd never let any harm come to her, let alone be the one who
inflicts it."

"Right." Just don't ask the woman I let die or the woman
in front of me who is in pain.

Mrs. Villafane picks up next. "It's not like Josh would ever
be so careless. He's always there for the people he loves."

I clear my throat, uncomfortable with this. "I fail too."

"We all fail, but you've always been the hero."

"I'm not."

A part of me wants to wail at these women, show them that
I'm not great. I wasn't there when she lost the baby. I wasn't
there when she needed me most. I let her down, and one day,
she'll see that.

Mrs. Garner nods. "Well, no one has ever died because of
you not being there."

If they only knew.

The walls are closing in.

I can feel the oxygen being sucked out of my lungs. I stand here, shaking as everything around me happens quickly.

Delia. She's in front of me, arms out, yelling for help as the water rises around her. The car is starting to move, the current's pushing her farther from me.

"Delia!" I scream. My lungs fighting for air because I'm tired. I've been trying to get to her, but each step forward comes with a loss of ground.

People behind me yell, and then a hand wraps around my arm, tugging me back. "I have to get to her! I have to save her!"

"You can't go out there, it'll take you with her!" the man yells as two other people form a chain, locking hands and arms.

I don't care. Let it take me because I can't lose her. "Josh! Please! I can't . . . I'm going to lose him!"

Her cries tear at my heart, ripping a roar out of my lungs as I go forward harder. I need to reach her. I can't lose her like this. Not when I know what it is to love her. She needs me, and I will do everything, even at the cost of my life, to get to her. I'll go down with her before I let her drift away.

"Delia! Look at me!" I yell as the car nudges farther down. "Don't leave me, goddamn it! Don't let go! Not again, baby. Don't."

She nods, and I inch forward. For once, the current isn't against me, it pulls me closer, but my hand, which was gripping the people forming the chain, weakens.

"Hold on!" the man yells, and the wind and rain whip my

face, making it hard to hear and see.

I try, but then a strong gust hits us, the car starts to move, and I panic. I need to get to Delia. I have to save her. I can't let another person die because of me. I will not fail her too. I will never allow another person to die because I loved them.

I rush, the water coming higher, up over my head, but I don't stop. I keep going, fighting, yelling, and kicking with all that I am to get there. I reach the window, but it isn't her in there. She's gone, swept away.

Just like everything in my life . . . lost.

"Josh!" Delia is there, shaking me. "Wake up!"

My eyes open, and I gasp for air. Her hands are on my face, and I'm covered in sweat. "What happened?"

"You were yelling my name. You were . . . I couldn't wake you."

It was a dream. Just a dream, but it was so fucking real. I could feel the water, the coldness seeping through my bones. My heart is pounding as though I were just back in that flood, fighting to reach her.

"You're okay?"

She nods. "Yes, we're here, and we're fine."

I move my hands, taking her face in mine, pulling her lips to me. I need her. I need to feel her, touch her, know she's okay. God, I lost her. I'm going to lose her because nothing I love is safe.

Delia tries to pull back, but I move quickly, not allowing her to break away. Then she stops fighting. She kisses me with every bit of need that I'm feeling. The two of us, broken and lost in our grief, cling to one another.

I want to drown in her because she is life.

She moves to her side, her hands going to my chest, and I

kiss her harder. While I know she's not in danger, it's as though my heart won't settle in my chest. The terror that's living inside me is too much, and I can't breathe.

"Delia," I say as if to call her back to me.

"I'm right here. I'm safe, and I love you."

Love. God, she needs to see the destruction it brings, but even with knowing that I'll be her demise, I can't stop myself from loving her. Everything good in this world is her, and I am going to extinguish that because I wasn't strong enough to stay away. I kiss her harder, deeper, with everything I feel, and say it all through my touch.

I love her.

I need her.

I'm going to lose her.

Her fingers slide through my hair, holding me where she wants me. I know she's in pain. The loss of the child is too much for either of us. I see the way she looks at me, the way she holds in her tears, trying to be strong. One day, she'll know the truth of why it all happened.

She'll hate me, and I'll deserve it.

So, for now, I kiss her.

"Josh," she says. "I . . . I love you. Please, just love me."

"More than I can say," I tell her. It's true, my love for her is real, but I also think that love should be freedom. It should give her a safe place. I can't do both, and it's killing me.

"Just kiss me. Kiss me until it doesn't hurt," Delia pleads.

I move quickly, shifting off the bed with my heart racing. It'll always hurt. I'm what hurts.

"Josh?" she says as I scramble farther back.

"We can't, Delia."

"I know, but . . ."

We can't have sex, and while that's what she probably thinks I mean, it's not. It's everything. The hurt and fear that lingers in her eyes are what keep me from saying everything. I don't know what way is up anymore.

I love her, want her, need her, and yet, I am fucking petrified that I'll lose her.

Not in the way that I just won't get to be with her, but that she's going to die. Morgan died. The baby died. It's always the people I love who are hurt.

Delia has to get through this pregnancy and birth. There's too much to risk.

I step back again. "I can't hurt you."

"You're not."

"I am! I'm . . . fuck. I can't do this. I can't live through watching you hurt."

She shifts onto her knees. "I'm trying! I'm trying to be normal, and when you kiss me, when I am in your arms, it is like I am me again. Now you're pushing me away?"

"I'm protecting you. Don't you see that?"

"You want to protect me, Josh? Hold me close. Take me in your arms and tell me it'll be okay. Tell me you love me, and you're here with me. We've barely even spoken to each other this week."

"What do you want me to say?" I yell, my hands flying up. "I can't fix this! Once again, I can't make this better. I can't give you back the baby we lost. I can't guaran-fucking-tee that you'll deliver our son safely. I'm sitting on the sidelines, watching all of this and hoping to God that nothing else happens."

She climbs off the bed, her hand moving to her stomach. "No one can do that. I'm dealing with the same fears, but we have each other. You're here with me, and we should be leaning on each other."

A shaky breath escapes my mouth. "I have to go."

"Go where?"

"I just have to think."

Delia watches me, and after a few seconds, she shrugs. "Then go."

I grab my keys and do exactly that. I leave, feeling lost and unsure of what the hell to do now. I'm losing her. I'm losing myself. I'm going to lose everything because that's what I deserve.

Thirty-Nine

DELIA

I t's been six hours since Josh left the house. He sent me a
text about an hour ago.

**Josh: I'm at the resort, checking on things. I'll be home
later. Call me if there is anything you need.**

I read it again, unsure of how to process this new turn of
events. I am fully aware that grief affects us all differently.
The fact that Josh is clearly not handling his is what worries
me. The dream and the way he screamed for me over and over
as though I were dying made my chest ache. I could hear the
panic in his voice, and when he woke, I could see that he was
not okay.

I asked him if he wanted to talk about it, and he said he
was fine.

Yet, for the last week, he has been here, but there has been space between us that I couldn't push through.

He looks at me, but it's as though he's a million miles away and I don't know what to do.

So, I'm sitting on the couch lost in pain, feeling less alone than I did when he was here.

"Delia?" Someone calls as there's a knock on the door. "It's me."

"Come in, Stella," I yell back.

She opens the door and comes in with a latte in her hand. "I come bearing gifts."

"You bring the right ones."

"After being your friend for this long, I should know at least this much," Stella says before kissing my cheek and sitting beside me, handing the coffee over.

"Thanks for this."

"Of course."

"Did your brother send you to babysit me?" I ask.

She shakes her head. "No, I was coming over to remove him and force him back to work, but then I saw his car was gone. Where is he?"

"Work."

"Glad I'm here then. The last phone call didn't go so great."

I heard it. Josh was yelling at her and his brothers, and even though I was inside and he was out by the tree line, I could hear him.

"He's struggling."

"I know, but he's biting everyone's heads off, and it's to the point that even Oliver wants to kick his ass."

I sigh, dropping my head to the back of the couch. "He isn't handling this well. I don't know what to do."

"Has he said anything?"

Telling Stella feels like a betrayal. Josh doesn't really talk about his feelings. He offers advice and is there for everyone he loves, but letting others take some of his burden isn't his strong suit.

I chew on my thumb and decide that I can't break his trust.

"He's just . . . feeling a lot and not really confiding in me about it."

"Sounds like him."

"I'm going to lose him, Stella." As I say it, my heart clenches and tears form. "I just got him, and now I'm going to have to go back to a life where we're not together. Each day, it's like he's pushing farther and farther away."

"You know he told me about the girl in New Orleans."

"He did?"

She nods. "I don't think he meant to, but once he started, it was like he just couldn't stop, you know? I was in shock, but how he's been for the last ten years makes a bit more sense. It's like he punishes himself for not being able to save her."

"I know, and now what? He loves me and he loved the twins. Now we're all going to lose. I can't take much more. I really can't. I love him, but this hurts. It is so hard to watch him shut down and act as though he's really fine."

"Don't cry, Deals," she says as her hand grips mine. I cry a bit, feeling overwhelmed, and then she releases me. "If you lose him because of this, then he never deserved you. Josh is . . . well, I don't know because he doesn't let any of us in. However, he can't use the past as an excuse to hurt his future. The loss you're both feeling is hard, but if he would lean on you, then you'd get through it."

"He's having dreams," I tell her.

"Of?"

"He won't talk about them, but he was screaming and thrashing. I think he was back in the flood."

She sighs. "I'm so sorry. I would offer help, but I think he'll just shut down. I've never been able to get through to him. Only advice I have is to talk to him and try to make him see how much you both need each other before it's too late."

"And if it already is?" I ask hesitantly.

"Then you let him go."

Day turns to night and still no Josh. My fingers have hovered over the call button, yet I won't do it. It's like a part of me already knows what's coming, and I'm putting it off.

The baby kicks, and I get up, pacing around the room. I don't know what to do, but it feels like each minute that passes is an hour.

Finally, I press send, only to have it go right to voice mail.

"Josh, I don't know where you are, but . . . call me."

I grab the blanket and curl up on the couch, unable to do anything else. After another hour, the door opens, and Josh walks in.

"You're still up?"

"You're finally home."

He tosses his keys onto the table. "I was busy at work."

"Busy avoiding me is more like it."

"Please don't start, I'm exhausted."

I get to my feet. "And I've been worried sick! You storm out of here this morning and are gone for over twelve hours with nothing. I called, no answer. I didn't even get a text after that cryptic one this morning."

"I shut my phone off."

I let out a puff of air. "Yes, why would you keep your phone on when your pregnant girlfriend might need you."

"You're fine. I'm fine. All is well. Not completely because we're clearly being punished, but . . . semantics."

My eyes widen as I stare at this man I don't know. "What do you mean being punished?"

"I'm going to bed. I need to go to work early."

He starts to walk away, but I chase after him, grabbing his arm. "No, what did you mean?"

"Exactly what I said. You're being punished because of me. It's clear that this is just the beginning, so I'm preparing."

I don't understand what he's saying. What punishment is because of him? "You're not making sense."

"What part isn't clear, Delia? You were fine before I showed up. You had the perfect house, new job, and life was great. Now . . . you're suffering."

I blink a few times because, yes, I'm sad. Yes, I'm struggling with the loss we're enduring, but I'm not suffering. "No, I'm not. I'm dealing with things. I'm grieving, Josh."

"And so am I, but at least you don't have the added layer of hell of knowing who is the cause."

"You believe that this is your fault?"

"Obviously."

I've always known he takes on the weight of the world, but this is crazy. I move toward him, my hand brushing his cheek, and he jerks back.

"You didn't do this. We lost a baby, Josh. That is nature and nothing to do with you. It isn't your fault any more than it's mine."

"How would it be your fault?" he bellows.

"I lost her! I did it! She was my responsibility, and now look at what happened."

"No, that's ridiculous!"

"What's ridiculous is that you think this is your fault! Don't you see that?"

He takes a step back, his eyes on mine. "I know what I bring. I know what my love does. Look at the body count around me!"

"You lost one person. One, Josh. That doesn't make you the master of destruction. It means that someone died—tragically—and you never dealt with it. You are no more at fault for what happened to Morgan than I am for Gina."

He huffs. "No, you're in denial. I destroy everything. I love and people lose. It's reality, and you failing to see that is only hurting you. I deluded myself into thinking that it could be different. That we were different. Now I see. I see what my loving you is doing to you."

"You're *choosing* to see it that way."

He laughs once. "Yeah, I chose it all. I chose to watch my girlfriend drown. I chose to fail you and lose our daughter. I chose it because that's what I want. No. I don't want this. I don't want this anymore. I don't want to watch you die because of me."

I try again, going toward him, but he backs up. "No. Don't. Don't try to fix me. I watched her die in front of me. I watched you cry as we lost our daughter. What's next, Delia? You? Our son? It'll happen because that's what always fucking happens."

"So, you're going to push me away? Not love me anymore?"

"I wish I could. I wish I could stop this feeling in my chest.

I wish I didn't love you so fucking much that it hurts to breathe. But do you know what hurts worse? This. This goddamn pain that never ends. Having to live with the knowledge that, any day now, you're going to hurt again."

I stand here, unsure of the next step. He is convinced that this is all his fault, and despite it being irrational, it's his belief. I can keep saying it's not, doing my best to convince him, but until he's ready to actually accept it, I don't know we'll ever get past it.

"And this is truly what you think?"

"It's what I know."

My heart breaks. "Okay then."

That seems to stun him a little. "What?"

"What now, Josh? How does this go? What is your solution to all of this? Are you going to get help or are you just going to walk away?"

"I'm going back to how it was before."

The air in my chest feels heavy. "Meaning?" I choke out the word and wait.

Josh presses his lips into a thin line. "I'm going to the RV for a few days."

"Just a few days or will you be back?"

"I don't know, but I need to put some distance between us."

Tears stream down my face as he shreds my heart. He really believes this is his fault and can't see that I love him and we can work through it. He's breaking us. "I see. So, you're leaving me?"

"I'm going to the RV a few towns over. It's not exactly leaving. I'm just putting some distance between us until I know you're safe."

Right.

If he wants distance, he's going to get that. I have always loved him, but I won't live like this.

"If you go, that's it. I'm not going to do this, and I told you that when I got pregnant. I can do this on my own, but you chose to love me. You wanted us to be a family. There's no way I can do it this way."

"You're giving me an ultimatum?"

"No, I'm giving you a choice." I soften my voice. "I'm giving you the option to choose me, Josh. To love me. To love the risks, the rewards, the possibilities, and the failures we'll endure. Nothing in life is perfect. Loss is inevitable, but I'm right here. I'm sad and hate that we lost our daughter, but we still have hope."

Josh goes to move forward but stops himself. "Hope for what?"

I always knew this would be the end in some way. That he wouldn't choose me. He'd walk away. The only reason we are even together now is because I got pregnant. Without the babies, there would never be an us. I'm not sure how I didn't see it sooner.

"Hope for our son! Hope for the life we were building. Hope for anything more than the shell of a fucking man you were before. I wanted us to be happy."

"I did too, but how the hell can we be? How can I love you when I know the ending?"

This time, I'm the one who pulls back, erecting a wall around my already decimated heart. "You created the ending. It didn't have to be this way. If you really believe that loving me is going to cause pain, then you should go. Not because I want you to but because I love you enough not to want that life for you. So, you choose, Josh."

He looks at me, his pain written all over his face. It all clears, and I have a sliver of hope that the decision he made is the right one, but he turns, his hand gripping the edge of the entryway table for just a second before he's reaching for me. Before he's kissing me. I close my eyes, the joy bubbling up that this isn't the end.

Tears this time aren't sadness as they move down my cheeks.

He pulls back, blue eyes staring down at me. "I'm sorry."

I blink, confusion now taking hold of me. "What?"

Josh grabs his keys from the table and walks to the door. "I'm sorry that I'm not the man you need."

The door clicks closed, and I feel a whole new ache in my chest as I hear his car's engine fade away in the distance.

Forty

DELIA

I keep trying to cry. I wait for the tears to come, but they don't.

It's funny how that happens. When I wanted to stop feeling sad, I couldn't make that happen, and now, I would give anything not to be drowning in this hollow numbness.

"I'll kill him," Jessica says, taking a seat on the couch across from me.

I didn't call her, but she just appeared. I'm assuming Grayson told her. Whatever.

"It's not like I didn't expect this."

"You expected the man you love to walk out?"

I shrug. "Maybe. He's broken, and I can't do anything about that."

"I'm going to break him."

"I don't think you could do much damage." I pull the blanket over me. I'm cold. I wonder if it's normal to be this cold.

"Probably not, but it would make me feel better."

"Thanks, Jess."

"I'm sorry. I really am. I thought he had changed, and . . . I don't know."

I did too. I let myself believe that he really loved me. That we could finally be a couple and build a life together. I was naïve and should've guarded myself better. I rub my stomach, feeling the baby moving inside me. It's him I'm sorry for. Our son who could've had a loving family with two parents. Not that there's anything wrong with non-traditional, but I wanted at least a chance at that.

"You know what the worst part is?" I ask absently.

"What?"

"That had he just talked to me, told me what he was feeling, we could've tried. Instead, he closed himself off. He was having nightmares and still wouldn't open up to me. I would've given whatever he needed to get his head straight. I thought the pain of his past was starting to ebb."

"You think this is about his past?"

I purse my lips, considering that. "I don't know. Maybe not. Maybe this new loss just pushed him over the edge."

She reaches out and takes my hand. "The Parkersons aren't exactly known for their exceptional skills in communication. Look at what happened when Grayson found out about his dad and his ex. He lashed out, pushed me away, and I almost died."

"I'd like that not to be the case here."

"It's why I'm at your house to make sure of it," she says with a soft smile. "My point is that these guys were taught to hide their pain at all costs and never show weakness. They do that by letting it all build up until they break."

"It's not an excuse."

She shakes her head. "No, it's not. It's not okay, and it's not healthy, but it's the reason behind it. I'm not saying to accept that behavior, but you should know where it's coming from. I loved the saying that anger is the outward expression of sadness. Dr. Warvel tried to explain to me that I was angry because I was so sad after the plane crash. I just didn't know how to feel the sadness because it was too much."

"You think he's sad?"

She nods. "I think he's devastated. I think he loved that baby you were going to have every bit as you did. He loves you, and he doesn't know how to handle that. I think he's also afraid. Stella told Grayson and I about the girl in New Orleans."

I jerk my head up at that. "She did?"

"I know she probably wasn't supposed to, but she had to tell his siblings so they could do whatever to help. My point is that he is still struggling with how he felt about her and that baby's death and now this. It's a lot easier to be angry than it is to be sad, but until he deals with that, really deals with it, I don't know that he's going to get his shit straight."

I lean my head on Jess's shoulder and sigh. "I love him."

"I know."

"I think he loves me too."

"I think he does too."

"But I can't watch him fall apart and live in this place where he's convinced that because he loves me, I'm going to die."

Jess squeezes my hand. "I know."

And then the tears come because the reality is . . . I can't help the man I love and get myself through this right now.

I upheld my part of the bargain with Josh, not that I felt I owed it to him, but I waited the length of time he asked me to, and today is going to be my first day back to work. I've spoken with Ronyelle, who I think is even more strict about what I'm allowed to do than Josh was.

She's set up my office so I can be comfortable, and everyone on the floor has been made aware that they are to come to me if they need anything. I'm not allowed to get up unless the building is on fire. Even then, I think she assigned people to come carry me from the building.

I head inside, waving to everyone as I pass, and enter my office to find Ronyelle already waiting.

"Are you feeling okay?"

"I'm fine."

"Yes, but you walked a lot."

My eyes narrow. "I walked from the parking lot. It wasn't a lot."

"I don't like this."

"Like what?" I ask.

"You being out of the house."

"Well, unless you want me to go crazy being trapped in a house, staring at all the things that Josh left, you won't fight me and you'll be understanding."

"I can be understanding without liking the situation. Speaking of that man, have you heard from him?"

I sigh. "He's called or texted me each day. I just haven't replied. He knows I'm fine because his siblings keep stopping by."

"Oh?"

"Jess came, then Stella was yesterday."

"And you don't want to talk to him?"

I want to talk to him more than anything. I miss him so much it freaking hurts, but I can't cave in and leave my heart exposed more than it is. We should be dealing with our grief as a couple, but we're not. I'm doing it on my own, and if I'm going to be a single mother, I should get used to it.

"What's the point?" I say with defeat. "Unless he suddenly got his ten years' worth of baggage under control, we're at the same point."

She gives me a sad smile. "I was really rooting for you guys."

"Me too."

"I think he loves you."

"Well, he sucks at showing it."

Ronyelle shifts her weight and chews on her lower lip.

"Say it," I encourage. We both know she's going to anyway.

"All right. I don't know what his deal is, but I do know you. You aren't a quitter. You fight for the people you love, and I'm going out on a limb saying that whatever the eldest Parkerson's issue is, it's not you. There's clearly something he needs to resolve, and, well, I can't think of anyone more capable of making him want it than you."

"That may be, but Josh has to want *me* more than his regret, and until that happens, we're never going to be together."

"I hope it changes." Ronyelle's soft voice trembles.

"Me too."

More than anyone will ever know.

Forty-One

JOSHUA

"**J**ust do what I say, Oliver!" I snap.

Oliver turns slowly, and the calm façade is a precursor to him unleashing his inner rage.

"I'm going to wait for the apology I deserve."

I close my eyes, wanting to fight him. It would be so much easier if he would've just punched me.

"Anytime, Josh," Oliver prompts.

"I'm . . . I'm . . ."

"Sorry. That's the word you're looking for, asshole."

"Sorry," I finish.

"You need to get your shit straight, brother. You're a damn mess, and I'm the only one who isn't ready to beat your ass."

"Why is that?"

Oliver puts the papers down. "Because I've been where you are. I loved a girl so much that I was ready to marry her, and I lost her."

He was so sure that Devney was the one for him. He had it all mapped out, and then she realized she was in love with her best friend. Oliver was fucking wrecked. I was able to convince our dad to get someone else to run the Pennsylvania bed and breakfast and send him to Wyoming. It was the only thing that kept him afloat.

"So, you pity me?"

"No, I just have been at that low spot you're currently sinking in."

"She won't respond to my texts or calls."

Oliver laughs. "Would you?"

I'd like to think I would. Today was her first day back to work, and I'm worried about her. She has a doctor's appointment in a few days.

"If I knew she was worried, I would."

He slaps me in the back of the head. "Of course, she knows you're worried. She is also pissed. For what you did, you deserve to have her cut your balls off."

"That's a bit harsh. I was upset and reacted poorly."

Oliver widens his eyes and blinks a few times. "I swear to God, you ate lead paint or drank out of a few too many hoses when we were kids. Poorly? Dude, you passed poorly seven days ago. You're now in the shit."

"And you're so damn perfect?"

"Hell no, I'm not. I have commitment issues and a broken heart, but I've accepted this. What I won't do is fall in love, get the girl, get her pregnant, and then leave her at the first sign of issues. I don't get you, Josh."

He sees what he wants and doesn't understand that it's not that simple. Things never are, and while a part of me wants to yell at him, explain that he's missing the entire point, it won't matter. I won't sway him or get him to see my side.

"No, you don't, and I pray to God you never do."

And with that, I walk away and dial her number again.

"You look like you could use a friend." Jack's voice causes me to lift my head.

"Wow, it must be really bad."

"Why is that?"

"My sister sent you."

Jack laughs and hands me a beer. "She was a little irrational. I volunteered."

I sit back in the lawn chair outside of what was Alex's RV but is now mine. "Lucky you."

"I think it's more like lucky you. If Stella were here, she would be bashing you over the head with a bottle."

He's not wrong. "I probably deserve it."

"You definitely do."

I let out a long sigh. "I keep wondering what exactly is going on. I've been staring out at the woods, waiting for a fucking answer."

"Don't tell Stella that. She seems to think all that's out there are weird hybrid bears."

"What?"

He chuckles. "Nothing. Look, I spent years out there, trying to find answers, and it turns out what I'd been looking for was in town the whole time."

"Stella?"

He nods. "It was always her."

"It's always been Delia."

Jack drinks from the bottle and then puts it down. "If she's the answer, why the hell are you out here searching for anything? You know where she is."

Yes, but it's been three days of radio silence. I've called, texted, and even drove to her work today. I didn't go in, but I stopped two of her co-workers in the parking lot and asked if she was doing okay. I wanted to go to her, beg her to help me, love me, fix me because I'm clearly a goddamn mess, but I won't. She is already dealing with too much, she doesn't need me dumping my baggage at her door.

"I fucked up."

"Is it not fixable?"

I shrug. "I don't know if it is."

He bobs his head. "I see. You know, I might just agree with your sister on knocking you upside the head."

At this point, I might do it myself. "I wish it were that simple, Jack."

"You think life is supposed to be simple?"

"I know more than anyone that it's not."

Jack's breath comes through his nose. "Dude, you don't know shit. I lost my mother, and then my father checked out. Your family was my only lifeline and, yeah, Mitchell is an asshole, but he was there. Your mother might have been burying her head in the sand about him, but she was breathing. You had four siblings who were always there. What did I have? Grayson and, by default, you all were my friends."

"It wasn't as easy as that," I tell him.

"No, you didn't have it easy, but it wasn't the worst life ever. Then you got to leave and move on with life. I was here, dealing with my choices and having to pretend I didn't love your sister. You don't have to do that. You *chose* that. Just like you're choosing this."

That fucking word again. Choosing. As though I want any of this. I didn't choose to lose our baby girl. I didn't choose to watch Morgan drown. I didn't choose to destroy the people and things I love most in life.

"If you think this is what I want, then you should leave before I hit you with this bottle."

"When we had to give Kinsley back to Samuel, it was literally the worst goddamn thing I've ever been through. A million times harder than when she was an infant. I didn't love her then. I didn't know her. Then we had her, and God, you see her, she's amazing. She's so much like her mother, and I couldn't keep her. I was breaking from the inside out, and the only thing that kept me together was Stella."

I look down, hating his words. "I'm what's breaking Delia."

"No, you *weren't*."

My eyes lift. "But I am now?"

"I can't answer that."

He doesn't have to. I already know whatever pain she's in now is because I'm a fucking asshole.

"I love her, but I keep thinking that it comes with a cost."

"Nothing in life is free, and love is no different. There are days when you're in the deficit and others where there's a surplus. You have to decide to love even stronger on those days when it feels like you can't fucking breathe because it's so hard to remember the good days and let that hold you over."

"Accounting love advice?"

Jack shrugs. "You get the point."

"I do. I'm a fucking idiot."

"You were scared."

"More than that, man, I was terrified."

"Fear is normal in love. Look at me and Grayson. We were afraid for a long time, but we chose not to live it anymore. I don't know if the fear will ever totally go away, but I know I'd rather be afraid loving her than without her."

It's as though he took the words straight from my heart. "I don't want to live without her."

"Then you have ten minutes to figure out what you need to do to fix it. Otherwise, I really will hit you over the head with the bottle."

"I have to go."

Jack gets up and smirks. "Me too, brother."

As soon as he's gone, I get to work. I don't need ten minutes to figure it out. I know that I need to grovel, beg, and refuse to give up. I quit on her, and I deserve to stand outside her door for days if that's what she requires. Whatever it takes to prove to her that I do choose her.

On the ride to her house, I start to make a plan, not a good one, but it's at least a start. First thing is to get her to talk to me. Since it's been radio silence since I left, that may be a bigger obstacle than I think.

After I get her to talk to me, I have to convince her that I'm worthy again.

When I get to her door, nerves hit me, but I focus on my goal—prove I love her. Show her that she's all that matters and I'll do anything. Life without Delia isn't worth living.

I ring the doorbell, but instead of opening it, her voice comes through. "What do you want, Josh?"

Maybe installing the additional cameras and stuff wasn't a great idea. Still, this is going to be opening myself bare to her.

The answer to her question is simple. "You."

She sighs. "I'm tired, and I have to work tomorrow. Please just give me time to get over this."

"I don't want you to get over this," I tell her, my hands braced on each side of the doorbell thing. "I want us. I want you. I want it all."

"You had it."

"And I threw it away."

"Yeah, you kinda did," Delia says, and I wish I could see her.

"Please let me talk."

I'm not really sure what the hell to say, but I want to look into her brown eyes and gauge something.

"Talk. I'm listening."

"Deals—"

"No, if you want to talk, then you can do it through the camera because I've learned that I'm weak when it comes to you. I let myself hear only what I want because it's so much better that way. Joshua Parkerson finally in love with the ugly duckling that was Delia Andrews." She laughs. "What a crock of shit that was. I've been so blinded by love that I've ignored the signs."

"What signs?" I ask.

"The one that said you never wanted this or me. You wanted sex, and you got that. I wanted your fucking heart, and I never got it, even when you told me it was mine. I got this sliver, and I convinced myself it was good enough, but it wasn't. I should've had it all."

"You do," I tell her, hating that she feels that way. "You are the only woman who has ever had it."

"Don't lie to me, Josh."

I have to do something quickly before she decides to stop talking.

"I'm not."

"I have been telling myself that, if I just gave you time, you'd come around. I bargained that you weren't just here for the babies. It was me too that you wanted."

I cut her off. "It is you."

"You don't leave the person you love to be alone as they struggle through the loss of a child by herself. You stand by her, and you left me."

My head drops down, and I hate myself even more. "You weren't alone. I was here, but I was so stupid and afraid that I was going to lose you. That you'd die because of me. Please, baby, come to the door. Let me try to make this right." She goes silent for a second, but the red light is still on. I know she's watching and listening. "We may not have started the way most do, but there was nothing about what I feel for you that is a lie. I have loved you for so damn long, Delia Andrews, and if I thought, even for one second, that I was worthy of you, I would propose now, but I'm not. I'm not good enough, not yet, but I promise, I'm going to try to be."

The lock clicks and then the door opens. She's so beautiful. Her long blonde hair is in a braid hanging over her shoulder. She's wearing a pair of shorts, and her hand rests on her swollen belly.

"How?" It's the only word she utters.

I lock my muscles, holding my arms at my sides to keep from reaching out for her. "By proving that I won't leave. I'll stand outside your door until you're ready to let me in."

She glares at me. "Really? You'll stay out here, in the freezing cold, just to prove you love me?"

"I'll do anything to win you back. I don't plan to walk away, Delia. See," I say as I point to the RV that's hitched to my truck. "I'll be right here, whenever you need me. I know I hurt you and broke your trust. I know that I don't deserve another chance, but I'm begging you for one."

She leans against the doorframe, chewing on her lip. "You're really willing to sleep in that thing outside my house?"

"I really am."

"Good. I'll see you in the morning." She closes the door and locks it, and now I'll show her I mean it.

Forty-Two

DELIA

"He's outside in the RV?" Stella asks with a laugh.

I peek out the blinds. "Yup. Still there."

"Good for you for not just taking his word for it. Did he connect to the house?"

"I don't know what that means, but most likely not."

"Even better. It means he has no water and is running the generator for power. Want to know how to sever that?"

His sister is diabolical, but I like it.

"For now, he can keep his generator."

"How long are you going to make him suffer?" she asks with a lilt to her voice. I really worry about Stella's enjoyment of her brother's penance.

"I don't know. Honestly, I can't believe I didn't have a Jerry Maguire moment where I was all . . . you had me at the doorbell."

She laughs. "I'm glad you didn't. We make it far too easy on these guys." Jack mutters something in the background. "Whatever, Jack, it wasn't like you had to really work for me. I was a sure thing."

I cut in. "Ummm, that's not really true."

She ignores me and continues talking to Jack. "I'm saying that, if you had come to my house with an RV, I would've dropped my pants. At least Delia has some self-respect."

"Do I?" I ask with a bit of confusion. "I mean, I slept with him—a lot—knowing he didn't care about me."

She scoffs. "I love you, but you're insane. Josh has always cared for you. He just was too stupid to recognize it."

I look back out at Josh, who is sitting outside his RV and looking at the house. I jump back, hating that he may have caught me peeking. And then I wonder what the hell I'm doing. He came back to me, and I'm in here pretending as if I didn't miss him every bit as much as he misses me. It's not rational.

We've both been grieving and struggling to be strong. Yes, he cracked and broke down, but I would be lying if I said I blamed him or really held it against him. The emotions are impossible to navigate.

"I have to go," I say to Stella.

"I thought you might."

I hang up, grab the blanket off the couch, and rush out the door. Josh is on his feet before I get down the steps.

"What's wrong?"

I don't reply as I crash against him. In an instant, he has me in his arms, holding me back. "You were out here."

"I was."

"And I was in there," I say, pulling back to look at him.

"I will stay out here if that's what you need," Josh says with all the honesty in the world.

"And if I need you with me?"

"There's nowhere else in the world I'd rather be."

I lift up on my toes and kiss him. "Let's go home."

He rests his forehead to mine. "Always with you."

Josh and I sit hand-in-hand in Dr. Warvel's office. The doctor helped Jessica after the plane crash, and we are hoping she can help us too.

We've gone through Josh's past, and he's been quiet since.

"What are you feeling?" she asks him.

"I don't know."

"That's okay, take your time and try to piece them out. Then I want you to name them aloud so we can work on each separately."

Josh looks to me, then to her. "Shame. Fear. Anger. Regret."

Dr. Warvel nods. "Those are feelings I would expect someone to feel after what you've endured. Is there anything else?"

He squeezes my hand. "Karma?"

"Tell me more about that."

The feeling in the room shifts. I can sense his discomfort, which seems worse now than it was when he was telling us about Morgan.

"It's hard to explain, but it always felt like this was what I was owed. All the bad things were because I failed the people I loved most."

Dr. Warvel writes something down. "Who did you fail before the drowning?"

"Everyone."

At that, I tense because it doesn't make sense. Josh has never failed the people he loves. He is there for them, always making sure they are okay.

"Specifically, who?"

"When I was little, it was always Grayson I failed. My parents were so hard on him, and I tried to make them focus on me. Then it was whatever girl I liked. I wasn't funny enough or have whatever it was they needed. Forget my parents because there wasn't a chance in hell I would ever be good enough in their eyes. When Morgan died, it felt like I was paying for whatever I had done."

"Josh, that's not true," I say quickly.

Dr. Warvel lifts her hand. "It may not be true to you, Delia, but what Josh is describing is very real to him. Emotions aren't rational, right? Sometimes we feel things that we might say to ourselves aren't rational, but they're still there. While the logical side of us knows it's crazy, the emotions don't care. That's part of what we have to work on together. It's getting you to feel what you feel, dealing with it, and then healing from it. That's the work. That's what I want to help you with."

Josh's thumb rubs the top of my hand. "I want that. I finally have this chance with her and our baby. I want to be a good dad and a good partner."

My heart clenches, and I kiss his cheek. "The fact that you're here shows that you are already."

"I agree with Delia. It's not easy to take the steps needed to overcome trauma. It's a very intense and sometimes long process, but I'll be here to guide you through it."

Josh's eyes meet mine. "For her, I'll do anything."

"I love you."

His lids lower as though he's absorbing the words, and then his blue eyes find mine. "I love you so much, and I'll fight every demon I have if it means a life with you."

"And all I want is your demons to go away so you can be happy and free of the past."

I lean into his touch, and we take a moment to just be before he turns to Dr. Warvel. "I'm ready."

She smiles. "I think you're going to be just fine."

Epilogue

JOSHUA

Fourteen Months Later

"I swear you're always late. It doesn't matter what we're doing." I pick up Everett, who's gumming one of his toys. "Your mommy is going to be late to her own wedding."

Delia peeks her head out of the bathroom. "Good thing this isn't my wedding then."

"No, it's worse. It's acceptable for the bride to be late but not guests. And keep saying that, you're going to marry me someday soon."

"Keep asking, and maybe I'll eventually say yes." She goes back into the bathroom, and I groan.

I ask her a lot. I ask her in different ways. And each time I ask her, she kisses me and tells me to try her again later.

It's become somewhat of a game between us. We live together, are raising Everett, and are ridiculously happy. I don't need her to be my wife for her to be my everything, she already is that. One day, she'll say yes, and then I'll whisk her away before she can change her mind.

After a few more minutes, Delia exits the bathroom with a huff as she fixes her earring. It amazes me that, no matter how much time we spend together, she never fails to take my breath away. Delia is the best thing that ever happened to me, and she gave me the greatest gift—Everett.

"Fine, I'm as good as I'm going to be."

"You're perfect."

She smiles even though I can see she doesn't want to. "Don't be sweet when you're a pain in the ass."

"Don't be beautiful when you're a pain in the ass."

"I'm not sure how to respond to that." She turns to Everett, who is now clapping his spit all over me. "Learn now, my sweet boy, that the woman you love is allowed to be late if that's her prerogative." Delia tickles his belly, and he smiles.

"We have to go, like, ten minutes ago."

"I did my best, but with him teething . . ."

I give her a look that says she's full of shit. "It wasn't him."

"It could've been."

I roll my eyes. "It wasn't. I took care of him while you soaked in the tub to prepare for the events of today."

"It's going to be a very long day. I needed to be relaxed so I don't ruin this wedding, if we can even call it that."

I laugh. "I still can't believe this is happening."

"I can't believe he asked you to be his best man."

"I *am* the best man," I say with pride.

"Yes, you are—in theory. At least to the groom." Delia pats my chest and takes Everett. "Let's go, slow poke, we have a wedding to get to."

We head out the door without further delay, which is a miracle in and of itself, and drive out to Melia Lake. Today is our soft opening for the resort. Somehow, Odette pulled it off and was able to have crews working nonstop to be ready for this event. Thanks to Oliver, we really had no choice since our soft opening is a freaking wedding.

When we get there, it's chaos. My sister has some weird headset on, and she's barking orders all over the place. "You!" She spots me. "You were supposed to be here an hour ago to help set up!"

I point to Delia. "Her fault."

Stella's eyes narrow. "I needed him."

Delia shrugs, clearly not worried about the strange twitch happening in Stella's eye. "I can't rush perfection. Besides, everything looks great."

Stella shakes her head. "No thanks to either of you. Whatever. Since you're here, you can do some damn work. We have a disaster in the kitchen, and the guest in 218 says there's an odor in her room. The only thing I can smell is the insane amount of perfume she wears. Oh, and the groom is flipping the fuck out."

Delia grabs Everett, her voice calm as Stella teeters on the brink of losing it. "I'll head to the kitchen, you handle the room issue, and Josh can take care of the groom since he's the best man."

"Shouldn't you be the best woman?" I ask Stella.

Again, she has that eye twitch. "God help me for having brothers."

"Where's Grayson?" I ask.

"He and Jessica are catering to the bride's family. They are very demanding since their beloved only daughter is getting married."

I grin. "But is she?"

"Not today, Joshua. Not today. I will kill you and won't feel bad about the jail time."

Kinsley comes running up. "You have to see this, Stella!"

"What?"

"Oliver is having a major meltdown. I tried to calm him down, I even brought in Amelia to do her magic, but nothing is helping."

Stella groans. "Must I do everything?"

"Yes," I reply and then a hand hits my chest.

My phone rings, and it's a video call from Alex. "Hey, brother. How's Egypt?"

"Hot as freaking hell, but the project is awesome."

Delia starts to bounce up and down. "Oh, oh, let me tell him!"

I shake my head and take a few steps back. Not a chance in hell. This is going to be my fun, not hers.

"Tell me what?"

"Nothing. Ignore her."

She fuses her lips together when I give her a stare.

"Something is going on there," Alex notes.

"Nope. Just our first big event here."

"I know, I'm calling to check on my investment."

I roll my eyes. "Right. It's all good. Stella has outdone herself with the preparations. I think this will be a great opening and test. We've already found some things to improve before we officially open the doors next month."

Alex grins. "That's awesome."

I turn then, Delia's eyes bulge and she's shifting her weight back and forth. She's going to blow.

"And how's working with Bryce?" I ask. His mentor and longtime friend, Bryce Peyton, is who got him the gig.

"It's great, but tell me more about today. How are Grayson and Oliver handling the stress?"

I smirk. "Gray is great."

"Ollie is losing it?"

"You could say that." I hold in the laugh.

"I feel like I'm missing something."

Oh, he is. He so is.

Delia grabs my phone, and before I can take it back, she's blurts it out. "Oliver is the groom, and that's why he's freaking out!"

She hands it back and walks away, blowing me a kiss as she goes.

"Yeah, so . . . I have quite the story for you . . ."

Thank you for reading Josh and Delia's story. Stay tuned for the final Willow Creek Valley book which will feature Oliver and Maren in A Chance for Us! I know that as writers or parents we aren't supposed to have a favorite child/character.

But . . .

Oliver is totally my favorite. (Don't tell the others)

Acknowledgments

To my husband and children. You sacrifice so much for me to continue to live out my dream. Days and nights of me being absent even when I'm here. I'm working on it. I promise. I love you more than my own life.

My readers. There's no way I can thank you enough. It still blows me away that you read my words. You guys have become a part of my heart and soul.

Bloggers: I don't think you guys understand what you do for the book world. It's not a job you get paid for. It's something you love and you do because of that. Thank you from the bottom of my heart.

My beta reader Melissa Saneholtz: Dear God, I don't know how you still talk to me after all the hell I put you through. Your input and ability to understand my mind when even I don't blows me away. If it weren't for our phone calls, I can't imagine where this book would've been. Thank you for helping me untangle the web of my brain.

My assistant, Christy Peckham: How many times can one person be fired and keep coming back? I think we're running out of times. No, but for real, I couldn't imagine my life without you. You're a pain in my ass but it's because of you that I haven't fallen apart.

Sommer Stein for once again making these covers perfect and still loving me after we fight because I change my mind a bajillion times.

Michele Ficht and Julia Griffis for always finding all the typos and crazy mistakes.

Nina and everyone at Valentine PR, thank you for always having my back and going above and beyond. I love you all so much.

Melanie Harlow, thank you for being the Glinda to my Elphaba or Ethel to my Lucy. Your friendship means the world to me and I love writing with you. I feel so blessed to have you in my life.

Bait, Crew, and Corinne Michaels Books—I love you more than you'll ever know.

My agent, Kimberly Brower, I am so happy to have you on my team. Thank you for your guidance and support.

Melissa Erickson, you're amazing. I love your face. Thank you for always talking me off the ledge that is mighty high.

To my narrators, Andi Arndt and Connor Crais, I am so honored to work with you. You bring my story to life and always manage to make the most magical audiobooks.

Vi, Claire, Chelle, Mandi, Amy, Kristy, Penelope, Kyla, Rachel, Tijan, Alessandra, Laurelin, Devney, Jessica, Carrie Ann, Kennedy, Lauren, Susan, Sarina, Beth, Julia, and Natasha—Thank you for keeping me striving to be better and loving me unconditionally. There are no better sister authors than you all.

Books by Corinne Michaels

The Salvation Series

Beloved

Beholden

Consolation

Conviction

Defenseless

Evermore: A 1001 Dark Night Novella

Indefinite

Infinite

The Hennington Brothers

Say You'll Stay

Say You Want Me

Say I'm Yours

Say You Won't Let Go: A Return to Me/Masters and Mercenaries Novella

Second Time Around Series

We Own Tonight

One Last Time

Not Until You

If I Only Knew

The Arrowood Brothers

Come Back for Me

Fight for Me

The One for Me

Stay for Me

Willow Creek Valley Series
Return to Us
One Chance for Us
A Moment for Us
Could Have Been Us

Standalones
All I Ask
You Loved Me Once (Coming 2021)

Co-Written with Melanie Harlow
Hold You Close
Imperfect Match

About the Author

Corinne Michaels is a *New York Times, USA Today, and Wall Street Journal* bestselling author of romance novels. Her stories are chock full of emotion, humor, and unrelenting love, and she enjoys putting her characters through intense heartbreak before finding a way to heal them through their struggles.

Corinne is a former Navy wife and happily married to the man of her dreams. She began her writing career after spending months away from her husband while he was deployed—reading and writing were her escape from the loneliness. Corinne now lives in Virginia with her husband and is the emotional, witty, sarcastic, and fun-loving mom of two beautiful children.

Made in the USA
Middletown, DE
01 October 2021